Praise for VALENCIA

"Wonderful storytelling . . . charged with reflection, anger
and the feeling of being alive."
—*The Village Voice*

"A spidery *roman á clef* for our times . . .
Valencia crackles with take-no-prisoners prose."
—*The Seattle Times*

"[T]here is immediacy in the stream-of-consciousness style, as if Tea
were in the room offering the reader a late-night confession."
—*Library Journal*

"An edgy, supercharged, supersurreal reality."
—*Booklist*

"What's truly inspired in this book is Tea's literary voice, an effort-
lessly controlled combination of ironic wit and romantic longing."
—*The Bay Guardian*

"The stream-of-consciousness narration is a delightful ride to be on,
shifting us into other registers of memory and relationship."
—*Rain Taxi*

"Tea's exquisite writing performs the miracle, dancing along
a razor's edge between humor and pathos, jaded exhaustion
and wonder. [I]n lesser hands, this material would simply be sad.
As it is, it's transcendental."
—*Girlfriends* magazine

VALENCIA

Michelle Tea

SEAL PRESS

VALENCIA

Copyright © 2000, 2008 by Michelle Tea

Seal Press
A Member of the Perseus Books Group
1700 Fourth Street
Berkeley, CA 94710

9 8 7 6 5 4 3 2 1

Library of Congress Cataloging-in-Publication Data

Tea, Michelle.
  Valencia / by Michelle Tea.
    p. cm.
  ISBN-13: 978-1-58005-035-7
  ISBN-10: 1-58005-035-2
  1. San Francisco (Calif.)—Fiction. 2. Lesbians—Fiction. I. Title.

PS3570.E15V35 2008
813'.54—dc22

                                    2007046879

Cover and Interior Design by Domini Dragoone
Printed in the United States by [TK]
Distributed by Publishers Group West

for Cari Campbell

introduction

What's more narcissistic than writing your own memoir? Writing an introduction to your own memoir. Welcome to it, people. Right before I began writing the stories that would become *Valencia,* I was coming down from an inspired poetry high that had allowed me to write one to five poems a day, all of them ruminations on my thoughts and my opinions and my experiences. I was twenty-three years old, had just moved to San Francisco, and these poems had allowed me to plug myself into the roiling early-'90s street poetry scene, a scene that overlapped neighborhoods, that erupted in crappy bars and coffee shops and art spaces, and that included anyone shameless and histrionic enough to clamber up to the stage and perform their life for the enjoyment of a bunch of romantic drunkards. I was psyched; I had found my dream community, and all I had to do to be part of it was run my mouth about what and who pissed me off. Incredibly, no one told me to shut up. They *clapped*. The mixture of butch dykes, shy girls, ex-bikers, crackheaded misogynists, recent hillbillies, slumming academics, former communist party members, junkies, bike messengers, waitresses, Gothic club kids, sex workers, tattooed fags, Kathy Acker acolytes, Bukowski, Ginsberg and Rollins wannabes, hardcore punks, shabby bon vivants, and other intellectual miscreants was astounding. Writing was often the only thing we had in common, but our obsession with it was profound enough to keep us bound together like a real tribe, if one that occasionally split into violently warring factions.

The inspiration for the poetry came out of nowhere and raged in me like a mania. As it started to subside I found myself wanting to tell longer stories, and was a bit confused and worried about what to do next. The thought that I could lose this excellent life in San Francisco—a place I'd moved to knowing only a single person, with nothing but $1,500 I'd earned hooking, an army bag stuffed with really ugly clothes, and a hand drum—was the worst. I felt compelled to scribble some short stories based on real things that had happened to me: vignettes about my nutso ex-girlfriend, about when I was so in love I ran away to Tucson on a Greyhound bus, about how I did speed at the Dyke March and picked up that girl from Canada. But was that literature? In the house I grew up in literature was Stephen King, Jackie Collins, Jacqueline Susann, and whichever horror paperback at the drugstore had the creepiest cover. A person didn't write about their own self and try to pass it off as *writing*; how egotistical!

Then I read Eileen Myles' *Chelsea Girls*, a collection of precisely such short stories, pieces that rang with detached but urgent truths and realities, written by a writer who handled the massive ups and downs of her past with coolness and style, never afraid to reveal harshness, seemingly oblivious to how she came off in the text, narrating herself like a god looking down at a fascinating life. It didn't hurt that the author was a dyke, or defiantly class-conscious, or that she hailed from the same slab of New England I'd recently escaped from. I'd found my literary soul mate. Reading *Chelsea Girls* was an electrifying experience. *I could do this.* I could write about my own life as if I were creating a character in a novel, letting my mind capture all the details it craved to capture, not giving a shit about how I or anyone else looked, just slamming a bunch of messy, crazy, fast life into my notebook. And I found that in the process of transforming my world, my life, my self into literature, my world, life, and self became elevated, seemed to occupy a space it hadn't previously, one more noble and romantic, the struggle of it all meaningful now, all past mishaps and future tragedies redeemed by this magical practice. Everything I touched turned to story, and it was golden.

And like the fairy tale, having everything turn to gold—or to story—has its downside, too. I think the weirdest side effect of

8

Valencia, and the memoirs I wrote before and after, isn't people getting pissed at the way you represent them—oddly, most people were tickled to find themselves inside a book, barely fictionalized. Iris, Valencia's main squeeze, was nothing but awesome about my compulsive rendering of her, even when our breakup was totally old news, but I still couldn't stop pouting about it and bitchily icing her and her girlfriend. Her girlfriend, Emma, was also psychotically generous about the way I not only wrote about her, but *read* about her, all the time, at events she was likely to turn out at. After one such reading she left the art gallery, kicked a bus shelter and broke her foot. Because I was a small-hearted, bad person, I delighted in this. Years later, reading an Emma excerpt from *Valencia* at a seven deadly sins-themed event (my sin was jealousy), I was horrified to learn she was in attendance. I'd prefaced the excerpt by telling the audience what a jerk she was, how she stole my girlfriend, blah, blah blah. This had all happened years ago, but because it had been cemented into narrative by this book, the character of Evil Emma lived on, forever trashing my love life. Except she was a real girl, there in the audience. I felt like the most stunted asshole ever, performing my ancient resentments. I apologized to her afterwards, and as always she was gracious, but my *Sorry* felt weak in comparison to the years of literary torment I'd subjected her to.

That's the strangest part of turning your life into a story—not the social fallout, the way you over-expose yourself, the way others will inevitably think you're a narcissistic egomaniac who can't get enough of herself. The hardest part is how writing it down petrifies your experience, freezes it in time. You have to believe the story is true to put it on paper, at least I do. But for normal, healthy non-writer people, the way you view your life ideally shifts with time and perspective. If you've rolled your history into a book, and then performed that book over and over, it can be hard for distance to set in and nuance the past. And when it eventually does, it feels confusing, embarrassing, and humbling. *Valencia* is a bug trapped in emotional amber. It's a snapshot, more or less, of my twenty-fifth year on earth, written not how it happened but how I *felt* it happened, and how I felt about it happening. I could not have written it without the inspiration and guidance unknowingly provided by Eileen Myles, who continues to be a mentor and favorite writer. And it could not have been written without Emma, who was a catalyst for drama the way we all are for each other, like it or not. Our lives make awesome stories, especially if you don't get too attached to the thread of your own narrative.

Michelle Tea
On a Plane Above the U.S.
September 2007

10

1

I sloshed away from the bar with my drink, sending little tsunamis of beer onto my hands, soaking into the wrist of my shirt. Don't ask me what I was wearing. Something to impress What's-Her-Name, the girl I wasn't dating. She had a girlfriend, she didn't need two. She needed someone to sleep naked with and share some sexual tension, and for that position I made myself available. Apparently it was a temporary position. Let me tell you right away, just so you understand the magnitude of my experience, that I was truly *obsessed* with this woman. This was no mere crush, this was some-thing huge, feelings taking the form of a hot, wet gas that filled the bar and I had to move through it with my drink, wading through the fog of my heart. I had met Petra back in February, at the start of the rainy season, at another bar on an intensely crowded dance floor that throbbed with the weight of so many slamming boots. My friend Ashley shoved me into her. Again and again. To this day Petra thinks I asked my friend to do this, but it's not true. Ashley would get this look on her face and *wham* her hands shot out and I would go sailing into this woman who danced so good, kind of bouncy, but contained. She had her hands balled into fists and she shook them in a discoey way like maracas, and managed to look tough while doing so. After a little bit of the shoving, people got the idea that I was trying to start a pit so everyone started shoving. Girls were just careening across the floor, into the wall, spilling drinks, burning each other with their cigarettes. This was at The Stud, so lots of boys were dancing too. I would beat them up. For dancing like jerks, all shooting fists and skanking kneecaps coming up and hitting the poor girls who were already slamming the shit out of each other, it's true, but that was different. They were girls. I would skip around the dance floor twirling and kicking in my particular style, looking very caught up in the music but really strategizing. And aiming. *Pow*—my boot flew out and connected with this tall boy's kneecap. Then another boy, right in the tush. They'd leave the dance floor, or grab me by the shoulder. *You keep kicking me!* What? It was so loud in the bar. Bikini Kill, L7, fucking Joan Jett. *Girl* music. The boys had no right. *You keep kicking me!* What?! What?! Sorry! A light shrug. I'd go back to dancing, kick them in their asses when they turned their backs. Laugh, hahahaha. I was doing the

12

goddess's work. A girl pulled me over, *I saw you kicking that boy.*
Thanks! Once, a guy grabbed Candice like a fucking piñata and just
spun her around, up high in the air because she is little. Just swinging her around. Candice *hates* to be touched. The guy ended up on
the ground and I was on top of him, my fingers knotted in his hair,
pounding his skull into the dance floor. Sweaty, my shirt off, hanging out my back pocket, I felt great.

But the night I met Petra I was being good. I was wearing
this really weird dress, red, pretty bright, with a couple of black
stripes. It was a knit dress, a sweater dress, tight with long sleeves
lazily unraveling at the wrist. And I had this wig on my head, which
was bald. A synthetic black wig, Cleopatra-style with a thick fringe
of bangs that bounced on my forehead as I danced. They were playing that Pixies song that is so fast, I was trying to dance just as fast
to it in my weird, kicky dance, really spastic, reaching up now and
then to straighten the wig. The dress was so hot, stupid for dancing, but it looked good. I looked different that night, so when Petra
asked me to go home with her I felt like an imposter. Maybe if she
knew how I really looked, bald head like a sick bird, she would not
want to take me home for sex. How could an attraction rooted in
such insecurity not result in obsession? Petra had a truck and since
I was her special guest that night, I got to sit in the front. In the
back were a couple of dogs plus five or six girls I had surmised were
Really Cool. They were very confident in their different fashions. I
knew that one of them was in a band, and another was a stripper.

I sat in the truck that smelled like dog, and fidgeted. All those girls knew Petra was taking me home to fuck me. They probably knew more about it than I did, in terms of what to expect.

Shortly after we arrived at her house, Petra pulled a knife on me. It was the scariest knife I had ever seen, a thick, jagged curve like a sinister smile, with a heavy black handle. *Do you like knives?* she asked. I Don't Know, I'm sure I whimpered. *I'm not going to hurt you,* she assured me, *I'm just going to scare you.* Sounded like a good plan. Petra passed me the knife so I could be on that end for a minute, feel its weight. It was very heavy, with that cruel, curving tip. There were things lodged inside my brain I had always figured would just have to stay there. Things I wasn't sure could stand to pass into the real world. Petra laid the knife to my throat and pressed it softly into the skin. She took the hooked tip and traced it down my neck, down to the dead end of my red sweater dress. *It's like a sexy Charlie Brown dress,* the boy at the thrift store had said. The front was laced up with red yarn that Petra worked at like a puzzle, pulling at the tangled thread so she could get at my tits. She placed the knife flat on my nipple and went at my throat with her teeth, all the while making these urgent little animal noises. Petra was really into the knife. I got the sense that I could have been any body beneath her, it was the knife that was the star of the show. I was really into *processing* the knife. Like, was I encouraging violence against women, was I "part of the problem," was she going to get frenzied and just stick the thing into my ribs? It was a hunting knife,

14

strong, made for ripping through gut and muscle and bone. I tried not to enjoy it too much. I would be an observer. I observed Petra. She was magnificent. She wasn't so much a person as an event, a gigantic presence. Long knots of hair scraggled over her shoulders, black with some red staining it here and there. A sharp face and clear blue eyes. Petra was older than me. Who wasn't? Thin lines fanned out from her eyes, and she was covered in tattoos, dark, murky claws swirling down her shoulders and curling under her tits like spindly fingers. Like someone spilled ink down her front, letting it make these precise, blurry paths. She put the knife away and we rolled around on her bed, banging into her dog, who was spread at the top of the futon, watching with her bored dog face.

Petra was fanatical about safe sex. She had a thick ball of latex gloves rolled up in each other, and she told me not to touch any part of her if I had my pussy on my fingers. I had never had safe sex with a girl before, but I acted like I knew what was up because I didn't want her to think I was diseased. I stretched the white clingy glove over my fingers, and I slid them one, two, three, four, up her cunt. *Put your fist up me.* What? I had read about this once, in a lesbian book. *Your fist.* God, the energy shooting off her chest was intense, she was a ball of electricity. This was the girl for me. This crazy girl with the crazy cunt that sucked my fist inside with a slow slurp. My whole hand. I saw my elbow, then my forearm, then her cunt. She had the fattest metal ring jammed through her clit hood. All you had to do was jiggle it and she went nuts. I thought about

15

the bouncy way she danced and thought about this chunk of metal tugging on her down there. I thought about my hand that had disappeared into her hole and I thought about the quantum physics theory that once something leaves our view we cannot prove what has happened to it, or if it even exists. I think too much during sex, my mind just whirs with the whole new landscape of body spreading out beneath me. I was barely moving my theoretical hand. I was afraid of breaking Petra. *Hard,* she groaned, so I started up some small thrusts. I still couldn't see my hand. *Hard,* she groaned, insistent. *Really hard.* I started punching Petra, her insides, the part I couldn't see. Thump, thump, thump. My clingy latex fist hit up against some strong, female part of her. She writhed and played with her tits, punched the bed beneath her, howled. It was pretty incredible. Knife-wielding Petra, more a force of nature than a girl like me, impaled upon my humble hand. I was really happy. I tugged on her jewelry until she had me stop everything. I don't think she came. I don't even know if that was the point. My fist left her cunt with another wet sound. I didn't know what to do with it. It was the hand of god. I turned the glistening glove inside out and crawled back onto Petra. *What do you like?* she asked. Oh god, how the fuck do I know? I had no more reference points for sex. Petra had destroyed them. I had never had sex before. Not if this was sex. I wanted the knife again, but I just couldn't bring myself to ask for it. I Don't Know What I Like, I confessed. Petra had a shelf piled with instruments, black rubber things, leather, studs, stiff handles, thin

16

straps. A perverse doctor's office. Especially with the gloves. Petra kneeled between my legs and tinkered around with my pussy. She tried to stuff her hand up it but there was no way that was going to happen. We fell asleep wrapped around each other, tightly smooshed together. My wig was tangled up in the sheets and her chin rested on my bald head. She had these piercings in her chin. They jutted out like sharp little fangs, and all night she ground her teeth and kept stabbing me in the head.

I can tell you more about Petra, but it's the aftermath I want to get to. We made out on a pool table at this really divey bar, and when we came up for air she told me she bought my poetry chapbook at this little cafe, and the poems were really intense. She couldn't see me anymore. She had a girlfriend vacationing in New Zealand. They could fuck other people but not have crushes, and she had a crush on me. I Have A Crush On You Too, I said. She drove me home in her truck. Then I saw her again at another bar and she asked if I wanted to go home with her. *I talked to my therapist about it,* she said, *and she said why couldn't it just be something light and fun and playful?* Yeah, Why Not, and I was in her bed again. Up in her loft. The walls were covered with pictures of Petra. With her dog and with her girlfriend, who was bleached blonde and really sex-radical. The girlfriend was a sex worker, and she did performances about sex, and she wrote about sex and talked about sex with a slight lisp from her tongue piercing. Me and Petra fucked. I had been so filled with regret after that last session with the knife, I knew it would never happen again and I wished desperately that I had gotten more into it. I was getting a second chance, and I still couldn't ask for it. The knife sat on the shelf with the other sex toys, gleaming its evil gleam. We did other stuff. When I launched my fist up her this time, I knew to do it hard. Petra can fist her own cooch. She told me. She can't really get the motion, though. That was the last time me and Petra did it. I guess she liked me too much, or she worried she would. So we hung out a lot. She had me come over to her house for dinner, and she fed me amazing vegetables, stuff you really had to use your hands for. We plucked petals from an artichoke and dunked them in thick melted butter. We tore into raw red peppers and peeled juicy fat pomelos. Her dog was there. She would get horny and Petra would stretch out her leather leg and the dog would hop up on her leather boot and grind. Petra laughed. I loved her. I don't know why she thought cutting off sex would extinguish the emotions. We were like boarding school girl-friends. In one last desperate act of seduction I wore the wig and a little majorette outfit to a party, and sat on her lap all night drinking tequila. She burned herself with cigarettes. On purpose. Held the smoking thing to her arm and gasped her little sex gasps. What a mystery she was. I was sitting on the lap of the sphinx. Unfortunately, Petra seemed immune to the majorette outfit's charm. It did smell like mothballs. She left the party with a quick hug.

18

Later, we would drive to the beach in her truck, and on the wet sand she would dance with all the dogs, let them dive and leap at her like she was the great dog god. We talked about books. When my twenty-third birthday came around, I was working two jobs, all morning at a courier company, taking orders on the computer, and all afternoon at an ineffectual anarchist labor union, managing the office. I didn't show up at the union on my birthday. Petra said she had a history of getting girls fired. She didn't work, and got her money through scams, dyke porn movies and occasional under-the-table work. For my birthday Petra took me for Thai food and then to the women's bathhouse on Valencia, where we sat naked in the steam and listened to this bitchy girl she knew go on and on about how one of her "slaves" was expecting too much emotion-ally, and the agreement was that the girl would just clean the house and that's it, do the floors and the dishes, and now she was just getting too needy and was about to get fired. I began to under-stand what I had gotten myself into. Petra's world wasn't my world. What had I been thinking? I watched her listen to the slave owner, her matted hair hanging damply. I still felt like an imposter. I wanted her so badly, my heart hung out of my chest like some hound-dog's tongue, pant, pant. We would see each other at bars and sit close and giggle. We'd go back to her loft and sleep together, no clothes, folded together. No sex. Then she stopped bringing me over and just drove me home in her truck after last call. Then came that final night, when I sloshed through the dark pumping bar with all the whirling girls. Petra was beside me and she was restless. Like she thought she had to be next to me but maybe she didn't want to. I was an obligation, the little sister she had to take around with her. On the dance floor in front of us was a girl moving like a belly dancer, gyrating her hips and extending her fingers like the wings of a bird. Petra was lusting after her. She wanted to take her home, I could feel it as thickly as I felt my own hopelessness. I was a lump beside her, a little pal. She couldn't cruise in front of me. We weren't going out but we sure were doing something. *I'm going home,* she announced. Yeah, Me Too. I tried to sound bored. We walked out of the bar. She had a leather cap on her head, all her scraggly hair poking out in tangles. Petra smelled bad. Maybe she never washed. Sour scalp, b.o. and pussy. My nose ate it up. Desire, I've been told, is all about stink. *Well. . . . bye,* she said on the sidewalk. *You can catch a bus right over there.* She pointed to a shelter at the corner of Haight and Filmore. A quick hug and then her little strut up the street. I knew where to catch the fucking bus.

I dove onto a plastic seat and cried. I hated San Francisco. All the sex-radical girls and their slaves and their leather. I cried and wished for cigarettes. I thought I would run away. To Tucson, Arizona. I'd only just left the place. Flipped a penny when I found out my Tucson girlfriend had acquired a boyfriend. "Heads" was Javalina-land, the plot of lesbian separatist land out in the Arizona desert where I could build a shack out of scrap wood and dead cactus and spend a few months falling to the dirt with heat stroke, avoiding

20

rattlesnakes and bonding with wimmin. "Tails" was San Francisco, where I could start smoking again and walk around lonely in the drizzle writing vague love poems in my head. It had come up tails, but I was losing my faith in the penny. Tucson would be bright and warm and slow. San Francisco was filthy. The rainy season had started and I'd be damp for months. In Tucson I would be dry, I could sit in a cafe and be far away from Petra. I would be in exile. I would need a Walkman. For the Greyhound.

I sank some coins into the pay phone. I had to let my friends know I was leaving. It was about two in the morning. Ashley's machine picked up. Ashley, I'm Going To Tucson. If You Wake Up And Get This, Can I Borrow Your Walkman? I called Ernesto. Ernesto, I'm Leaving. Called Vinnie. Goodbye, Vinnie. A bus came and I got on it. I arrived back at my bright little bedroom in the Mission, a small, carpeted square. All my money was in a hiking boot in my closet, a tight little bulge in the toe. I took about half of it, grabbed some clothes and stuffed them into my black army bag. I took tapes, but nothing that would remind me of San Francisco. I was out of my head and probably a little drunk. The light in my room was so bright, it was manic. I called Greyhound, How Much For A Bus To Tucson? *One way or round trip?* Outside my window I heard some noise on the street, a woman yelling. Hold On, I said to the Greyhound lady and threw the phone on the rug, flung open my window. I saw a car, some men trying to pull a woman inside. I grabbed one of my candles, a pink candle in glass I had bought to magically seduce

21

Petra, and I hurled it out the window. Leave Her Alone! The glass cracked on the pavement and the people at the car all laughed. They were just kidding. The pink glob of wax rolled sadly into the gutter. I got back on the phone. Sorry, I said to the Greyhound lady, who now thought I was insane. Seventy-two bucks for a round-trip bus to Tucson. I'll Take It, I said. Who else did I have to call? My jobs, fuck them. The labor union was driving me nuts. I left a message on its machine, Sorry, I'm Going Nuts, I Have To Go Away. One of my roommates worked at my morning courier job. I left her a note to give to our boss: I Know These Are The Type Of Shenanigans That Get One's Ass Fired, But I'd Really Like To Work Full-Time When I Get Back. I called Gwynn to tell her I was running away, and she picked up the phone on the first ring. Gwynn, I'm Going To Tucson. *I'll come.* For Real? Oh, Gwynn was tragic. *Michelle, there's blood everywhere.* Gwynn sometimes cut herself. Not in a suicidal way, just when she was really sad, which was often. She'd been up all night digging into her arm with a razor. Over the girl in the apartment upstairs. Oh, I wanted Gwynn to come so badly. It changed everything. It would be an adventure. Gwynn was a warrior, she was deeply wounded and she was beautiful. And indecisive. *Oh, I don't know,* she said, picking crusty blood off her razor. She kept cursing as she nicked the tips of her fingers. Oh Gwynn, It Will Be So Good For You! *Where will we sleep?* I told her my friend Julisa would put us up, and if that fell through we could sleep outside, by the dried-up creek that ran through little tunnels beneath the city.

22

I'd heard the Manson gang had hung out in those tunnels. Hide-aways for outcasts. *Oh, I don't know.* Gwynn didn't like the idea of sleeping outside. It'll Be An Adventure, I promised. You Can Write About It. Gwynn was a poet.

I took a cab to her house, on the toughest block of the lower Haight where boys grabbed her ass and threatened her with pit bulls when she walked alone. I found her on her mattress with the yellow sheets, her arms slowly scabbing. There were brown smears by the pillow. What Happened? I asked, hugging her. *Justine,* she said sadly. I had been in love with Gwynn once. I had wanted to save her. Then I realized Gwynn wasn't meant to be saved. At least not by me. I got her out of the house, which I couldn't believe. Gwynn is difficult to impossible to inspire. She was just so sad. Her whole face hung with it, like sadness was her personal gravity. We walked to the Castro to catch a train. The morning was taking shape around us, the sky slowly brightening into the deepest blue. It was the color of hope. We stopped at a gas station for cigarettes. If I was going to take a Greyhound, I was going to smoke. Roman-tic cigarettes on the side of the road. I was thinking that maybe I should leave for good. I'd never meant to stay in San Francisco. By the time we got to the Greyhound station Gwynn had decided to go to Oregon. Oregon? What The Fuck Is In Oregon? *Eugene,* she said. A town, not a person. Oh Gwynn, I sighed weakly. I knew how hopeless it was to persuade her. My energy was waning. I hadn't slept, I was in the same clothes I'd worn to the bar, my feet squishy from sweat and last night's rain. Before we'd left the ticket counter Gwynn decided not to go anywhere at all. We bought Cokes from the machine and smoked cigarettes while waiting for my bus to board. I'm Going To Get A Tattoo, I said. A Heart. Right Here. I touched my chest. *Oh Michelle,* Gwynn said mournfully. *Don't get a tattoo that's going to remind you of a girl.* The heart I wanted came from a deck of fortunetelling cards. A real heart, not a valentine. I got on my bus. It wasn't so crowded, I got two seats for myself. I stretched out to sleep and woke up in total greenery. Outside, the earth rolled gently and there were lazy drooping trees and sunlight. This is where I belonged, this in-between place. I dozed back off. I could have stayed on that bus forever, someone else driving, always on my way, never arriving.

In a Burger King parking lot I smoked my romantic Camels. A guy from Florida told me he was on his way to Phoenix, to quit heroin. Greyhound is the coach of the desperate. He had his own cigarettes to smoke. We sat in our stories and stared out the windows. I realized I hadn't brought any socks. My boots, these plasticky things I had bought at Payless when I was vegan, were falling apart. My toes felt pruny. It took sixteen hours to get to Tucson, we pulled into town around four in the morning. Half-asleep, I stumbled with my stuff to the Hotel Congress, where the Dillinger gang once hid out and was nearly caught by the law. One of the outlaws was shot out front and died in a puddle of blood. It was a hotel for fugitives. I got a room in the hostel part of the building. An old room. I imagined a band of bank robbers holed up behind the plaster walls. Army-style bunk beds and a porcelain sink with a hazy mirror. White toilet and a narrow shower, a radiator to hang my soaked socks on. I climbed up into the top bunk and stretched out, wondering if I was legally allowed inside the Hotel Congress, and if there was a warrant for my arrest in the state of Arizona. When I'd lived here I got in a brawl with a bouncer at the downstairs nightclub. It was my ex-girlfriend's fault. She had been out on the curb waiting for me and heard the bouncer call some boy a fag, so she started arguing with him. By the time I came out the scene was really heated. Liz was a compulsive liar and loved to start fights, but I really believed in Liz, so I hopped right in, harassing the bouncers, calling them macho men, mocking them with a swishy little tap dance and muscle-man moves. They were trying to kick us off the sidewalk, but we were waiting for our friends. Liz sarcastically applauded their toughness, clapping her hands about an inch from the big one's face, and finally he grabbed her and went to push her off the curb. Instantly I was on him, kicking with my patent leather pumps. I got him good in the crotch. I tore at his shirt and his hair, until his friends grabbed me in this police hold and I couldn't fight anymore. This was life with Liz. Violence could erupt at any minute like a big song and dance number, a musical of seething rage. *Y'all wish you had penises, huh?* chuckled the bouncer. He was real rednecky-looking. They called the cops on us, assault, so we called the cops back on them, assault. We went home. The police cars pulled up to the orange trees outside our quaint southwestern adobe, and the trustfund deadhead roommates went crazy trying to hide the bongs and the pipes. Three mustached men leaned coolly in our doorway. I showed them the bruises on my arms from the redneck's fingers. I was wearing this flowered little dress. *Look at her!* Liz shrieked. *She's ninety-eight pounds, you think she assaulted them?* My little sister, who was visiting, cried in the corner. It was too much for her. This was her vacation. Me and Liz split town before our court date.

When I woke up in the morning my socks had dried into stiff boards on the radiator. I would have to go without. I put on some shorts and a flannel I regretted once I left the hotel. Tucson just never gets cold. It was February and had to be about ninety. I dragged my stuff over to Julisa's house. Her house was beautiful. A little adobe with a porch that cradled cats and futons and hammocks. Majestic cacti and tall stalks of okra grew in her garden. It was magical. Julisa was happy to see me. She was this voluptuous, earthy chick who threw potlucks for Earth First! and worked at a day-care center. I went to work with her and hung out with the kids. They thought I was a boy. I had no hair, I'd left my wig in San Francisco. With Petra. I couldn't stop talking about her, and Julisa wanted to know everything. She was curious and fascinated and judgmental and then insisted she wasn't being judgmental. We were eating cheap delicious food at a Guatemalan restaurant. *You had rough sex?* she

26

asked plainly. Yeah. *You liked it?* Yeah. *I do not like rough sex,* she said to her boyfriend, a hippie. He didn't either. That's Great, I said, and drank my beer. Around the corner from Julisa's house was a little tattoo shop called Denim & Doilies. I went there with my little fortunetelling card and some money. The tattoo guy's name was Picasso, this big biker guy, his hair held back with a studded piece of leather. *Now that's a* real *heart,* he said appreciatively. He took me around back to the private room with the reclining chair, and stuck the outline of the heart onto me with some Speed Stick. I had no reference point for tattoos, I didn't know how much they should cost or what they should feel like. Now I know that Picasso ripped me off and he was sadistic, digging the needle in deeply. I held on to a stuffed kittycat with a pierced septum and tore the fur from it. It really hurt. I felt the stinging in my nipple, which Picasso was trying to get me to pierce. One Thing At A Time, I said. He took frequent cigarette breaks, and I talked about Petra. He brought in some magazines to distract me. I picked up one of the modern primitive ones. That's Her, I said numbly, staring at the cover. That's Petra. She looked sharp and dangerous, her fanged chin jutting out like a dare. *No shit!* Picasso called out to his wife, a skinny, chain-smoking biker lady. *That's her girlfriend,* he bragged. *Petra!* the lady cooed. She's Not My Girlfriend, I pouted. Petra was never my girlfriend. *Did you, like, fuck her?* I nodded. *She fucked her,* he told his wife. *Petra!* she exclaimed again. *Do you know Zanya too?* She turned to a photo of another pierced and tattooed naked girl,

Petra's friend. Yeah, I Know Her, I said wearily. *Zanya!* she shrieked. *Zanya's her favorite,* said Picasso.

You could get stuff pierced at Denim & Doilies, by this really hip, good-looking fag. His ear was a slinky of stainless steel, his hair was long and dark, he was about seventeen and he was already much too jaded for Tucson. He invited me to a party the next night. *A dyke party,* he said with a little tinkle in his voice. When Julisa came to the shop to pick me up, she had the boy give her a tour of the piercing area. He showed us all the gleaming needles and I thought of Petra's knife. *So you stick these into people?* Julisa asked. *Oh, yeah,* said the boy. *Grrrrrreat,* she said. Julisa had this really sarcastic way of saying "great." She looked at the pictures on the wall, cut out from magazines. *They chain themselves together by their bellybuttons?* she asked, pointing to one. *That's not code-pendent?* Before I went to bed that night I covered the new tattoo with Saran Wrap, so the goo wouldn't get all over Julisa's sheets. It nearly looked like a real heart, hanging rawly outside my ribs the way I wanted, a mess of wet red and pus and salve. Gory. But when I woke up in the morning it looked like I'd been shot in the chest. I'd sweated out bunches of the ink. *Why'd you do that?* Picasso cried when I called the shop. His masterpiece. He'd been so proud. *Now you can tell everyone you own a Picasso,* he'd said, taping a square of gauze to my chest. And now I had ruined it.

That was the morning Julisa was taking me to a rodeo protest. There were all these kids at her house, kids from PETA, Earth First!,

Voices for Animals. I used to protest the rodeos when I lived in Tucson. We stood with our signs and were abused by the cowboys. At one point Julisa lay down on her back and had us hog-tie her. *I want to know what it feels like,* she explained to the crowd. Her skirt came up around her waist, showing her white cotton underwear. The cowboys didn't know what to make of it. It was performance art. Actually, it made me think of sex. Petra had ruined me. That night I went out for drinks with my other Tucson friend, Laura. Like Julisa, Laura was theoretically bisexual. She always had a boyfriend, but her friends were all dykes. We drank beer at this bar that had a big candy dish full of free cigarettes. Free buffet, too. The living is easy in Tucson, if you can find a job. These kids were all students. Laura's new boyfriend was from Israel and was leading a toast in honor of a Jewish holiday. What's The Holiday? *Well, these people were going to kill us but we killed them instead.* That's Excellent, I said, and toasted. A girl sitting next to me kept hitting on me harder and harder the more she drank. She was a medical student at the university. She gave me cigarettes, eventually she was giving me hickeys, chewing on my neck right there at the table. I still had the hazy ghost of a hickey from Petra, and I figured if I could keep getting it touched up by other girls it'd be like it never went away. *I have beer in my car,* said the girl, so I went. I don't remember her name, it started with a vowel. Let's call her "Edie." Edie had a six of Newcastle in her back seat but no way to open them. I ended up breaking the neck of one on the curb. We strained it for glass with our teeth as we drank.

Come in the car, Edie urged. I Have To Meet Someone In An Hour, I said. The boy from the tattoo shop, who was going to take me to the dyke party. *Don't worry, I'll drive you,* she said. *Come on, come in.* It was a Camaro. I figured I should do it. For artistic reasons. I climbed into the car and Edie climbed on top of me and we made out. She had a Luther Vandross tape playing and she was singing it to me and it was really gross. What did she want me to do? Stare longingly at her? Somehow Edie found a way to kneel on the floor of the front seat and she got my pants down and put her face in my cunt. I kept thinking about how I was in a Camaro. I was doing it for Petra. She would really appreciate it. She did recently tell a crowd of people *Michelle had sex in a Camaro once,* and for a second I had no idea what she was talking about. Then I remembered. Edie. Edie, I Have To Go. I was wearing this necklace made of small fragrant beads of myrrh, and in our fumbling it snapped and fell between the car seats. *Oh,* Edie moaned. *I'm going to find that some day and it's going to make me really sad.* Jesus. She was worse than me. Edie drove me to the tattoo shop and walked me inside. I'm sure she was hoping I'd bring her to the party but I did not want her hanging on me all night. *I'm just another one of your conquests, huh?* she demanded as we approached the shop. *I'm just another notch on your belt.* She was pretty drunk. The piercing boy closed up the shop and I said my goodbyes to sulking Edie. I never saw her again. Since the piercing boy was only seventeen years old I was elected to buy liquor for him and his friend. They wanted Zima. Really? You Guys Drink

30

Zima? They insisted it was good. We were late getting to the party, which was a birthday bash for this girl, Daisy, who had phenomenal hips. I've never seen anything like it. She was very sexy. A few girls were in tuxedos, and Piercing Boy abandoned me pretty quickly for some other boy. I recognized a couple of girls from when I had lived in Tucson and started a Queer Nation, but they were involved in their own romantic intrigues, rushing in and out of rooms, huddling and confiding. No one was very interested in me. There was a lot of liquor and food, so I sat at the table and drank vodka and picked at the remnants of a chocolate coconut cake that was divine. I wrote a poem about Petra and her stupid girlfriend, and this lumberjacky girl in a baseball hat came over to see what I was writing. I told her all about Petra and her dumb girlfriend. I Guess I Shouldn't Be So Mean About Her Girlfriend, I confessed. *It's ok,* she said authoritatively. *It probably keeps you from turning your anger and criticism inward.* She was a therapist. I hated her. I thought we would never leave the party. Dykes are really sceney everywhere, not just in San Francisco. Anybody who doesn't think so is just part of the scene. I went home to Julisa's. She had a futon in every room in the house. I grabbed the one on the porch and slept outside in the warm cactus air.

I made a friend on the Greyhound back to San Francisco. Tony from Texas. I didn't ask for him, he chose me. He had long, permed hair and had been playing keyboard in a metal band before hopping the

Greyhound. His girlfriend had just broken up with him, so he went to the McDonald's where she worked, intending to kill himself in the men's room, but then decided to go to California instead. He had twenty bucks and a bag of psycho-pharmaceuticals. He called them his happy pills. They were in a little brown paper bag, and he'd shake the bag and say, *Let me know if you get stressed. I got happy pills.* Every time the bus driver took a break Tony would hand me a cigarette. I didn't even have to ask. Carltons. At one stop the driver announced there was a snack truck in case we were hungry. Oh Great, I said sarcastically, Skittles. Tony went and bought me two bags of Skittles. Tony, You Don't Have Any Money! *Take the Skittles, Michelle.* He was my boyfriend. I thought about all the Edies and Tonys. I didn't want to be anybody's Petra. Or was I an Edie? I was tired. Tony had this great shirt, Bikers For Jesus. It had a big motorcycle and it said Pray to the Best or Die Like the Rest. I could have gotten him to give it to me. I thought about trading him my ACT UP shirt, since he was in San Francisco now. At the Greyhound terminal I put Tony on a bus to Haight Street and waved goodbye.

I saw Petra at The Stud, rolling her fists and shaking her clanging wallet chain to that Nine Inch Nails cover of that Rod Stewart song. Could she be wearing spurs on her boots? Was she that cool? I heaved a sigh. One of burden, not romance. Hey, Petra. I showed her my new tattoo. I Was In Tucson, I explained. *Cool,* she said.

Maybe she hadn't noticed I was gone. Her girlfriend was back from her vacation down under. She was running around the bar with the slave owner from the sauna. They both had these Pebbles Flintstone ponytails on top of their heads. *I'm Tabitha,* she said, accosting me at the bar. *I just thought we should know each other.* She had this big, plasticky smile. Or maybe it was genuine. Yeah, I said, and shook her extended hand. She lingered awkwardly for a minute, and left. She looked a little disappointed.

2

Maybe I should tell you some more about Gwynn, sad sad Gwynn, the tortured poet who did not come to Arizona with me. Gwynn was an alcoholic, or had been once, I wasn't sure how the whole alcoholism, Twelve Step situation worked. Couldn't you simply have alcoholic periods, when you are sad or reckless and drinking for pathetic reasons, and then you get past it and cheer up and can drink again because it's so much fun to be drunk? Sobriety seemed a real stick-in-the-mud stance to take, but I guess drinking was a problem for Gwynn. It pushed her onto airplanes to follow different sad women from state to state. She had been to a few A.A. meetings in the Tenderloin, which just depressed her and increased her desire to drink, so she stopped showing up. Gwynn, she was always talking about wanting to be drunk and honestly I did want to encourage that, I wanted to go to a bar with her and let all the stuff sobriety pushed down be released so I could catch it in my palms and finally kiss her. She was just so sad. Melancholy was a fleshy wave permanently cresting on her face, she had to speak through it when she talked. I found her beautiful, but it only made her sadder to hear it. Gwynn liked women who were on the edge and dangerous or else really sad like herself, giving me an inferiority complex. I'd never been a drug addict or anorexic or even an alcoholic, never compulsively cut up my arms or puked secret after-dinner pukes. I'd been a prostitute for a little while, but that hadn't been self-destructive enough to count. A row of scars laddered down Gwynn's shoulder. She'd put them there herself. She'd trail her fingers up the scars making harp noises, and laugh. I wanted to take care of this woman. Get her to stop eating so much meat. Gwynn was very unhealthy. She smoked cigarettes in her apartment with all the windows shut until her cat stank like an ashtray.

Living right upstairs from my sad poet Gwynn was Justine, the older woman who had mangled Gwynn's heart off and on for the past four years. I'm sure it was mutual, but only Gwynn got my sympathy. I didn't know a lot about Justine, just that we shared the same birthday, a good omen, and that she sang in the choir of a progressive church, which I thought was inexcusably weird. It took me a while to realize how epic their affair had been. Gwynn didn't talk about it much. The stories she told were always about the

35

others, the drinkers she stalked at parties and begged to run away with her, to head for Nevada in her black and shiny VW Bug that really did look like a bug. Being a poet, Gwynn told beautiful stories about these unstable women. I would sit and listen and regret being so normal and well-adjusted, unable to be the challenge she seemed to need to keep her love life exciting. It was a doomed crush with some nice moments. We went to the movies once, we saw *The Piano* and hated it, cringed through the whole exquisitely shot thing mumbling *no oh no oh please don't make her fall in love with the rapist.* We drove out of San Francisco to the Serramonte Mall on the freeway because she was craving an Orange Julius. I got one too, but it was a big letdown. I didn't remember them as tasting so much like Creamsicles and I really hated Creamsicles. Gwynn ate an Orange Julius hot dog loaded up with so much garbage, I wondered if it was even vegetarian to kiss her. That trip to the mall was the first time I ever saw a Hot Dog on a Stick stand at the food court, and I gazed in horror at the high school girls who worked there, the towering striped hats that were their uniform. There was something really obscene about them jumping up and down on the old-fashioned lemonade press. Gwynn told me about how she tried to get a job at Hot Dog on a Stick when she was a teenager in southern California, but they wouldn't hire her because she wasn't slutty enough. We went to the surreal candy store where tubes of sickeningly bright candies cascaded down the walls and I bought a little bag of really toxic gum, blue gum and green gum, incredibly

36

sour. It raised your taste buds and made you wonder if your tongue was bleeding. We would chew a piece six or seven times then spit it out the car window and try a new one.

We were in Gwynn's Bug the night I told her I liked her. I Have A Crush On You, I said, and bit her arm. *Oh, Michelle,* she said sadly. She was especially depressed that night, driving us aimlessly around San Francisco until inspiration struck and she decided to take me to Pacific Heights to see where Danielle Steel lived. I had been told that Danielle Steel was invented by a bunch of heterosexual men who actually wrote those melodramatic books my mother and aunts loved. But Gwynn insisted she existed. *No, she's real, she lives in this big house right around here somewhere,* she said as we wound around the huge, expensive homes with floodlights and professional landscaping. I wanted to ring Danielle Steele's doorbell and tell her to stop oppressing my mother, but we couldn't find her house and I was starting to feel sick because I had forgotten to eat that day, so we went back to Gwynn's apartment and she fixed me beans with rice that weren't really cooked but I ate it all anyway because I was starving.

So the crush withered and died the way things that aren't being fed usually do. We became friends, good poet-friends, and one day I climbed the paved hills to her home for a visit, hazy and dejected because I had started the cycle of unrequited love anew, with a different sad poet, Willa, who also lived on Haight Street. Gwynn had a present for me, a t-shirt with a glitter decal of Yoda from *Star Wars. Do you really like it? I had a dream you didn't like it at all.* Yes, I Like It. I Love It. It was a baseball shirt with blue sleeves down to my elbows. I wore shirts like this in junior high, and then in high school worked in a shop at the mall making them, searing names and who-loves-whos onto the backs of t-shirts with this steamy huge machine that melted the white makeup I wore on my face, 'cause I was goth. *I thought it was so you,* she said, pulling up a chair. Gwynn had lawn furniture in her kitchen. I was sitting in this metal chair painted white, it looked like she stole it from an outdoor cafe. The ashtray cat was there, playing with a fake mouse with real animal fur glued to it, batting it under the radiator then smashing her feline skull trying to dig it back out. Gwynn told me about a wedding she'd gone to in Sacramento the previous weekend, and how she had had sex in the shower with the bride. And then the bridesmaids jumped in. *They were all straight, all strippers,* she said. *It was one of those straight parties with a lot of weird sexual energy. Ever been to one of those?* I Can't Believe You Had Sex With The Bride! *It wasn't really sex, we were just groping.* And then the phone rang as we talked and it was the bride and she wanted Gwynn to take her to the beach. Oh, I wanted one of Gwynn's cigarettes so badly and she wouldn't give one to me. Winston's are what my dead grand-mother smoked. I loved her so much, Aquarian like me, big round glasses she wore even while swimming, a gauzy kerchief tied under her chin to keep the chlorine off her hair. She took us south from Boston every summer, a long, hot ride to Disney World via the swampy trailer parks our Louisiana relatives lived in. My jovial grandfather, tearing over state lines, and Nana, who didn't know how to drive, clutching the dash like she was trapped on a carnival ride. Me and my little sister fighting sweaty in the back seat until our grandmother snaked her talon-tipped fingers our way, pinching up a bit of little girl leg skin to shut us up. She'd buy cartons of Winston's for cheap at Carolina gas stations and I'd steal a pack to smoke in the bathroom at Stuckey's.

Come On Gwynn, Just One. *No,* she said with that big sad face. *You said you weren't gonna smoke.* It was true. I wasn't going to smoke or drink or eat dairy or have sex, and I wasn't going to go visit Willa, who was only a block or two up the street. Willa, who did not love me. I asked Gwynn if it was bad to keep with a relationship that had you in love with someone who didn't love you back and she said yes. She was trying to be supportive, holding out on me with the cigarettes and telling me I shouldn't walk up the street to see the girl. Everything inside me felt chemical. Nicotine blood pushing me at the cigarettes. Phenylethylamine pushing me out of Gwynn's house to Willa, phenylethylamine being the neurotransmitter your body produces when you're in love, making you chase down the object of your desire because the mere sight of her activates the chemical and gets you high.

That's what Willa told me. She was so brainy, it's why I loved her. She also told me I didn't trigger her phenylethylamine. And there I was in withdrawal, thinking, she's just up the street, I'd only stay a minute. That's why I took Gwynn's bike that day, so I could change my life and stay away from Willa. Gwynn didn't want it anymore, her lungs couldn't pull it up the hills to her home. It was a black one-speed, a zillion years old with foot brakes and a big grated basket. Ok, I'll Take It. I thought it would help me get healthy since I'd pledged not to smoke or drink or do much of anything anymore. And I could ride with Dykes on Bicycles in the parade. And I couldn't go see Willa, 'cause there was no way in hell I could pump that relic up the hill to her house. I dragged it out of Gwynn's apartment and coasted home. It was fun being on a bicycle in San Francisco, cutting across Market Street to my home in the Mission. I took it by this bookstore to visit my friend Tatiana at work. She loved my new bike. She pedaled it up and down the street wishing she owned it. I was so sad that day. My heart was trying to climb from my body. Tatiana was sad too. She was with a woman who'd been straight her whole life and just couldn't fall in love with a girl. Are You In Love With Her? *Yeah.* That Sucks. *Let's make up rumors about each other and spread them all over town.* I made up a great one about her answering a suspicious help-wanted ad and it turning out to be an assistant-in-training position with a dyke bounty hunter. You know, a gun for hire. A killer. Everyone believed it because Tatiana's kind of psycho

40

and would maybe take a job like that. She told people that I was flying to Los Angeles to lead a feminist action protesting *The Love Connection*. That's So Stupid, I told her when I saw her again.

Oh, and then the bike got stolen. I rode it to work once and it made me feel like I'd swallowed fire. I'd been keeping it in the back hall because it was too heavy to be lifted up the stairs like some lightweight mountain bike. Then the alcoholic guy downstairs who lined his windows with empty vodka bottles fell down during a bad drunk and got shipped to the hospital. When he came home, he had a scab on his forehead and a wheelchair that could only be wheeled out the back hall so the bike had to go. It wasn't important to me, the bike, and it did not keep me away from Willa. So I didn't feel I owed it anything, and I wasn't about to buy a bike lock. I pedaled it over to my friend George's house on Sycamore and left it parked on his stairs behind the tall locked gate. George was one of the first kids I ever met in San Francisco, at a protest in front of a Baptist church where that reverend who made *The Gay Agenda* video and said gay people eat poop was cowering inside. Outside, me and George and bunches of other queers blocked traffic, got shoved around by unsympathetic dyke cops, pounded on the church doors and screamed *Nazi!* Someone wrenched the dreaded american flag from the flagpole and ran a happy homo rainbow flag up instead. George and I were both exhausted by activism, it was the last action we'd go to for a long while and probably the last time we submitted to chanting, ever. We had lost our idealism, but gained a friendship. Willa said I wanted the bike to get stolen or else why would I leave it on Sycamore, where George's own bike was stolen by the Stolen Bike Ring that lurked on the corner. She said it was like how I call in sick a lot when I want a job to fire me. That wasn't true. I didn't want the bike stolen. I just didn't care if it was. I only cared later when I was tripping on mushrooms and this girl Iris said, *You know, I really loved that bike, I knew it was going to get stolen and I just loved it. I thought about stealing it myself but then I thought that would be weird.* Oh Iris, you should have. Now it's gone forever. If any of you ever see me treating something badly, carelessly, you can take it. Honest, it's yours.

3

I was trying to get fired from my job at the courier company. I was doing it for Willa. It was incredible, the effort it took. My entire history of employment, starting back at the fluorescent-lit supermarket where I swished, Catholic-school-skirted, through the sawdusted aisles to collect my drawer and insert it into my register with the proud purpose of one who has never worked before, has always seemed full of horribly precarious arrangements. In my heart I knew I wasn't cut out for it, employment. I was irresponsible, had no work ethic, was raised by parents who called in sick regular as weekends, and it was only a matter of time until I made The Big Fuck-Up and got canned. But this job would just not fire me. The courier company used cars, not bikes. I sat at a computer and took orders from different financial district companies, occasionally deleting calls from companies I disagreed with politically. I was flat on my futon with the girl I loved with a fierce and holy love, I had the phone at my ear and in my weakest tone possible was explaining to my boss why I couldn't come in. I was really sick. *Michelle, you have got to come in.* I had just done this last week, probably the week before. *Your job is seriously in jeopardy if you don't show up.* Well . . . Ok, I said, hurt. What if I really had been sick? They didn't know. I'm On My Way, I said, and rolled back over to curl around Willa. She was this thing, this marvelous thing too good for this world that had tortured and tormented her, locked her up in stale institutions and driven her to slice up her skin, run barefoot through New England snow 'til her feet were dead slabs of meat from the freezer. She was my job. I didn't have time for two. *Are you going to work?* she asked, and I pressed my cheek to her scalp's clammy stubble. Her neon mohawk curled up from her crown like something from a Dr. Seuss book. No, I was not going to work. I was an artist, a lover, a lover of women, of the oppressed and downtrodden, a warrior really. I should have been somewhere leading an armed revolution in the name of love and no, I was not going to work. Willa didn't work. I mean, she did, but it's a stretch to call it work. She bartended at a dyke bar a few nights a week, drank free beer, and bummed all her cigarettes. People paid three bucks at the door to have the same experience she was having at her job. All week she was free, writing angsty brilliant poems, drawing comic books, painting gi-

44

gantic painful pictures, you know, *living*. I wanted to live. With my tortured tormented girlfriend who, incidentally, still forbade me to refer to her as my "girlfriend" and was pretty sure that she would never fall in love with me, although she did think she would fall in love again, sometime in the future. I had ceased to care. My love for her was religious, it was patriotic; like god or country it was something I pledged myself to in service of something huge and perfect that I was honored to have anything to do with. Our sex was adolescent, shy and blanketed, done through layers of flannel pajamas that rarely came off. In a very Catholic way I felt this made it more special, reaching out to the pile of cloth that was her body and pushing deeper, finding the sharp jutting bone of her hip or the softer ball of her breast. She was a message, a coded message to be deciphered with careful intelligence. With time I would under-stand all of her and she would love me passionately, but that would never happen so long as I had to pull myself away from her every 8:00 a.m., leaving her fully clothed and sleeping, to wake into the day without me.

I grabbed the cordless phone and dialed up my job again. My boss wasn't in so I talked to the dispatcher, this scraggly, overworked bearded guy with a martyr complex that was fitting considering he did in fact look like Jesus Christ. Listen, I said, Tell Clarisse I Tried To Come To Work, I Was On My Way, And . . . I Just Started Puking, Right On Muni. I Had To Get Off The Bus, And I Was There On Mission, Just Puking On The Sidewalk, So I Had To Come Home . . . Tell

45

Her, Ok? Big sigh from Jesus. I hung up. *Michelle,* said Willa, her tone mildly disapproving, *are you going to get fired?* I Guess So, I sighed bravely, and lay back onto the futon. I had an awful time quitting jobs. It was so irresponsible, and being inherently irresponsible, I knew I had to be vigilant. So instead I would make them fire me. I have had girlfriends who employ this strategy in relationships, which is bad, but in regards to employment it is ok. *What are you going to do?* she asked. Oh, I Don't Want To Work, I whined. I Want To Hang Out With You. Maybe I Should Start A Nightclub. There was still a decent wad of bills stashed in my hiking boot, the result of a successful traveler's check scam. You get a bunch of traveler's checks, big bills, and cash them one by one at little shops, pocket the change, then tell the check company you got robbed. I Was Pickpocketed On BART, The Checks Are Gone. *Oh, you don't know how many people that happens to,* said the teller as she flicked the crisp bills at me. *It's really terrible.* So I could live off my illegal profits for a little while, but eventually I would need true employment. Something mindless and occasional, leaving me lots of time to write and further the seduction of Willa. I could whore. I had done it, vowed I would never do it again because it was so gross and weird, and I had actually indulged in a little New-Agey prayer to the cosmos, promising to never again participate in such a negative profession if it would please send me a job, and the universe did in fact get me a job, the one at the courier company that I was trying to get fired from.

So I was by my phone in the living room, poring through the seamy back pages of the local papers, circling opportunities under the Adult Employment heading. Only one house was hiring, International Variety, ladies from all over the world, right, a pseudo-erotic spice rack. I figured I could be the Polish girl. Was it ok for me to do this? When I thought back to what it'd been like, my memories were soaked in a hazy liquor of confusion and panic. I realized how much better I was now, my shit was really together, and if I had done a pretty good job of handling it back when I was such a mess, now I'd be a champ. I rang the lady up. I said I wanted a job. Oh, Yeah, I've Worked Before, I told her, all cosmo-like. In Boston And In Tucson. *Oh, that's great,* she said, relieved. *What do you look like? Do you have any tattoos?* No, I lied. We arranged an interview at a cafe around the corner from my house and I went to work wrangling up an outfit that looked feminine and wasn't ripped. I had a wig, the black Cleopatra-style one, pretty basic but it would hide my hair, which was now choppy and green. My turtleneck was certainly a little stuffy for a whore but it would hide the heart tattoo on my chest, whose aorta stretched above the neckline of every other shirt I owned. A nice skirt. Obviously if I were hired, I would have to go shopping. I had thrown out all my old whore clothes, thinking I would not be doing this again, but life is full of surprises.

And I did get hired, despite my doubts about the authenticity of my wig. And I did go shopping. High-heeled shoes, ten bucks at

Payless. A couple of cheap ten-dollar teddies, lace and mesh, from this store on Haight Street that caters to rock stars, strippers and drag queens. The place was packed with feathers and lamé and sequined spandex. The register guy asked, *Are you a performer?* and I said, Yeah, Actually, and got the ten percent performers' discount. Dresses that were sexy but didn't reveal the forbidden tattoo were rare, but I did find this skintight green velvet number with a neckline that raised into a cute little hood, and a hot pink retro dress that fit oddly but hid the ink. I walked through town with my special purchases. The best part of whoring was the secret preparations, when you were alone with your occupation, feeling like an outlaw. At Walgreens I grabbed a bunch of condoms and a thing of lube. Since arriving in San Francisco I had discovered real lube like Probe or Wet, stuff you dripped onto gloves and used with girls, but for this purpose I chose a tin tube of K-Y, like old times. Back in my little room it all sat, a pile on the carpet topped by my wig's heavy tangle as I leaned out my window, smoking. My roommate Laurel came in and poked at the pile with her toe. I felt funny telling people about my new old profession. Before, I was so angry and hated everyone and relished disclosing such information, daring whoever it was to judge me or ask a dumb question. I ached for a fight, but usually the information just scared people, made them act small somehow. *Maybe I should do it,* Laurel said thoughtfully. *How much will you make?* One Hundred And Ten Dollars A Call. Technically an hour though it rarely took so long. I figured I'd make about $350 a day,

48

more while I was still new. The house was in Marin and I would work only one day a week, less than Willa even. The woman who ran the house would pick me up and drop me off. I was set. Laurel sat and smoked with me, fingering the weaves of my new lingerie. You Don't Want To Do It, I said. It Fucks You Up. *Well, why are you doing it?* It Doesn't Fuck Me Up. But It Fucks Lots Of Girls Up. It's Fucked-Up Work. I blew my smoke out the window. I Don't Know, Maybe You'd Be Fine. Or Maybe You'd Spend All Your Earnings On Therapy. I tried on my new look. The mesh teddy was cool but it slid up the crack of my butt and drove me crazy. The dress fit cozily over it, I wobbled in my heels, and the wig looked like a wig.

Willa called, from a party around the corner—why didn't I come? Well, I said, laughing into the mirror, I've Got All My New Work Clothes On. *Wear them over,* she said lightly. *Come show us.* I Am Not Leaving The House Like This. *Oh, come on, please,* she pleaded. I did, I walked around the corner like the whore of Babylon and rang the bell. Lots of girls were there. *You look beautiful,* they said, and I hated them for thinking it was pretty. It was wretched. I was a fool. Instantly I wished I had not done this, brought this weird decision out into my life like it was nothing more than a funny costume, watching everyone treat it so lightly and me right there with them, laughing in my lipstick. Everything's cool, don't get '70s feminism on me, ok? At least I'm not paying taxes, yeah fuck you uncle sam. Everyone seemed subtly uncomfortable as I sat on the floor like a sick centerpiece, drinking mimosas. Willa didn't say anything.

Later it was night and millions of questions hung in her eyelashes as I turned off the light and climbed on top of her pajamas. My tiny room was lit with bunches of candles that I fervently hoped would warm the freezing space. It's like whoever built the houses in San Francisco figured it was California and always warm and installed no heating systems. Every winter you woke up with frozen clouds of breath above your face. I thought of my candles as little fireplaces that would keep me and my lover warm. As life and sex with Willa progressed from a few weeks to a few months, my PJs had made it down to my knees, then ankles, but hers remained snug to her hips. After much begging she joined me in the shower only to burst into tears beneath the wet spray, moving her arms desperately around her body, wishing they were large enough to hide it. Oh Willa, Willa, I Didn't Know, I Had No Idea. You're Beautiful, I said stupidly, and grabbed gritty handfuls of some smelly exfoliation product and lathered her up, like I could scrub her feelings away. I didn't understand. Willa was smart, she was the smartest person I knew. In bed by the candles she read to me from old diaries, taking me slowly through the pages of her life, solidifying what I always knew, that she was a genius, a vessel for some kind of wonderful wisdom that I was born to serve. How could she not know she was beautiful? In bed I slid my leg above her flannel crotch and tried to find a rhythm, and she would grab my hips and shift me, shift me again, pull me so that my pubic bone came down on the layers of clothes that I could only assume cushioned her clitoris. *Like this,* she'd hiss, and I would lose the rhythm or the location, I couldn't tell where anything was with all the fabric, and she would get frustrated and snap, *Forget it.* Willa, I said helplessly. I didn't know what to do when it all turned so sharp, the sex, her, the candles that now seemed like fire hazards, burning all night in a city prone to earthquakes.

I can only explain the whorehouse in Marin by reference to what I knew before, the house in Boston filled with jaded, money-hungry women, sarcastic and cynical, moving the tricks through the door with artistic efficiency. They bonded over cigarettes, about how stupid the men were, how weird were the things they liked or wanted. I couldn't wait to meet the other hookers, make some special new friends. Linda, the Marin boss, picked me up on the corner in her little car and drove into the Haight to grab another girl, who climbed into the car with an enormous suitcase, this blonde woman in a cute, country-bumpkin outfit. I recognized her immediately. My very first job in San Francisco had been reading tarot cards at a little shop on weekends. The owner was a British girl into the rave scene. She sold rave music and incense and oils and people would come and hang out and talk about raves and DJs, and this woman was one of them. I Know You, I said, excited. When I first started whoring, I suspected that maybe all women whored, all of us doing it and keeping it a secret, thinking we were the only ones occupying this silent landscape. I Was The Tarot Girl, I said, and recognition hit her face and quickly bled into horror. *You can't tell anyone,* she snapped, mad at me for knowing her. Who Would I Tell? I asked. She stared at me, suspicious. I was trying to bond and now she hated me. I Never See Those People, I assured her. I'm A Dyke, I Only See Dykes. *Yeah, you're gay,* she said, remembering. *How do you like working?* Well. . . . It's A Job, I said. The boss stared ahead, driving. *I am wired for this work,* said the woman, stretching out in the back seat like a big cat. Really? *Yeah . . . I was made for it.* Oh, I said. I never knew what to think about whores who liked it. I rarely met them, and when I did, I could only think that they had low expectations of life or sex, but that seemed so judgmental I didn't trust it.

We drove over the Golden Gate Bridge, my first time. It's actually orange. The house was this quaint little cabin practically in the woods, with a wooden deck that overlooked thick tangles of blackberry bushes. The boss told me there were raccoons and even deer out there. I stayed outside on the porch as much as I could that day, smoking in the cold with a book of poetry, trying to make it romantic somehow, but I felt like a train had come and taken me out of my life, leaving me in a secret country where no one could find me. I immediately understood that I had gotten myself in over my head. This was no cynical slacker cathouse, these girls were professionals. On the coffee table was the house handbook, the rules all the new girls were expected to read. Inside were policies on appearance and conduct, a section that elaborated on how we were there to serve the client and make him happy and absolutely spend the entire

52

hour with him, it would be noted if a girl's calls ended early. My stomach splashed down to some watery part of my guts. Angie, the blonde girl, and a beautiful, sullen, dark-haired girl kneeled on the floor by suitcases packed with incredible collections of exquisite lingerie and elaborate sequined dresses designed to showcase bodies that a lot of work went into. They entered the bathroom, shimmering smocks in hand, and exited something bigger than female, shining like Las Vegas in the homey little cottage. My shabby thrift store outfit was no match, my wiggy wig that I soon learned was intolerable to have on my head eight hours straight, itching and slipping crooked. Linda, I confessed, My Hair Isn't Real. It's A Wig. *It looks real,* she shrugged. Well, Can I Not Wear It Between Calls Because It Really Makes My Head Itch. Linda didn't care. She was pretty amused by my butchered, unnaturally colored hair, as were the two girls sunk into the couch with a copy of *Hustler,* talking about their future tit jobs. *You need it in this work,* Angie said earnestly. This was her career. The sulky girl didn't talk to me. We got off to a bad start when I told her my real name and asked for hers. *Here I'm Veronica,* she snapped, and looked at me like I was crazy. Because I was the new girl I got a lot of calls that day and made over six hundred dollars, three weeks' wages at the courier job that, can I tell you, would not stop calling my house leaving messages like, *If you don't call us soon and tell us what's going on, your job is really going to be in jeopardy.* Oh God, I wailed, Why Won't They Just Fire Me? *Why don't you just quit?* asked Laurel. I

53

Can't, I moaned. This upscale Marin whorehouse allowed the men to come and pick from the lineup of women like we were donuts in a pastry case. It was so humiliating and insulting. The other house I worked at would never allow that. This Isn't A Candy Store, we'd bark at the men who tried. In the cottage foyer I stood, hands at my side, staring at the man as he stared at Angie and Sulky-Face, deciding which one he would have. So competitive. The lucky girl would grab his hand and pull him into a bedroom like they were going to have some big party.

That night I took my roommates out for margaritas. I Made All This Money, I said guiltily. They gasped when I said how much. *Are you ok?* Yeah, I'm Fine, I shrugged. Was I shallow? How come I was ok? Willa came to my bed like she did every single night, still insisting she was not in love with me, and I believe that she was not. Why was she there? What was going on inside her, inside everyone, the invisible motors that kept us chugging toward all the things we didn't want? When she started to touch me, she curled up into an autistic ball of flannel, face smashed into the pillow. What? *I don't want to touch you like they do.* Oh Willa, You Couldn't, I said, pulling her back to me. You're Nothing Like That, It's Not At All The Same. Everything was slightly off, like a tab of acid melting slowly into my bloodstream. The same but different. I went somewhere she would never go and brought a loneliness back and I had to climb over it to reach her. The fact that we had never had safe sex worried Willa now and she made sure to wear gloves, which I thought was smart

54

but I suddenly felt contaminated, and upset that I brought her all this worry. So I wrote a poem about it and read it at an open mic and she got mad at me because now everyone would know she'd had unsafe sex and would think she was dumb or diseased. And the woman who ran the open mic realized from the poem that I was whoring and she freaked out and told me all the horrible things that would happen to me, and if I came and worked for her at her small press I could get experience and be able to find a real job, though of course she couldn't pay me. And my period was late. Every day my panties were clean, spotless, and Willa would ask again and again, *Did you get your period yet god it's really late did your period come yet?* She didn't say anything else and she didn't need to. I went to the local lesbian Walgreens and bought a pregnancy test, completely paranoid that one of the eight hundred dykes who lived on the block would bump into me as I handed over my cash. I went home and pissed on the little strip. I had absolutely had safe sex with these men, although not as safe as Angie, who, in addition to condoms, stuffed one of those horrible, frothing contraceptive sponges up there, but I was safe. And I wasn't pregnant. This is fucking crazy, I thought as I triple-bagged the evidence and threw it in the trash. My period came and Willa was calmed.

One day Linda booked me a call with Novato Bob. All the tricks gave regular names, then some word to distinguish them from the roster of Bobs, Johns and Mikes. Linda gave me some vague disclaimer beforehand, like he was intense but harmless and she had seen him and all the girls had seen him. Novato Bob pinned me to the bed and held my head to the mattress. Don't Do That, I snapped, and he snapped back, *Come on,* annoyed, and it makes sense that I don't remember much of the call except that he was rough in a way that scared me. And I knew he wouldn't hit me, just fuck me, and did it matter that he hated me while he did it? It's not rape if I knew I was going to end up fucked when I walked in the room. And I did not stop the call, I took it because that essentially was my job, to take it, lie still until it was done, take my money and leave. I was waiting on the corner the next week for my boss to pick me up and I felt my throat go thick like I'd swallowed something big that stuck there and I knew I couldn't go. I went home. It was early still so I climbed back in bed, alone, without Willa. I quit my job. I quit Willa too, eventually I did, because she was not in love with me and I was an artist, a lover, a lover of women, a warrior really, too noble to stick it out in a dead-end job 'til they saw fit to fire me.

4

Pride Weekend was the perfect weekend to leave a lover and hop right into a new one. The city was buzzing, and I was gliding up 18th Street with a brand new girl and a 40, while the June sun was still high and shining. Passing the bottle back and forth, snug in its wrinkled brown paper. I just love to be drunk in the daylight. Everything turns liquid and golden with me moving right through it. The air's bright shimmer washed away the dead feeling I'd had since that last night with Willa, when she'd slammed her head against my plaster walls again and again, the awful dull thud of it louder than my own shrill voice sounding out the terms of our breakup. I hated the sight of her small body lurching toward the wall, it made me furious. Willa, Stop. My room was like a tight dark box, there was hardly room for air with all the terrible motion and mania, a crazy whirling like bad weather moving in fast. I didn't understand. Willa loved me, but it was a friendly love we could keep between us while we both went off in search of wild crazy love. It was best for both of us—didn't Willa want to fall in love? Each bash of her body up against the wall made me think of her scars, her diaries, all the things that made me think of her as too precious and fragile, the thing that sewed me to her, and here it was unfurling its awful pages into my bedroom and it made me want to kill her. Willa, Stop. It was so unnecessary. Not romantic. I was crying. Her boomerang face was too much a dark blur to see if she was too, but her voice was a warble. I Can't Take This, I said and walked into the hall. It was so late, how could my roommates be sleeping through this? *Fuck you!* Willa cried, and that was it. Get Out! I screamed. I heard motion from behind Laurel's door. Willa ran down the stairs. In her pajamas. *Fuck you!* she yelled again, crying. The door slammed and rattled. My room was still. Something should have been broken, there should be shards on the carpet or plaster dusting off the walls, but everything was fine. Like nothing had happened. Laurel's door creaked open. *Michelle?* I went into her room and smoked with her in the dark, our bodies folded out the window, leaning over the empty street. She Was Slamming Her Head Into The Wall, I said. Laurel smoked. I didn't know how I could go back into my room and sleep on that futon, everything vibrating with Willa. Her energy had reached an intensity capable of imprinting itself forever on the place, a ghost, Willa forever hurtling toward my wall. But the next day, it was gone. My room. Bits of everywhere I'd been so far sitting on the shelves, shriveled cactus bits from Tucson, a tiny sparkling geode from the Grand Canyon, broken bits of china from ships crashed off the coast of Provincetown and washed into the harbor. All I could see of Willa was the gigantic bag of thrift store socks she'd bought me, horrified at my tiny collection of five. A bright and jumbled pile, like Willa with her Crayola mohawk and mismatched clothes. I couldn't think about her. I thought about the new girl. Her name was Iris.

Iris was the quiet girl on the bike outside the club everyone went to. I knew her roommates, sort of. I first met her a few weeks before ending it with Willa, on Harrison Avenue at three o'clock in the morning, with a neon sign blinking above our heads and people roaring out of the nearby alley on motorcycles. A little farther down the street was the steady hum of trucks and buses filling up at the diesel station on the corner. Iris was on her bicycle, the big wheels lifting her off the ground. She had her helmet on and she looked about eleven years old. Some kind of striped shirt, orangey stripes, and jeans. Then I saw her again the very next night, at a party Willa had brought me to. There she was again. I was on the back porch where Willa's last girlfriend, a notorious drunk named Kitty, was smashing teacups on the wooden floor. I thought she was great. Iris's roommates, who I was sitting with at a little table, thought she was obnoxious. Candice was like the head roommate, kind of cold I thought, critical and detached, with different-colored eyes, like David Bowie. She had lived in Georgia with Iris, and the two of them were gossiping about people I would never know, the women's studies professor they had had a crush on, girls who were dumb or girls who were cool. They made no effort to include me, yet I couldn't bring myself to leave the table. I just knew that if I could find the right entry into the conversation I could say something brilliant and captivate Iris. Can I Have A Cigarette? I asked Candice, and she nodded coolly and passed me her pack. Another teacup sailed above our heads as Kitty howled and stomped down the backstairs and into the party. *Who is that?* Candice asked, and kind of glared at me like I was responsible. Iris smiled, a little smile. She was pretty. Her face looked young. I ran into her later in the evening when I was raiding the hostess's refrigerator. I had found a jar of pickles, and nothing is better when you're really drunk and kind of dehydrated than a pickle. I think I was even shamefully stealing sips of the salty green juice. It seems like such a gross thing to enjoy, like beef jerky. There was Iris. Want A Pickle? I asked. Maybe she took one. I remember I kissed her hand. My seduction technique is best filed under Obvious. I told her to meet me the next day at the Bearded Lady for waffles and neither of us showed up. But she turned up a week later, part of the late-night gaggle of kids I was smuggling into the anarchist labor union that had forgotten to take away my keys before firing me so many months ago, for running away to Tucson and leaving the office unmanned. With a lack of Willa freeing up my time, I spent my evenings sneaking into the closed-up office building, which was above a strip club on Market, to use the xerox machine and the computers. First all by myself, chain-smoking and gazing out the windows at the esoteric glowing eyeballs and clouds on the Oddfellows Temple across the street, at the drunken brawls outside the check-cashing place on the corner, following with my eyes the saunters of ponytailed girls on their way to work at the peepshow downstairs. Later I got lonely and started throwing zine parties. The kids I invited would stand on the street six stories down, the lively corner of 7th and Market, and they would scream *Revolution!* and I would take the elevator downstairs and let them scurry in. It was really fun. After getting completely wired on coffee I would start in on wine, Rene Junot, six bucks for a wide bottle, or some squat green grenades of Mickey's, or whiskey, or whatever people brought, and everyone who came would have to write something and it would get printed out on the computer and I would stick it all together with a gummy yellow glue stick and crank it out on the xerox machine.

The final time we did this Iris was there. She made me so nervous, as she sat at a glowing computer and hardly talked. I am always compelled to fling myself at these quiet girls whose quietness only makes me talk larger, talk faster and faster to fill up the nervous silence they seem to sit inside so comfortably. I would babble to Iris until I felt a warm flush rise and I felt like a jerk and settled back into my computer. Then Iris would say something simple and I would launch into another grand show and finally some more kids shouted

Revolution! out on the street and I was saved. I think that Iris presented herself to me as some kind of writer, or maybe I just made her into one, the way I had assumed for the first half of my life that my mother was a writer, simply because I loved her and identified with her and figured since I was a writer she would have to be one too. Iris did write a little. She wrote good. Her contribution to that night's zine was a rant about how she hated her grandfather. She was inspired by the solemn portrait of the union's grand martyr, Joe Hill, that hung above her computer, and she wrote about how her bourgeois grandfather probably hated Joe Hill and was glad that he'd been killed by The Man during the general strike long ago. I was impressed that Iris knew who Joe Hill was. I hadn't. The only reason I got hired by the union, which kept only two paid employees, was that a dyke in the union who knew me from my Queer Nation/clinic defense/queer street patrol/AIDS outreach days in Boston had snuck me into the computer system as a five-year East Coast union organizer, and told all the old guys who ran the outfit a big fat lie about how I had successfully organized exotic dancers in Boston. I didn't feel so bad about taking the job since I did want to be an anarchist labor union organizer and had big dreams of returning capitalism to the workers. But the union turned out to be nothing but a historical society of irritating gray-haired bureaucrats dedicated to preserving Joe Hill's ashes, and little more. The ashes sat in a film canister inside a gold paper bag, locked up in a glass case. See That? I asked Iris. That's Joe Hill. His Ashes Are In There. Once when I was really mad at the union for not letting me involve us with Food Not Bombs, I concocted a great plan of revenge. I would steal Joe Hill and take him on a road trip, free his restless, noble spirit from the gilded cage they had locked him in. I would take photos of him in front of famous statues and landmarks across the country and publish them in a zine about the sad state of anarchist labor unions today. I would steal the union's membership roster and do a daily raffle in which some lucky worker won a pinch of Joe. I loved imagining the gritty bone and ash between my fingers as I dropped a pile of the man into an envelope and set him free. The best idea I never acted on.

Iris chose a really cool font for her anticapitalist tirade. It looked very handsome folded into the book and was my favorite page. Bobby wrote a funny bitch about the O.J. Simpson thing, Laurel wrote a love manifesto for a girl she had a crush on, George xeroxed his tongue and wrote about stealing from his job, and Suzanne wrote about waiting in line for food stamps. It was a great zine and it took us 'til six in the morning to finish it. I was just so blasted, moving around the office filled with cigarette smoke, collating the pages, and then boom the xerox machine ran out of ink and I went into some kind of mania, determined to finish producing this zine that we had put so much earnest love and creativity into. There didn't seem to be any more ink cartridges. A bunch was actually on the shelf right above my head but I never looked up. Instead I found a plastic jug filled with the leftover toner of other dead ink cartridges, a fine black powder, some inches of it. I removed the spent cartridge from the humming machine, and I stabbed a good-sized hole into the plastic. I made a crappy funnel, and I poured in the recycled toner. I did this in the back room that served as a storage area for volumes and volumes of historical writings on socialist and anarchist labor politics, and also cardboard boxes full of t-shirts, which my friends stole. They were pretty cool shirts, they had black cats on the front and said An Injury to One Is an Injury to All. I was so bitter and disillusioned with the union I didn't much care about the theft, and I took one as well. But in this back room was a little porcelain saucer of a sink, above which I transferred the toner, creating small but potent clouds of toxic black dust that settled in thick clumps to be washed into the bay. A bunch got on me, too, on the red calico dress I loved even though people said I looked like a Deadhead in it. I had chopped the dress up here and there to give it an edge, but it still looked kind of crunchy. I patched up the gash in the toner cartridge with masking tape, plugged it back into the machine and finished all the zines. The head of the union called me for weeks afterward, needing to "talk to me about something." I never called him back. Ultimately he changed the locks and that was the end of the zine parties.

I thought maybe I would fall in love with Iris. She was new to San Francisco. Of course. Everyone was. She came from a little part of Georgia where she'd been constantly fighting the way you constantly have to fight when you're queer in a small place, starting direct action groups, getting up in the middle of the night to vandalize the town, things like that. Iris had some good stories, but most important she was revved up for love. That Pride Weekend we went to a party up on someone's roof. It was small, a group of girls sitting around on the pebbly tar paper drinking their small bottles and chatting. I had my big bottle and Iris close enough to give me shivers, and I was much too manic for such calmness. Nearby, thousands of dykes were convening to march through the city. It was exciting. The beer made me glow so I felt like a god, that powerful, up high on a roof with the city stretched out beneath me. We were cuddly, holding hands or walking with arms slung around each other like we were girlfriends already. We left the roof party and met up with a gang of girls in front of the gay cafe on 16th Street that wouldn't let us use the bathroom. A big problem. Fucking elitist cafe. We were dykes, we had to pee. George had made long neon stickers that said Assimilationist and we were sticking them on the cafe windows, and also on any nice cars we came upon. There were also stickers that said Trash and Smelly Dyke and those got stuck on asses and t-shirts. The march took so long to get started. We were standing in the street at 18th and Castro surrounded on all sides by millions of lesbians, trapped. Everyone needed to pee or else needed to get more beer and you just couldn't move. It was almost too much. Someone handed me a drum, a bucket on a rope, and I beat it with a wooden spatula. Iris was getting me winks of approval from friends and acquaintances. I showed her off like a new tattoo. She was awfully cute, and her southern voice drove me crazy. It sounded both tough and charming, and then there were her slinky blue eyes, and her big lips like a crimson pillow with a pearly corner of tooth poking out. She had that rakish look I die for, and when she opened her mouth, forget it. We were marching around, slapping on the fake drum. I could see Willa's glowing head bobbing in the crowd up ahead. The need to avoid her perfectly tempered my bliss with drama. We were trying to be friends that weekend, but I couldn't handle it. I'd think that I could and then *whomph,* right in the stomach. Why hadn't she loved me the way I wanted her to? Had I given up too soon? It had been such a manic breakup, it almost felt like I'd imagined the whole thing. And there was a post-breakup law in effect that I couldn't be affectionate with anyone in Willa's presence until her adjustment period passed. This was understandable but also mean because she bartended at the only bar worth going to, so I might as well have stayed home.

The march wound its way back to a stage set up in the middle of the Castro, it was amazing. The night stayed warm, and all these dykes were jumping around in the street. Girls were performing on the stage, there was a fisting demonstration. A dramatic green-haired girl did a convulsive dance until she fell off the edge. I had my shirt off, I was sweaty, blitzed, everyone was. Girls were tugging down their pants and squatting to pee in the middle of everything. I had moved from beer to wine and back. I figured I could make out with Iris if Willa wasn't paying attention and of course that got sloppy. I opened my eyes in the middle of a big tonguey one and Willa was standing right there. Naturally she acted like she didn't care, why bother, everyone was having such a great time. I think she bummed a cigarette from me. I remember a highchair right in the middle of the street, and a really drunk woman locked in it, banging on the tray, making people feed her Coronas. The lesbians started to disperse, but we decided to take the party back to Iris's house. We were looking for a cab to deliver us to the Mission, and there was Willa, kind of sulking, very drunk and wanting to come along. Well, Ok, If You Think That Would Be All Right For You. She was moping, quiet, her face wrinkling down toward the ground. *Well,* do you *want me to go?* She was so indecisive, it drove me crazy. Listen, Do What You Want, But Make Sure You Can Deal With It. She climbed into the cab like a kid being taken to a hospital or her grandparents', someplace awful. Then there was this strange woman in the cab with us, no one knew who she was, she just wanted to join us so we let her. She was older and had a long drunken story about her ex-lover and a Greyhound bus and how she had no place to go. I think once she opened her mouth we realized it was a mistake to let her come along. She had the driver stop at a store, where she jumped out and returned with more beer and a *Hustler.* She was showing us all the pictures and asking what we thought. *Check her out, that one's hot.* She was like someone's drunken father. At Iris's we threw the magazine out the window while she was in the bathroom. *Hey, where's my* Hustler? Laurel gave her a lecture about how *Hustler* was gross, not suitable dyke pornography. We all started arguing about politics and this woman was definitely the target. She was for all the Wrong Things. Willa slumped on a chair looking rather autistic. Eventually she got up and sat by herself in the hallway. People were looking to me for an explanation. I shrugged. She wasn't my responsibility anymore. Someone finally called her a cab and she left without saying goodbye.

I spent the night at Iris's. Her futon was beneath a windowsill that these pigeons lived on. They made loud cooing noises the whole night and I was enchanted. You Have Pigeons, I said. It was like being in the wilderness or something, sleeping beside this pack of loud birds. The awkwardness of not knowing someone's body, I had no idea what to do. I shoved my fingers into her. *You can do it harder,* she said, and I did. These girls. I couldn't believe I wasn't hurting her. I remembered Petra, the last place my fist had been. The vagina is not a delicate place, I was learning this slowly. I worked my hand into Iris, who sucked and chewed on the inky red heart that marked the place my real heart churned. She was so intense. *I feel like you're squeezing my heart,* she said. I pressed myself against her and bit her neck, my hand grasping. Things with Willa had been much more intellectual than sexual, so this was a nice switch.

68

We must have slept only an hour or two when Iris's room-mates woke us up. There was a brunch, and then we were all sup-posed to ride with Dykes on Bicycles in the Pride Parade. I was still drunk when I woke up, sick but with all this hazy energy. I had to go back home to change. Laurel had spent the night on the extra futon in Iris's kitchen and she was still drunk too. We stumbled home through the Mission together, stopping for coffee and car-rot juice and a bagel I could hardly get down. Out in front of Esta Noche, drag queens were teetering into a decorated convertible. Their makeup was detailed and flawless. They must have gotten up at dawn. Back at my house I found a message from Willa on the answering machine, saying venomous, unbelievably mean things. It was horrible, the things she was saying. *Why don't you write a fucking poem about it!* I was so upset, I sat on the toilet crying and Laurel assured me that yes, my ex-girlfriend was crazy but I should just get over it because we were late for the parade. I got up and wiped my face and changed into my marvelous Pride Day outfit, a yellow terry cloth sundress, strapless, with rainbow elastic that held it to my body. I had big purple hair, a green studded collar and roller skates. I looked insane. The guy at the BART station wouldn't let me on wearing the skates so I had to ride the train in my socks.

Market Street was mobbed, it was wonderful. I was over-whelmed with tender feelings for my community, but I also hadn't slept and was seriously worried about not making it through the parade. Laurel had her bike and no shirt on. She had stickers saying This Is Sexist stuck over her nipples. We waited at the front of the parade and watched Dykes on Bikes roar by, then jumped in with Dykes on Bicycles, pedaling behind the motorcycles like little sisters. Ashley had a milk crate rigged to the back of her bike. I grabbed it and she pulled me the whole length of Market Street. We were a fabulous team, people were cheering. I managed not to wipe out, though it was scary going over the grates. Iris was there on her bike, topless, turning around and grinning at me. Willa was also there, pretending I didn't exist. Fine. If she wanted to act like a child, that was fine. Down by the water where the parade ended I drank more beer, got stoned, managed to digest a veggie burger and some rice, and left. I went home to change into something less ridiculous, shoes without wheels. I dragged Iris with me. She collapsed on my futon with an astrology book. She was reading Aquarius and verifying my personality. She wanted to take a nap. No Way, I said, and put on *Live Through This,* loud. There was a free Tribe 8 show back at the parade, we had to catch it. Come On, Get Up, You Just Need Some Coffee. I threw on a housedress with a Strawberry Shortcake pattern. You know, the cartoon character. Come On Now, Get Up. Iris looked kind of sick, but I was determined to get the most out of this weekend. We got tall cups of iced coffee and headed back down toward the water. We stopped at a liquor store, which was out of beer, amazing us, but I grabbed some whiskey and stuck it in the pocket of my housedress. *I can't believe I'm with a girl in a Strawberry Shortcake housedress with a pint of whiskey hanging out of the pocket,* Iris smiled, like she was dreaming an entertaining little dream. I was happy to be with a girl who appreciated such things.

What a blurry weekend. We missed most of the concert, went back to the Mission for more beer and coffee. I changed again and we went to Willa's bar in the lower Haight. A real dive of a bar, dark and cramped with girls. Something was always wrong with the toilets. You'd wait in line forever, bursting with piss, and once inside the smelly little room you'd see that the bowl was thick with soaked clouds of tissue. One time I pulled up my skirt and sat on the little porcelain sink to piss there, and it fell right off the wall, a heave and a croak and I fell onto the mucky floor, the sink hanging from a broken pipe that spurted water. I pulled down my skirt and left the bathroom. That particular bathroom also had a urinal. One time a girl named Robin Hood tried to teach me to piss into it stand-ing up. It was gross. She did it so well, whipped down her jeans and reached into her pussy like there was a secret button hidden among the folds. She pulled the skin tight, bucked her hips, and piss shot out in a fine, strong stream. Wow, I said. I knew I couldn't do it. Robin Hood was telling me about a certain muscle up inside me, groggy and underused. If I could find it I could piss a hard arc like she did, and I'd also be able to ejaculate during sex and all kinds of fun stuff. I pulled down the black cotton leggings I wore beneath my dress, a fashion staple since high school. They hung in saggy loops at my ankles. I reached down between my legs and grabbed

71

fingersful of skin and hair, yanked it taut. *Come on girl, you can do it!* Robin Hood and the five other drunk girls who had crowded inside to witness the spectacle cheered me on. There was an initial, promising squirt and then an infantile dribble of pee that splashed down my thighs and puddled into my leggings. Eeew. Someone handed me toilet paper and I mopped up. *Keep practicing,* Robin Hood advised, and I did for a while, in the shower and stuff, but I couldn't get my parts to work right.

But that night, after the Pride Parade, me and Iris walked gutsy into Willa's bar, her territory. She was there lining up shots of tequila, she smiled at me all pleasant and friendly. I was dressed up like a superhero, big boots, Wonder Woman underwear, a wig and a gun. I shot Willa. *Did I call you last night?* she asked innocently. Yeah, You Sure Did. Well, she was blacked out. She didn't remember any of it. She was full of shit. Ok, Sure, Whatever. We had to have a talk, it was more of a fight. She didn't want me at her bar with Iris. She wouldn't come right out and say it, she just made all these impossible rules, like that me and Iris couldn't dance together or kiss or do anything. I started yelling at her. *Why do you always pick a fight with me when I'm working?!* she cried. Forget It, I'm Leaving. I grabbed Iris, and we split for this S/M fag club South of Market, very LA and pretentious. I was winding down and beginning to feel sick so we didn't stay long. Back at my house later I think we just passed out. We had our first sober sex in the morning, and it freaked me out. My hands were confused, used to Willa's body. I got panicky. I missed my ex-girlfriend. What was I doing? I gave Iris an insincere compliment on the faded daisy tattoo on the back of her shoulder. It was a teenage Bad Judgement tattoo, and I hadn't noticed it until we were naked and sober together in the afternoon sun of my bedroom. I told her it was cute, and then I told her I had stuff to do, and she left. I called Willa and begged her to go out with me again. I was crying. We got back together, but that didn't make anything better. We were doomed. I was back in her bedroom with the body I knew and it didn't mean anything. It was desperation and pure confusion. Iris got really sick from being so fucked up all weekend. She was hypoglycemic, and I hadn't let her eat or rest. I just kept pumping her full of booze, sex and action, then sent her home to puke, pass out and alarm her roommates into carting her off to General to sit among the rest of the gay revelry casualties. She was lying on a cot with needles in her arms and doctors asking her what were all the dark red marks and scratches at her neck and if she thought she might be pregnant. And she didn't even know I had broken up with her.

5

I almost didn't eat the mushrooms. Because I was in a performance and I was busy. The performance had a theme and the theme was "pep rally," and for my perkiness and for my spunk I was chosen to organize a kind of joke cheerleading squad. I had been a cheerleader once, not in high school but in junior high, seventh grade, before cheerleading suggested anything about integrity. I knew some cheers: R-O-W-D-I-E, Devil's Attack, Uh! Ungawa! Devils Have The Power!, which originally, back in the '60s, went Uh! Ungawa! People Have The Power! and was a Black Power chant, though nobody told this to the cheerleaders. Imagine having your righteous mantra appropriated by some scrawny shit-town cheerleading squad. For the performance I rewrote Devil's Attack into Summer's Here/We're Glad We're Queer/Time To Have

Fun And Drink Some Beer! I taught all the flailing arms and spread-eagle leaps to my squad, which consisted of Ashley, who was kind of manic, and Bobby, the cross-dressing straight boy who got a lot of play off dykes, and a third girl I didn't know very well but who was so quiet and introverted that I worried she'd not do ok with the cheers. Then I thought that was probably a fucked-up cheerleadery thing to think—am I falling into some bad cheerleader mindset? I was rehearsing with my squad in this tiny performance space run by a really cute boy who wore those plastic riot-grrl barrettes in his hair and heavy black glasses on his face and who was always very excited and gushing over everything. He made art with liquid jello and twinkies and pink sugar frosting. On the outside his theater was metallic silver and on the inside it was a one-room schoolhouse or maybe a small chapel, the kind you find in a hospital. Wooden pews against the wall.

My roommate Laurel came by with Iris. This was about a week after I'd ended the brief but hauntingly passionate affair. And I had ended it so poorly, in her car with the motor running after we'd gone to look at the buffalo in Golden Gate Park. It was weird that there were buffalo in the park. Behind a regular chain-link fence, grazing among the eucalyptus trees that also didn't belong in San Francisco. The buffalo were thick and morose and their fur was coming off their backs in long strips, like the bark that was falling off the eucalyptus. I've heard this shedding is normal for buffalo, but it made them look so mangy and miserable. We stood at the fence and stared at them and then we got back in the car, and Iris dropped me at my house, and I said, Iris, I Can't See You Anymore, and Iris just looked kind of blank and said, *Ok* and drove off. I honestly didn't know what she thought about it, but I figured she couldn't be too heartbroken if she was willing to do mushrooms with me. You have to be pretty all right with someone to get that unstable around her. I hadn't ever done mushrooms before. Supposedly they were better than acid, in a hippie way, natural, no rat poison, but I've always liked those cramps you get when you're coming down off LSD. They felt interesting, and made me really know I'd done drugs. I'd heard that mushrooms taste disgusting and I believed it, because even non-hallucinogenic mushrooms made me want to hurl. So earthy and slimy, with that weird texture you feel deep inside your ears as you chew. Like bugs. A taste like mold but worse, human mold, like musty armpits or asscrack. My other roommate, Denise, had the mushrooms. She lived at the end of the hall by the only heating vent, which blew warm air straight into her room and no place else. She brought us a plastic baggie filled with shriveled brown nuggets of fungus. We chopped them up on a cutting board on the counter and *ulp* swallowed. Not so bad. It took a while to hit so we ate more.

We sat outside on the front stoop, a great place to sit, maybe the best in the city. You were connected to the absolute hub of 16th Street, but you sat in a dark corridor, apart, quieter, like 16th Street was this incredible secret and my street was the moment before

76

you told it. You had the sense that something was building, sitting in the subtle glow of the streetlights facing the bottlebrush tree sprouting freakish bristly blossoms that actually looked like bottle brushes. I had seen a bottlebrush tree once before, when I was a prostitute in Tucson. I had a call at a hotel by the freeway, and when the guy took off his pants, there was clearly something wrong with his dick, so I left. In the parking lot was the tree. I picked one of the brushes from a branch and put it on the dashboard, where the skinny scarlet needles dried in the Arizona heat and fell off. Now I had one right outside my house, growing all the way up to my window, filling the frame. A great tree. The one from which Laurel hung upside down in the rain the night she learned her friend died from heroin. Laurel was with George that night, who always had a lot of angst, and I had just discovered Eileen Myles. I was reading her little green book at my window when I saw those two moving through the wet night, the street shiny like a polyester shirt, and I yelled down to them, Wait, You Have To Hear This, and I read them "Mai Maison," my favorite, a kind of reverse serenade, calling the words out my window, and Laurel cried and George smoked a damp cigarette and then Laurel hung by her knees from the bottle-brush tree. The tree also served as a kind of toilet bowl when you were out on the stoop drinking 40s and smoking and felt too slug-gish and congested to climb the stairs to the bathroom. Or maybe you didn't want to miss anything, so you pulled down your pants and squatted over the patch of dirt the tree grew out of.

So the mushrooms tasted like a trunk of moth-eaten clothes, and after we ate them we went out to the stoop and waited for the world to turn weird. Laurel swinging from the tree again helped, like if we just started acting silly the stuff would kick in faster. We were impatient for the little chunks to get all shot up with acid in our bellies and leak into our bloodstreams. Can You Drink On Mushrooms? I asked. Laurel and Iris shrugged. There's a whole purist morality that goes along with mushrooms, like it's so good and holy, unlike LSD or cocaine or Valium, and so you should be holy and ritualistic about it and not wash it all down with beer as if the point were to get bombed, not to have a natural, enlightening experience. I bought my beer at the store around the corner. I liked walking around with the beer in its ratty paper bag. I had a teeny black tape recorder with me so I could record all the amazing things everybody said while they were high. Right when the drug was kicking in, a certain shifting behind the brow, a light zinging down my sternum, we ran into this dancer, Jorge. He was on a bicycle and he talked into the recorder about this sick made-for-TV movie with Melissa Gilbert he'd been watching. It was about rape or incest or forced prostitution or something, I couldn't figure out which, or how he felt about it. Did it upset him or did he think it was funny or was he just putting on a show for me because he knew I was on drugs? Jorge rode away on his bicycle. He was high, too, on pot.

I had him on tape, so I could play the conversation back later and see what it all meant. I thought about all the situations I've walked away from that I would never be able to rewind and understand. It gave me a sad and anxious feeling, like when I worried about not having gone to college, and I thought maybe I should carry the tape recorder around all the time. Would my friends find that irritating?

Me and Laurel and Iris walked toward the Castro, hungry for visuals. We passed a storefront that displayed art made by developmentally disabled adults, and in the window was this big fantastic dragon, dark green goofy with ragged crayola flames and googly eyes and huge teeth and immediately we understood it was some kind of spirit. A power animal or a guide or something. I moved close to the glass, pressing myself against the cold pane. It looked at me, it had such a personality. We Need To Leave It Offerings, I said, and dug through my pockets. I had some change and the jagged cap to my beer. I thought about leaving the change, but I was pretty broke and figured the dragon was a benevolent spirit who loved me and would want me to have my change. The dragon was pleased that I had even considered leaving it my change. I had passed a certain test, like Charlie returning the gobstopper and getting to keep the whole factory. I kept calling the dragon a "she" but that felt like a lie. I tripped on that for a little while. Like, did it need a pink bow on its head for me to really see it as female? But it just looked like a boy to me. A boy dragon. In the Castro we walked into the Baghdad Cafe because Gwynn was working, and I wanted to tell her I was on drugs. She gave me the fattest cinnamon roll, it was like a bed, soft and white with tunnels of cinnamon winding beneath it. You know how you can't eat while you're on acid? On mushrooms eating and that kind of stuff seem ok, though the cinnamon roll was more an adventure than anything. I didn't want to share it with anyone, but I did. I just knew nobody was going to appreciate it as much as I would. Gwynn also gave me a crisp white cup of the coldest, blackest coffee, chunky with ice. It was some sort of juice, I sipped it slowly, feeling the cold stream down my throat. The three of us huddled together on the little stoop in front of the Life Garden and watched everyone. It was nighttime but the shops were still open and the streets were crawling with people. There was a guy selling stuff on the street. We asked if we were in his space. *Well now I'd say you're in your own space.* Then, *I was in a tiger trap in Nam for ten months, and the cops are going to give me a ci-ta-tion? Fuck the po-lice.* Yeah, we all agreed. I tried to smoke but it felt gross, stale and hollow, and I thought maybe mushrooms were in fact so holy and natural that they made you want to be that way too. I crushed the cigarette on the pavement and kicked it away. I wished I could get its smell off my hands. It felt gross touching the beautiful cinnamon roll with my dirty cigarette hands.

What were we going to do? It seemed enough just to be on drugs. We thought maybe we needed to pee, it's hard to tell when you're tripping. If you think about it too long you start wondering if perhaps you already did pee, right in your pants, or maybe you're peeing right now. A girl named Chloe walked by, she had a brown mohawk and a leather jacket with Hopey from *Love and Rockets* on the back. She was visiting from London, we learned, housesitting around the corner, and we could pee there. On the way we found a box of food. Things like that always happen when you're on drugs, and it's so meaningful. It was munchie food, candy and a box of crackers called Chicken in a Biskit. Oh My God, The Boy I Lost My Virginity To Used To Eat Those! What did it mean? The house seemed confusing, too many hallways, a real maze. We contemplated whether we should eat the found food. What if it was a trick? Where did the whiskey I held come from? I took a burning gulp and wondered if I was pushing it. I decided just to hold on to the Chicken in a Biskit, as a kind of talisman. Its meaning would come to me. *Are you going to Toybox?* Chloe asked. Willa's bar. Willa who I'd persuaded to go out with me again. Because it wasn't going so well, I felt I should show up at her bar and pretend to really Be A Girlfriend. I would keep her company while she poured beer from the taps, fetch her cigarettes and go home with her. In my state. Willa wasn't against drugs, she tripped sometimes, but mostly she was the kind of girl who took care of you while you tripped. Maybe I'll Swing By, I said casually. *You will?* My drug comrades sounded surprised. Maybe a little betrayed. I was abandoning them. Yeah, I Want To See Willa. Iris maybe looked hurt at that. In her face for a minute and then it was gone. Who was Iris? I didn't really know. I felt peaceful about it. It was fine that I didn't know who she was. I convinced the druggies to come to Toybox with me. We walked to the Haight, pausing to light cigarettes in doorways, checking if it was still gross to smoke. It was. I had a revelation about everything both being very important and not mattering at all. It was such a beautiful thought. It both pulled you in and released you. Iris agreed, but insisted in an intense voice that there were some things that really were important. She said she didn't want to bring the trip down but some things just were. Yeah, But Even Those Really, Really Important Things Aren't. *No,* she shook her shaggy head, wet blue eyes. *Some things are just very important,* and she told us about a girl she'd slept with back in Georgia who'd just killed herself and that was what she meant. I felt a little insensitive but silently maintained that even that, in all its importance, was still equally unimportant, and if we each did as that girl had done it would also not matter, ultimately. This didn't depress me, it felt joyful. It meant that none of us could ever fuck up.

We were in the lower Haight, the dark corner of Haight and Filmore and ahead was the shitty little dive bar that allowed dykes to plow in each Sunday night, fuck in the bathrooms, pierce and sew their pussy lips on a makeshift stage, all kinds of things going on. Spankings, girls peeling their clothes off on top of the bar. Are You Sure You Want To Come In? Iris and Laurel shrugged. It was important, but it didn't really matter. We pushed into the bar and found it empty, with that cute rocker DJ with the black hair heaving milk crates full of records toward the front. Suzanne was there, and

Willa was clearing glasses from tables. Hi, We're On Drugs, I told her. *Oh,* she smiled this great smile. She didn't care that I was hanging out with Iris, and that was nice. She was a Libra, pretty detached although she had jealous moments, like the day before when she discovered that the box of latex gloves beside my bed was empty. *Did you use them all with Iris?* she cried. *How many times did you guys fuck, like, the whole time?* Not A Lot, I said truthfully.

We left the bar, and our whole bunch walked over to Duboce Park. Suzanne was wearing a wig, a ratty brown and yellow bouffant with a tattered pink bow fixed to the middle. It was pretty great, the Whiskey Wig, we called it. To take a hit of the whiskey you had to wear the wig. We sat on the ground by the swing set and passed the bottle and the hair around, talked into my tape recorder about, you know, childhood teachers who'd hit us or funny stories of being too drunk. Laurel had a great story about smoking crack in an abandoned barber shop with this guy who almost raped her. Everyone had a couple big stories that kind of defined them, and sitting around the dark park, the dead subway tunnel gaping behind us like part of a big face, the shady boys skirting by our small group, checking us out, it was the moment to deliver your stories. Laurel had smoked crack and had been a speed freak plus had grown up poor in Maine picking potatoes with a crazy mother. Willa had been institutionalized and had parents she called "educated poor" and her dad was a minister. Iris was from the South, where she was persecuted in high school and put on Prozac and had a tumultuous affair with this really controlling girl who brought her to California. Suzanne was the most mysterious, but she had been a heroin addict and used to hit her girlfriend. I of course had been a prostitute, and had a girlfriend go straight on me and a peeping tom stepfather. That was my story. Laurel got on a swing and swung really high, tilting her body backward as she zoomed up. If she had had hair on her head it would have trailed on the ground but Laurel was bald. We were all bald or slowly recovering from recent baldness. *It looks like death!* she howled as she rushed upside down. *It looks like skulls!* I tried it. The oddly lit sand rolled in curves and shadows and did look like skulls. Willa wanted us to have sweaters, worried that we were too cold but didn't know it, being so high. I couldn't tell if this was annoying or sweet. We trudged up sloping Haight Street to her house. Willa turned the heat on right away and went to work toasting us slabs of raisin bread and globbing them with butter. The plump raisins bursting under my teeth were slimy and good. I ate walnuts out of a bag until my mouth stung, sitting on the worn couch in a living room that looked and smelled like that of a very old woman. We sat in the dark. Everyone had plates of warm bread and nuts. Willa moved in and out of the solemn darkness, serving us. I wanted to sleep, not to walk all the way back to the Mission with Laurel and Iris. I wanted to sleep there, in Willa's bed. I did. Laurel and Iris slept on the little living room couch. They were really uncomfortable. When I woke up in the morning in my girlfriend's bed I felt normal, and the girls had gone home, emptying the living room.

84

6

I may not have any right to talk to you about Suzanne. We were never that close. She was somebody else's friend, big and smiley, and she always told me she liked my poems. In George's bedroom she smeared purple dye on my head with a toothbrush, moving it cautiously over the bristly hairs at the nape of my neck. That night I was reading at an art gallery and she picked through a stack of my bratty rants, selecting which pieces I should perform. She read me a piece of her own, lying on a futon, with Ani DiFranco whining out from the stereo. Her poems were strong, fired with the yearning achy goodness that made her seem young. She'd told us about doing so much heroin back in Seattle, but it all seemed far away from this shiny girl who stuck a nail through her ear and wrote about it while waiting for her food stamps at 8th and Mission. One night I was at a party with her and other friends, one of those parties you hear about thirdhand and you get there and don't know anyone and the host drunkenly accommodates you and you stake out a little corner and sheepishly drink her alcohol. Actually I think we stole the alcohol. I remember having a heavy bottle of Absolut tucked awkwardly under my jacket and thinking, well if they can afford Absolut then I'm not going to feel bad about swiping it. A Robin Hood gesture, I thought. Walking home, Suzanne kept loudly trying to get me to recite one of my poems, and I was embarrassed. *Come on, please*, she said. We all went back to my house.

That night a prostitute got beaten up in the parking lot across the street from my house. A different night I would've slept through it, it happened at about three in the morning, but we were all there, awake, mixing the stolen Absolut with tap water and ice, sipping it from my roommate Denise's coffee cups. Lulu was there, and Vinnie. George and Brad had gone up to Dolores Park to make out behind the fat leafy palm trees. And Suzanne, we found her later, out front on the sidewalk, sprawled drunk and spinning in her head. We weren't the only ones who heard the woman screaming, a guy a few doors down rushed into the street with a two-by-four held thickly in his hands. He looked bewildered and completely unprepared to use it. I had tried to find a weapon too, but looking around my room saw nothing dangerous and took only my body out into the lot where a pickup truck stuffed with men peeled out onto 17th Street and a broken-looking whore dripped tears and blood onto the sidewalk. They had raped her, of course. Stabbed her too, in the hand, it looked like, and not too bad, but it was hard to tell because she was fucked up and freaked out, one minute doubled over and howling like a shot animal, then sprinting away like she was scared we'd hurt her too. We told her we'd help her, told her we'd take her to the hospital, and when she said she wanted to just go home we told her we'd take her there. She slung her thin arms around my and Lulu's shoulders and we walked her toward Mission, pausing when she stopped to double over again and scream. Vinnie walked to the side, uncomfortable and scared, and the blood from the woman's hand dripped onto my shirt. At Mission Street a cop car pulled up and the woman spun her head to them, her crazy red face streaked with tears and makeup, yelling *Where were you when I needed you! Where were you when they. . . . you don't give a fuck about whores!* She was planted on the sidewalk in her worn-down heels and I was trying to steer her away from the slowing cruiser. Come On, It's Ok, We'll Get You Home. The cops drove up onto the sidewalk, flew out of the car, left the door open so you could see the lights blinking on the dash, hear the sputtery static voices from the radio. *What's the problem here. Does she need medical attention? What's going on? You don't give a fuck about me, fuck you!* Come On, I whispered, and to the cops, She's Fine, She's Not Hurt Bad, We're Going To Take Her Home. *She may need medical*—GET THE FUCK AWAY

87

FROM ME! We'll Take Her To The Hospital If She Needs To Go, Really. *Come on, I think you should come with us.* GET THE FUCK AWAY FROM ME! Hey, She Doesn't Want To Go With You. Her arm was wrapped around my shoulders, her fingers clutching. She Was Just Attacked, Leave Her Alone. *Let go of her,* said the cop. There were two of them, both men, mustaches, the blue shirts, the hats, the waists hung with guns and cuffs and other coply accessories. They told me I was interfering with an officer. Don't You Get It? I was crying. She Was Raped, She Doesn't Want To—The cop just grabbed her, pulled her arm off my shoulders, and the other moved behind me and scooped my arms up behind my back and held them there, painful and immobile. *Now you just calm down,* he said to me, while the other shoved her screaming into the cop car. Let Me Go! I was screaming too, Let Me Go, I've Done Nothing! *It's ok, Michelle, it's ok,* Lulu said gently, crying, telling the cop to let me go. You Are Going To Hell! I screamed at the cop holding me. It was all I could think to say, watching the other pig stuff the bleeding woman into the car. You Are Going To Hell! I screamed again and again like a crazy woman. Another cop car pulled up to the curb and yet another cop climbed out, a woman, sent to calm me down. *Now just calm down,* she said, *calm down.* You Tell Him To Let Me Go, I said to her, my jaw tight. *Now you just calm down,* she repeated, *and he'll let you go.* Fuck You, I said. *Thank you!* yelled the prostitute from the window as the cop car pulled out into the street.

But really I wanted to tell you about Suzanne, who was passed out on the sidewalk as the cop bound my arms to my back and I screamed. Suzanne, who shared a house with George and with crazy mean Chip who brought tricks home to pay his cheap Mission rent even though everyone knew he had a trust fund. Until everything broke and George moved out, all three of them lived in this house that crawled with cats and drama. George then asked if I would go with him to get his things. Laurel and Iris helped too. It felt like a bad high school hallway, loading out crates of books and blankets while Chip and Suzanne whispered and cackled and hurled things against the wall, making us jump. George decided to leave most of his shit on the curb out front for whoever wanted it. I grabbed some thermals and a blanket. He pulled from his pocket a fat magic marker and wrote Chip Is A Rapist on the sidewalk. George was really into appropriating the word "rapist" and applying it to different circumstances. It was a good word to fling at someone when your feelings were hurt. Suzanne ran down the stairs and shouted all kinds of mean things, not just at George but at Iris and Laurel and me. I guess we became enemies then. It was pretty dumb since we were never super-friendly in the first place. She was this unstable girl who hated me now so ok, whatever. At a Tribe 8 show the next week she tried to get this fucked-up gang of girls to beat up Iris. She was crazy. And then after moving out,

George started talking to her again. I Wouldn't Ever Talk To Her Again, I snapped at him. After How She Treated You? She's A Bitch. George shrugged. I hate when you hate someone in solidarity with a friend, and then they make up and you're left feeling weirdly betrayed and unsure how to act. *She's whoring,* George told me. We were driving around in the silvery-blue station wagon that was his temporary home. He would pull it up to the dunes at Ocean Beach and somehow curl his tall body up in the back and sleep. *She's working on Capp Street.* On The Street? I asked. Jesus, Why Is She Doing That? She Should Work For An Agency, Girls On The Street Aren't Safe. Some freak pulls up and opens the door and that's it. *She says the women all look out for each other.* Still. She Could Get Killed. But she didn't. At a crowded party, I was leaving the bathroom and I walked right into her. *Can I talk to you?* she asked. Sure, I said, apprehensively. The bathroom was dim, lit by a single blue light, and she said, *I've been whoring.* I Know, I said uncertainly. She was crying. *Can I hug you?* She knew that I had worked before too. *I just needed to touch another whore.* Listen, You Should Work For An Agency If You're Going To Work. If Some Psycho Wants To Kill A Woman, He's Going To Pick One Up Off The Streets. I told her about the woman we tried to help months ago, the bleeding lady the cops took away while Suzanne herself lay drunk in the street, feet away. She nodded. She had had a weird trick, she told me, this weird guy. She spent the day with him. Yeah, It's Weird, I said. It's A Weird Fucking Job. The guy was a regular.

Regulars Are Weird, I told her. If You See Someone On A Regular Basis It Turns Into A Relationship. I was hugging her, talking to her, and she calmed down, wiped at her eyes with her wrists. Then she was hostile again. Backed away, her face all stone. *I don't know,* she snapped, *I still have issues with you.* She left the bathroom, shut the door behind her. Fuck you, Suzanne. She needed a whore to hug her while she freaked out and then, fuck off, I'm her enemy again. I barely knew her. She was crazy.

So she was doing heroin again, and whoring on Capp Street. Her roommates kicked her out. They couldn't deal with her friends and her shooting up in her bedroom. At the house meeting she said it was like they were racist, making her leave because she was a junkie. I don't know where she went when she left. And then she died. She was trying to kick and the people at the hospital sent her away, full of malnutrition and hepatitis. She was so sick that she died. She did not OD. The workers at General don't care about junkies, everybody knows that. Her poems were good, I thought. She was young and she'd get older and be different. I had a dream after she died that she brought me to the point of death and then shot me up with electricity, pure sex and oatmeal. *Oh, she ate oatmeal every day,* her friends told me. *She thought it cured depression.* I didn't know that. I barely knew her at all. She was on hold, someone I'd be friends with when she got her shit together. And then she died.

7

On Valencia Street I discovered coffee. Life became expansive, it grew outward. My insides bubbled over onto the Mission streets I walked, high on my new beverage. I hadn't known it was a drug, that you didn't drink it so much as you did it. I had always thought it another bitter beverage that adults drank, like alcohol, only I understood the purpose of liquor, while coffee was a hot, dark mystery, a nasty stew. I don't know why I started drinking it except that there were so many coffeehouses in San Francisco and it seemed right to sip the stuff while sitting there, hunched over my papers like all the scruffy students and poets, each at our own round tables with warm cups and purpose. Then *bing wham zip,* my blood became charged, became something else, and I was smarter, my brain some kind of cornucopia of thought. And I was happier. Not that I had been depressed, but you can always take a good mood a little further. I felt joyful, and excited, very excited, as if the sidewalk outside the cafe were about to erupt into some magnificent carnival and I was on the edge of my seat, brimming with thought, sinking it into my notebook quick before life bumped up against me like a big animal and took me in its jaw. It is a fact that people who drink coffee are less likely to commit suicide. A study somehow came to this conclusion. But Willa was trying to get me to quit my new friend Coffee. She said it made my eyes get all buggy like I was on drugs for real. I am hyper enough already that people have mistaken me for a speed freak and avoided making my acquaintance. Willa was one of those people. I tried not drinking any coffee because she promised that once you got past the first three days off coffee you could wake up in the morning and drink a glass of orange juice and have all this energy and inspiration and it was great. I'd been drinking orange juice off and on my whole life, without coffee, and had never experienced any druglike sensations from it, but since Willa actually started to avoid me during the earlier part of the day, when the effects of the caffeine were strongest, I figured why not give it a try.

I was in the Castro on like the second day without coffee, a beautiful sunny day with millions of gay people shopping and I was walking down Market with Willa and Ashley and I just started sobbing. Everything slowed down like I was sick, talking was hard and not fun, and I hated having to lift my legs to move forward.

It was miserable, life was suddenly terrible and I felt like a chump, like I had been viewing reality through some inauthentic window that made everything look nice when really it wasn't. The worst thing about depression is how true your vision seems, like misery is the only correct perspective and everything you think when you're happy is a sham. I didn't even want to be happy anymore because I'd rather live in honest misery than fake bliss. I cried openly through the throngs of cheerful lesbians and boys with neat haircuts and why does everyone in the Castro look so fucking healthy? *Maybe you should drink some coffee,* Ashley suggested. All this pain just to be more sensitive to the subtle uplift of orange juice didn't seem worth it. I remember Willa was especially unsympathetic. I had a dramatic arm slung around each of their shoulders like the grand martyr, and Willa was obliviously window shopping in the awful stores. Actually she was deeply in love with Ashley and undoubtedly consumed by her own tragedy, but I'll write that book another time. I drank some coffee and my outlook improved immensely. I was ready to write some poems and, I don't know, get drunk, run around, take my shirt off and get kicked out of someplace. You know, live a little. But I wondered about being with someone who tried to stop me from drinking coffee. Once the caffeine hit, the analytical part of my brain went haywire trying to figure out the nature of my so-called relationship with Willa. I'd grill her again and again, arranging everything nicely, intellectualizing it all. But it was getting a little thin. Even I was bored with trying to convince her that she was in love with me, or that she should be. When I ended our relationship again a month later it was a lot nicer, no swearing or headbanging, civilized. Two caffeinated air signs, me the wired Aquarius, and Libra Willa delicately perky on a little pot of tea. I was haunted by the thought that maybe Iris had been my True Love. What a concept. A *Where's Waldo?* of the heart. I don't buy it anymore, true love. But I decided she was. It had been so passionate, so intense. I had to get Iris back. Would she even have me, after I had put her in the hospital and coldly dumped her in front of the sad displaced buffalo? Lately Iris's house had been the fun place to hang out. The house was unusual for San Francisco in being new, small, with carpet in the bedrooms and linoleum in the kitchen. A regular house, not a Victorian. It had an ugly modern lamp on the ceiling, very bright. This night it was me, Laurel, George, Iris and her roommate Candice, who was still kind of bitchy, but I pretended like we were best pals. It broke her down a little. The other roommate, Lucille, was always depressed and would shut herself in her room and stomp about loudly whenever she heard people having fun. Laurel was mysterious in seeming to give so much of herself away in conversation, yet keeping whole important chunks of herself under wraps. You engaged eagerly in her conversation hoping it would be the moment she gave it all away, and she never did, but you never felt ripped off. Laurel made you believe in the subconscious mind. George was an event. He was tall and obnoxious in that newly queer, newly punk way, over-compensating for his recent history of academic hippiedom in Iowa where he'd joined a fraternity and had to memorize the text from the Budweiser label. The best was when he pierced his tongue and made a big show about soaking it in salt water, stretching his six-foot-something frame across Iris's linoleum, his protruding tongue dangling into a cup of the stuff. He could've simply rinsed. Every conversation was a vehicle for George to demonstrate his stellar political consciousness, which was fine because everyone's political consciousness was very fresh and important and we loved to dress them up and trot them around the ring. Sometimes Candice's recent ex-girlfriend, Lulu, was there. That was a little embarrassing for me since she was one of the first people I met in San Francisco, when I was just slowly coming out of the coma induced by my banquet of '70s-flavored feminism, and I would argue with her in bars about S/M and pornography. *I like being objectified,* she said daringly in the dark over beer, and she really had me. I mean what do you say to that? "Me Too" would've been nice, but I just wasn't there yet.

In Iris's house we drank a variety of beer. Laurel and George drank Oatmeal Stout because they were vegan and it was the only beer that wasn't prepared by straining the stuff through animal bones or something. Candice drank nice German beer because she had lived in Germany until she was five and was reclaiming her ethnic heritage, and everyone else drank Mickey's or split a 40 of something cheap. And we talked and we smoked a lot. We gave each other tattoos with needles and india ink. That was the night

Iris tried speed for the first time and didn't tell anyone. She was just terribly efficient and smart with the needle. She tattooed the number 13 on her own shoulder, and it looked real good. She tattooed Fag on George's wrist, and the letter S at his temple. Supposedly if you have a tattoo on your face you are legally recognized as unemployable and it's really easy to collect SSI from the government. The S didn't have any kind of meaning, George just liked the letter. Each day after this he would choose a different whimsical S word and say that's what the letter stood for. I tattooed a little triangle on my ankle, surrounded by three little circles. It was the Wyrd Sisters. I got the design out of *The Woman's Dictionary of Symbols and Sacred Objects,* which I had stolen from the library. It symbolized general feminine weirdness, witchery, fate, destiny, synchronicity, and it seemed a good way to mark the moment. I put a pool of dark ink into the cap from my Mickey's, and I dunked my needle and began to poke. A drop of beer mixed in with the ink and I thought that was funny. A Mickey's tattoo. Laurel and George were fairly impressive potheads, and dreamy Piscean Iris was recruited into their habit with ease. Though I didn't enjoy pot all that much, I joined in because they were having so much fun. The idea was to smoke until we lost the pipe. The four of us, me and Iris and Laurel and George, were kind of a gang. We were going to get matching flasks and engrave Queer Drunk Punks on it. When the pipe was finally lost in the cracks of the pull-out sofa, me and Iris decided it was time to go out to buy some potato chips.

I remember standing in the brutal fluorescent light at the corner market and not knowing how to act around her, I was so high. We had had an affair, and now there was all this thick awkward tension. We were two stoned girls peeping clumsily at each other around racks of shrimp-flavored chips and squat tins of nacho cheese. We bought our chips and left. Another good stoned thing to do was play Uno, the card game. The four of us had these epic Uno games that went on for hours, and we talked incessantly through them, processing our childhoods and how shitty the world was and thank god we had figured it all out and found each other. *She is really belting it out,* one of us said about the song on Iris's stereo and we all stared in horror, comprehending in a united stoned consciousness that the phrase "belting it out" came from the cries of someone being hit with a belt. Holy Shit. Then Iris realized that it was abuse when her father used to hit her with his belt, and we all had a moment around that. The card game went around like a carousel, primary colors and simple numbers. At one point Laurel and George left the room, and Iris looked at me, and I knew it was going to happen. I did a soft lunge at her and she caught me with her mouth and it was such a thrilling kiss, knowing that our friends would come into the room any minute, making up with intensity what we were losing with time. We detached, and George and Laurel were back with more beer. It was so late that me and Laurel just decided to sleep there. Which meant the three of us on Iris's narrow futon, Iris, me, Laurel, wall. Did Laurel fall right asleep? It seemed so. Me and Iris faced each other in the dark cigarette smog of her bedroom, kissing these secret kisses, careful for squishy noises. Very desperate kisses fueled by the frustrating presence of a third party who may or may not be asleep. Very cautious touching, no rustling sounds, no noticeable movements. The restraint was terrible because it was obvious how incredible it would be to just fall into her, this terrific girl, but surely the restraint was actually better, drawing our attraction into a taut wire, electric and humming. We slept.

In the morning we were girlfriends. It happened that quickly, and immediately the excellent group friendship died. We killed it, me and Iris. We couldn't stop staring at each other. It was a real problem. Laurel would be in the middle of some great story and then—*forget it.* A big annoyed sound. What?! I Was Listening! *I can't talk to you if you both keep looking at each other.* But I Was Listening! *Forget it.* The word "codependent" was fun for everyone right then. We're Not Codependent! It's a useless thing to defend yourself against, like alcoholism. I had only been codependent with shitty, kind of mean people, so it was fun to get all codependent with Iris. But the lofty and elaborate group plans we had made went kersplat. Like train hopping, something me and Laurel and Iris were going to do. We would dress like boys and bring nothing but cans of beans and matches, use each other's bellies for pillows and arms for blankets. Duck beneath still hunks of train, escaping the trainyard cops who shot hard pellets of salt at our butts. *I'm not traveling with a couple,*

Laurel said darkly. What About New Orleans? We had talked about that too, about living in chipped wooden homes that crawled with slow roaches the size of turtles, drunk on the heat. I would sit on iron balconies in thin slips that clung, humid, to my skin, writing stories while Iris and Laurel smoked their pot and ate vegetables. *I am not traveling with you two!* I shrugged. Finewhatever. Then Candice decided Iris wasn't spending enough time with her, or in the house, and plus she was a big slob and wasn't taking care of her wedge of the chore wheel. The Michelle-Iris romance blossomed as we became misunderstood outlaws, cast out from our circle, each the other's only ally. The Shakespearean peak was Laurel's announcement that she was in love with Iris. *I need to talk to you,* she said, all heavy, one afternoon in the house where we shared our drama. We made plans to meet later at a cafe on Valencia, and I didn't want to because it meant an hour or two I would spend pried apart from Iris. Time I could spend at a bar with her, looking into her eyes. It was that gross. We would just stare at each other, run home to have sex at her house, run to the bar for last call and just gaze at each other. It was very meaningful, we shivered with it. Get stoned and make out for hours. Once, when I was very high on pot, Iris raked her fingers up my back, and I had a vision of the world being born, dry land splitting into rivers. I was out of my mind.

At the cafe with Laurel, I had a tasteless little bagel with a thin layer of cream cheese on it, and I couldn't eat because my stomach was tangled and heavy with this sense of impending

100

doom, like I was ten years old and in big trouble. I hate people being mad at me. I wanted to start crying and apologize for whatever I'd done before Laurel even opened her mouth. *I'm in love with Iris,* she said. You're Not, I replied. *I am,* she said. I nibbled at my lousy bagel. Supposedly there had been a moment when Iris liked Laurel, thought she was cute, maybe had a crush on her, and I came in with my dump-truck presence and mowed down all the possibilities. What do you do? I had a deep, adolescent understanding that you do not let a boy come between you and your girlfriends, and I supposed this noble notion had to transfer from boy to girl. And there was Laurel, looking very grown-up and even businesslike about the whole thing, the Laurel who'd gone to Brown and had a responsible job at a software company in Berkeley, the Laurel I rarely glimpsed, seemingly years older than me though really she was younger. I was about to cry and she was contained. I thought about one recent night, Iris waiting in my room, when in the dark parlor I had bummed a latex glove off Laurel and she was so pissy about it. *It's my last one,* she said, irritated. I'll Get More Tomorrow, I said. You're Not Going To Use It Tonight. She handed it to me and stomped back into her room. Everything was clear now. I'll Break Up With Her. Laurel raised her eyebrows. *I'm not asking you to do that.* Her tone was not kind. It's The Right Thing, I said. You're My Friend.

I left her in the cafe, walked down Valencia Street, crying. Finally I had found a girl who really just liked me so much, and now this. A girl who was nice and let me drink coffee and wasn't waiting for anybody but me. I was supposed to call Iris and I didn't. I went to a bar where a poetry night was going on because I knew I could talk and cry to my poetry friends and they would buy me beer since I'd spent the last of my money on the uneaten bagel. I told my story again and again. *You're crazy,* the poets said. I cried in my beer. Once I was drunk I made my way to the pay phone at the front of the bar, sunk my change into the slot, called my Iris. Candice told me she was gone, was looking for me, what was going on? I was trapped at the bar. I couldn't go home, it was Laurel's home, she would be there with George, who was also trying to ruin this great love. Both of them would be smoking cigarettes out Laurel's window, talking about me with the Ramones cranked loud so I couldn't hear. Then Iris came in, into the dark red and trashy bar, she came in like a young prince with her bike at her side like an obedient steed. She had no helmet on her head. Her hair was black, dyed that way, a gorgeous scruffy mess on her head. I Have To Talk To You, I said, leading her back to a little round table. My face was red and hideous from the crying, bloated and runny. I Can't Go Out With You Anymore. It was an awful, delicious moment. Watching her pretty face crumple. She'd been searching for me, on her bike, riding through the city. Knowing something was wrong. Laurel's In Love With You. She's My Friend. *What?* Iris looked seriously confused. She had just started smoking again, and pulled an American Spirit from a mangled blue pack. *But I don't want to not go out with you,* she said. *I like you so much.* Maybe she was crying now too. *I like you more than anything.* At the bar the poets, all of them older, mostly with drinking problems, sipped at their beers and rolled their eyes watching us. We made them feel old. I could not break up with Iris. How could I walk away from this girl who liked me so much she could easily waste whole chunks of this, the prime of her life, simply looking at me? We would be fugitives together. We could go nowhere, not my house where Laurel lurked, and not Iris's with that bitchy Candice. We would go to Ashley's, the friend who miraculously never became involved in the intense group friendship that was more codependent than me and Iris ever were.

Ashley had a beautiful backyard, oddly big, planted with flow-ers and a cluster of cactus and a big pine tree and the plum tree with the blossoms that smelled so good. Her house used to be a Chinese restaurant, and if you dug into the dirt of her yard you would find old bones of ducks and pigs. Iris had a tent, we would pitch it and live there in Ashley's backyard. With the chain-link fence that separated her Taurean greenery from the Big 4 Rents lot full of huge cranes and wrecking machines and metal dumpsters. I left this hysterical message on Ashley's machine, and she called me back right there at the bar, the Casanova, a great bar, dingy and red, the bathrooms smelling like vetiver. It's gone now. Swal-lowed up by the yuppies who are swiftly ruining my neighborhood. The bartender handed me the phone. *I'm in love with you,* Ashley gushed in a stricken voice. *Ha ha just kidding.* Yes, we could live in her yard, but she thought we were acting like idiots. *Just go home,* she said. *You and Iris are in love and that's that.* Very simple. We drank at the bar 'til it closed, then Iris rode me home on the back of her bike. Her home, not mine. Laurel found out I didn't end it with Iris and gave me a big Whatever. *You were trying to do the integrity thing,* she said cynically and I hated that slur on my initial pledge. I'd meant what I'd felt. But what did it matter anyway now that the friendship was so ruined? It was just gone. Laurel wasn't ever going to show that deep and shadowy place way inside her, you couldn't even glimpse it now, it was just hardness, ruined. And George wasn't going to stop being annoying and Candice wasn't going to start being pleasant. It was just gone. Eventually Laurel went off to Europe alone and George carried on solo as a soldier in the war against love, trying to get Iris to break up with me because, I don't know, I'm a social climber, and not really an environmentalist because I always got nachos from El Farolito in the big styrofoam containers. And Laurel got a girlfriend in Amsterdam, and George got a boyfriend who wouldn't top him, and eventually Candice did like me, and eventually Iris no longer did, and my older poetry friends from the bar left behind secret addictions as they moved to far away states to dry out, and Ashley got a boyfriend and disappeared completely, and here I sit with my coffee.

8

But back to when it was thick and glisten-
ing and alive. I mean life, never knowing what was going
to happen. That's what I was full of one night. Gliding up 16th
Street, heading home, past the old guys selling syringes, the lines
of kids waiting to get into the Roxie, waiting to get a falafel or a
burrito. Moving toward my house with the windows open wide like
big mouths eating the sky. You could sit in the window and be its
teeth, my favorite place to be. The house felt like a squat then, because we were all moving out. The landlord had refunded the last
month's rent, making that month free. And the uptight roommate,
Denise, who went to est-like gatherings in the mountains and made
me go out into the driveway once and tell the two women shooting
up behind her car to leave or else the cops would come, she had

finally moved out, and the whole place had really fallen to shit. We were smoking cigarettes all over the formerly nonsmoking house and tripping on moving debris, crates, clothes, bundles of blankets that were really beds. Dozens of keys to my house seemed to float around and I never knew who'd be camping in the hallway when I got home. That night it was Iris, lying on her back on my floor, music on big and bright as lightbulbs. She flashed me this smile, *Hey,* like she was surprised to see me even though it was my house. I kissed her and tasted beer. I have to tell you that Iris looked like all these different people, a glamorous model, a fifteen-year-old boy, a fairy or elf or little kid. Big lips like a sofa you could plop right down on. Eyes all blue and slinky. The eyes were the glamorous part, all girl. No boy could have eyes like that, lashes long enough to swing from. She told me we were going to Tower because her friend Josiah liked a boy who worked there, so we headed up to the Castro drinking beers and I still had my glide. Josiah brought this really cute love note to give to the boy, he was passing it around, creasing it nervously in his fingers. Josiah was from Athens, Georgia. He'd only been in town a day or two and already he had all these leads on work and sex. He pursued each need with an admirable Virgo ambition.

Tower was so bright and Josiah's boy wasn't there. His Name Is ChiChi? Oh, I Know Him. Everyone Knows Him, He's One Of Those Club Kids. Kind Of Shallow. Well, That's Cool If You Don't Mind. Iris stole a CD. She didn't want our trip to be for nothing. She shoved it right down her pants. I didn't even know until we were blocks away and she lifted her shirt and there it was, pressed against her belly, that space between her jeans and skin which often hid stolen goods. Usually beer but once a whole bottle of wine and was that a score. Josiah wanted men so we stayed in the Castro. For the Boy Bars. Smug little clubhouses, I know about them. The Bear was a leather bar, denim really. I went there once and all these fags were paying a dollar to spank Mr. Leather-Something-or-Other. It was for charity. The Midnight Sun, the Phoenix, the Jackhammer. Twin Peaks, but you certainly didn't want to go there. Uncle Bert's was pretty good. Then that one where you had to pass through a heavy leather curtain to get inside, what's that one called? That's the one we wanted. The guy checking IDs smiled at me like, *Cute, a girl!* and I smirked at him and attempted to lift the curtain, which was the weight of a whole dead cow. Inside, it was dark and a chain-link fence lined one wall, an attempt to make the place seem dangerous. Please, I've been to sleazier places than that. The Paradise in Cambridge, where Patrick got fucked on the pool table while dick movies played on TVs above the bar. The Nine Circle in New York. It had dick movies too and the floors were wet and sticky, no doors on the bathrooms. Like someone's scuzzy basement.

The three of us were up against the bar. Josiah's eyes roamed and me and Iris ordered Long Island Iced Teas, such a high school drink but we had very little money between us and wanted to get the most booze for our buck. The drink always makes the bartender look put-out and want to see your ID. The only other women in that bar were two fag hags and a couple of drag queens. Josiah was pouting because Iris was the one getting all the looks. For real. She looked like the most beautiful teenage boy, baseball hat a little crooked, t-shirt baggy so you couldn't see her tits. I moved away from her. We wanted to encourage the attention. We wanted a guy to pick her up and then buy her a drink because we were so out of money. Those Long Island Iced Teas were like five bucks each. And were watery. We were hunting for a nice middle-class NAMBLA guy, one of the older potbellied ones. It was delicious not to touch Iris. The more I watched, the more she became a boy. Amazing. I studied her expression. She cruised the guy to her left shyly, she's young. She moved her eyes like Josiah, silently hungry, and I became her fag hag, standing a little to the side, looking bored, watching the boys admire her. An older guy with a moustache came over, real jovial, trying to get a cigarette. I was friendly but he ignored me completely, focused on Iris. That night was the noisiest, all blaring disco and would you believe I knew most of the words. I leaned against the bar and sang, waiting for Iris to hustle a drink off the daddy. Josiah was gone, off walking through the chain-link, his long black braids swinging down his back. He was telling people his name was Nicholas, and it occurred to me that Josiah probably wasn't his real name either. I wished I looked like a boy. There wasn't anything for me to do. The sugar daddy up and left before Iris could get that drink off him. Our iced teas were

108

gone, and then Iris had to pee. I followed her to the bathroom, pushing through so many men. She really was a boy in that place. What was I? I was in love. We reached the restrooms and the girls' room was locked, of course, the key back at the bar. We went into the men's room, one long urinal lining the wall like a slop trough for pigs. Iris dropped her pants and squatted over the little drain on the floor, peed right into it.

We grabbed Josiah and moved across the street to San Francisco's self-proclaimed "only lesbian bar." Mostly men. It was unbelievably crowded and so many smells, hair spray, perfume. What about environmental illness, the lesbian disease? We moved toward the outdoor patio, Iris stealing drinks along the way. The music was awful. What were they playing? Madonna. "Holiday." Iris was yelling. *Oh yeah, if we just took a holiday, it would be all right! All the homeless people just need a little holiday! All across the world. In every nation. This one's for you, Rwanda! Go Cuba, Go Cuba!* If I took my shirt off I'd be kicked out of the city's only lesbian bar. I couldn't stop thinking about it. My nipples were twitching. I was coveting an abandoned Corona, half-full with a little lime bobbing at the top. I was planning my move when two men sat down between me and the bottle. Hey, Can You Hand Me That Corona? They weren't fooled. They did it, though. They liked us because we were making fun of everyone. The two men were our new friends. We loved them. Their faces were bright red from drinking and they kept telling us to fuck off, I don't know why. It was really funny.

They hated men. Oh, We Hate Men Too, we said, and bonded on that for a little. Then the barbacks came to herd us out, prodding us toward the door, snapping and yelling, totally useless because it was so packed you couldn't move. We swiped more drinks and knocked them back. One had Kahlua in it, now that's a mom drink. The bartender was demanding that Iris put down her drink and leave. *You've got two minutes before I rip it out of your hand,* she growled. The meanest bitches worked there. I Hate This Place, Why Did We Come Here? We walked home, Iris drinking the beer I smuggled out beneath my coat. She smashed the glass on the sidewalk and laughed. She spit on parked cars and kicked them. Iris was a bicycler. One of those Critical Massers. About a month earlier she'd been doored and had to go to acupuncture, so she was righteous in the harm she did to automobiles. Plus she was against capitalism and all that. She started climbing on them, these nice shiny cars. She tried to hop off the roof of one and fell on her ass, legs up in the air and her head by the bumper. My Uncle Charlie broke his leg that way when he was a kid, but Iris was all right. She was just a troublemaker, that's all.

9

September in northern Georgia, way out by Tennessee, and I was trapped in Iris's childhood home with absolutely nothing to do. Iris's schoolteacher sister was getting married. I was there to pretend to be straight to a wide family of strangers, and to watch my butch girlfriend walk through a church in a hideous dress and a faceful of makeup. The dress was raw silk, deep maroon, with little rosettes on the sleeves like a morbid birthday cake. Dyed-to-match pumps and pearl-drop earrings. Somehow I had thought this would be fun, back when we were aiming the fat blue station wagon George lent us, in exchange for a month sleeping in a real bedroom, Iris's, through the country, stopping in Mexico, Tucson, Austin. Hot places. Sleeping in the back of the car and waking so dehydrated our tongues were like socks stuck thickly to the roofs of our mouths. Two dykes at a big Southern Baptist wedding. To Iris it was like playing a little trick on her extended family, sneaking her lezzie girlfriend in under their noses. For me it was an anthropological study and also kind of zany. Sure. Iris's sister took one look at my hacked green hair and burst into tears. *You've really gone too far this time,* she hissed at Iris, beginning a passive-aggressive hair war with everyone but me. The bride was screaming and crying all week long. To my face she was real charming and pleasant. She would say hello and ask me empty questions, then take Iris's poor mother by the hand, lead her into another room and get hysterical. I just lay on the couch and tried to stay out of it. I hadn't been inside a family for years, and I'd forgotten how inherently dysfunctional it was. I watched TV. Iris sat beside me. We were both so bored, what else could we do? We watched MTV, catching up on videos we had missed in San Francisco where no one had cable. We watched *Beavis & Butthead* and agreed that it was funny. We felt deranged. It was making us sick, Georgia, physically sick. Something about Iris's mom's house. The new carpet in the living room had chemicals that made us fuzzy and lethargic, or maybe it was all the Folgers coffee. We just could not get our asses off the couch. Daisy, the excitable cocker spaniel who later would meet with unspeakable tragedy, would bounce over with her spitty braid of rope and Iris would raise a weak arm and toss it into the kitchen. Daisy would slide across the linoleum like a kids' toy come to life and bring the braid back, beaming.

112

I thought Daisy was cute, but she smelled bad, like a dog, and she was using up too much of my girlfriend's precious energy. I ignored Daisy and watched TV, this documentary about a girl who was like a feral child, locked in a closet for years by cruel parents and eventually discovered by greedy psychologists wanting to be the next what's-her-name, the woman who taught Helen Keller to sign. Anne Sullivan. The doctors dumped the girl once they realized she wasn't catching on and might be retarded from birth, which may be why her parents shut her in the closet in the first place. It was sad. She was a thin, haunted girl who had sunk so far into her brain, all those years in the dark, how could she ever come back? She grinned huge when the doctors played catch with her. There was also this great made-for-TV movie with the blonde girl from *90210* playing this wild child who gets locked up in a terrible institution. I loved stories about incarcerated girls, but I was still bored out of my skull, and the mysterious chronic fatigue had us both on perma-lounge. Me and Iris had thought it would be fun to have sex there, in the house where she grew up, Mom sleeping lightly at the end of the hall, and we did attempt some weak teenage boy–teenage girl seduction in front of the television, but really we were exhausted. And the lighter fluid for Iris's mudflap-girl zippo had leaked in the suitcase and contaminated the latex gloves, and the replacement ones we bought at the drugstore weren't regular clingy latex, they were these enormous, boxy plastic things that felt dorky to fuck in. And we couldn't smack each other or play around

113

with the recycled bicycle tire whip because it could wake Mom. We tried it once and traumatized poor Daisy. Even the sound of Iris's hand landing on my ass had her whimpering and scurrying across the linoleum, cowering in the sewing room. Depressed that our sexual violence disturbed the dog, we resumed our sluglike positions in front of the television.

We were trying to stay removed from the pre-wedding drama erupting around us, and we did, except Iris indulged in a terrific fight with her mom about how no one was ever going to spend six thousand dollars on a wedding for *her* now, were they? A true complaint, but Iris was being so bratty and mean that her mom started crying and it was terrible. Iris was furious at all the gifts her sister was getting. They were arranged in the spare room like a set from the home shopping network, all spread out on rose-colored tablecloths. She got everything, even doubles and triples of some items, like multiple toaster ovens and iced tea makers and espresso machines. *She doesn't even drink espresso!* Iris yelled. *I drink espresso!* Her whole thing seemed pretty babyish. Iris was, by my standards, adequately spoiled, despite the avenues of heterosexual privilege that had been shut off to her. The fight went on, with Iris raging and her mom sputtering, and then we jumped in the car and drove into Tennessee to go to the movies. Half of me felt I should've stayed in the poisonous house hugging the mom. She was a sweet lady with that bad-mom complex about trying to please everyone in the family, creating a house full of spoiled whiny children. She had her hands full with the prima donna bride, and I think she was counting on Iris's simple lesbian nature for support. She had bought us bags of tortilla chips to eat on our visit. She was really excited about them. I guess they weren't her usual snack.

So we escaped to the movies, the new *A Nightmare on Elm Street*. We nearly got kicked out of the ladies' room afterward, for being boys. I had all that pent-up energy from sitting so long in the dark, my ass numb and tingly, and I was trying to shake it out by jumping all over Iris, horsing around in the big empty bathroom. An old lady with hair like a chlorinated pool came in and burst out, all terror-stricken, *You're in the wrong room!* I paused mid-leap and said to her, What? What Did You Say? Not to be challenging but because I really hadn't heard her. I guess I seemed threatening, so amped up and hopping in her face. She stood there horrified until Iris said, *She thinks we're boys,* and I started laughing, and said, We're *Girls* and the old woman looked even more frightened and said, *Oh my, oh I am so sorry,* and darted into a stall.

Me and Iris were trying hard to come up with activities that kept us off the couch, preferably out of the house, away from the sad codependent mom and the wicked-witch sister. We drove one night to Chattanooga to see Donna, Iris's childhood friend who, miraculously, was also a dyke. Donna was sweet with frizzy brown hair, a round face and that thick syrupy accent I hoped Iris would take back to San Francisco. Donna worked in Chattanooga's only sex shop, really more of a novelty shop, with wind-up penises that hop and naked lady toothbrushes. I was picking up different items and threatening to buy them for the sister's wedding present. Love-cuffs. Edible body oils that tasted like melted popsicles. A French maid outfit. Donna was wild. She told excellent stories in that southern voice, her daddy and his gun sitting on top of their roof, waiting to shoot some boys who were bothering her at school. Now, I had always thought drugs were the property of urban living, but apparently they're a big problem everywhere, especially in quiet southern towns where everyone's bored. Donna had had a big drug problem, but supposedly she'd calmed down and was aiming to move to San Francisco in the winter. She took us to Alan Gold's, the big gay spot in Chattanooga, and we saw the best drag queen ever with rhinestones pasted to her cheeks like tears, and a fat sparkling tiara. She was mouthing the words to "Miss World." Alan Gold's was packed, everyone was dancing and carrying on. Donna bought us pitchers of beer and asked if we wanted some coke if she could find it. Iris did. She was very into drugs right then. During our overnight stop-over in Athens, on the way to the wedding, she'd smoked opium, sucking the melty black liquid through a straw off the edge of a Waffle House ashtray. I declined. We were at this filthy, smoke-thick apartment inhabited by the straight boys Iris used to play music with in college. All these guys were there and I just wanted to sleep. For a while I tattooed the glyph for Uranus, my ruling planet, onto the inside of my ankle, dipping the burnt tip of a sewing needle into a puddle of ink and poke poke poke while Iris "jammed" with her old band, whacking the shit out of a crumbling little drum kit with split heads and a foot pedal that kept slipping off the rim. Eventually I conked out on the scroungy pull-out couch while Iris stayed up watching *The Jeffrey Dahmer Story* on video and smoking. She was pretty alert for someone who had just done opium.

So back to Donna darting around the club trying to score drugs. Me and Iris went into the girls' room and I ate her pussy in one of the stalls. We were still in that phase of the relationship, barely. Back at the bar Donna was drugless, going on about the Butchest Woman in Chattanooga who thought she was so tough and cool and kept stealing everyone's girlfriend. I was dying to see her. Show Me, Show Me! *She's the one in the red vest over at the bar,* Donna said, flicking a dismissive hand in the woman's direction. Donna was bitter. I guess she got a girl swiped, one with long red hair that curled thick like a princess. The Butchest Woman in Chattanooga had come and swept her away. I had to see. I sashayed over to the bar and spotted a red leather vest like the one Billy Idol wore in the poster I had above my bed in eighth grade. Here it rested on this woman with the biggest blonde hair, bleached and teased to brittleness. Heavy eye shadow and gobs of lipstick. Amazing. This was the Butchest Woman in Chattanooga, the set of her jaw affirmed it, the way she stood and the way she held her cigarette. I watched her slug her beer at the bar and then went back to Iris.

Alan Gold's closed and Donna, having failed on the cocaine quest, was determined to at least have pot. We drove in her car to the home of some paranoid lesbians who were up watching a talk show. They didn't seem to like me and Iris. Their suspicious scowls kept us hovering by the door, squinting at the television. They gave Donna a bulging bag of green and we left. *It was free!* she squealed happily, climbing into the car. *They owe me.* Back at Donna's house Iris rolled joints and I was at the television, trying to find the talk show the drug dealers had on. Pot makes me feel like I forgot to drink my coffee. I did not want any of the smoldering cigarette, and I did not want a sniff from the tiny brown glass bottle Donna had brought out of her bureau drawer. Poppers. They sold them at the porn store where she worked. Iris and Donna were holding the bottle under their noses and falling back against the wall. Like in grade school when we all made ourselves pass out by hyperventilating and squeezing the sides of our throats. It was head cleaner for videotapes, making them giggle all slumped against the wall. Something like that. I felt old and cranky. I wanted to sleep. For some reason I was actually caring that poppers killed brain cells. I don't know what was wrong with me. Donna had an original Howard Finster and that was kind of impressive, a wooden animal like a giraffe, all covered with his rambling scrawl, stuff about god and visions. But I hated Donna's house. The kitchen was under construction, with a plaster-filled sink plopped in the middle, and the bedroom had this depressing yellowy lightbulb. Donna was fanatically trying to get Iris to smoke more and more pot. *I'm really stoned,* Iris said weakly, her big blue Pisces eyes full of smoke and water. *I never see you!*

118

Donna protested. *Come on, finish the bag with me.* It was kind of twisted, the obsessive hospitality of a southern drug addict. Donna gave us her bed and went off to sleep somewhere in the kitchen debris. Me and Iris climbed under the blankets and she started up this little role play that disgusted me, pretending we were two slobs in a filthy apartment watching crappy TV. I'm Really Not Into It, I said, and went to sleep before I got any grouchier.

The next day we hopped into Iris's mom's car, nicer than George's unregistered station wagon, and drove to this Fort Oglethorp tattoo shack, the one with the air-brushed sign advertising Cherokee, Lady Tattooist. Inside was Cherokee, nodding out on a busted naugahyde seat, a mile-long ash burning in her hand. We came back the next day, and she was looking more alive, so I had her put a flaming heart on my arm, the word "lezzie" stretched across a banner in shaky script. Cherokee didn't even flinch at my request. She and her chatterbox husband told us stories about these legendary lesbians who dropped by occasionally to "get some work done." One in particular was real rough and tended to get into fistfights with men. I was dying for her to walk in, but it was just me and Iris in Cherokee's cramped little tattooing space. She burned incense and played a tape of Celtic chanting music as she sank the colors into my arm, saying, *Don't try to be a hero. This gets too much for you, just let me know an' we'll take a break.* A nice switch from sadistic Picasso of Tucson, Arizona. Talking about how big burly men bust out crying at the sound of the tattoo gun,

119

but women, they're stronger. *Lezzie?* she asked. *L-E-Z-Z-I-E?* I nodded. There I was in the middle of nowhere, having to play straight for an aging Baptist family I didn't even know, tattooing "lezzie" on my shoulder. Crying out for help, obviously. I thought about the peaceful Virgin Mary while Cherokee ran the burning gun over my arm. She bandaged me up, and I gave fifty dollars to her and fifty dollars to Billy Joe in the other room, who had tattooed Siamese fighting fish on Iris's shoulder. Back into Mom's car and home with our newly ornamented bodies.

We were deeply bored. We went to the homecoming parade. Iris's schoolteacher sister worried about our little adventure and warned us to behave. She did not want to be known as the girl with the lesbian sister. In a campy way I was excited about homecoming, a piece of Americana I had never experienced. It was fall in Georgia and the air stank of it, the sweet rot of discarded leaves. It smelled like being a kid picking apples in New England, and felt good to be out of San Francisco where the weather is so complacent, to be in a place where seasons actually change and time is in motion. There is something very traditional about fall, so it felt correct that this home-coming thing was happening. To show my momentary support for alienating American traditions, I put on Iris's old varsity jacket, blue satin with "Trojans" on the back. I wore it and my green hair to the high school. No one knew what to do. They were too surprised to beat us up. Iris had a good-sized piece of steel stuck through her eyebrow. Maybe they thought we were

120

crazy and felt no pain. We watched the "floats" go by, cars filled with members of all the high school clubs—the future home-makers, the different levels of cheerleaders, the young blocky boys on the football team, all tossing candy. This was not my high school experience. I went to a vocational high school, a purgatory where losers go to learn a "skill" before being released upon the world. You took plumbing or cabinet-making or sheet metal. If you were a girl you did data processing, cosmetology or graphic arts, like I did. You smoked pot in the courtyard. If you were a girl you got pregnant. No shiny carloads of future homemakers and wholesome cheerleaders tossing bits of candy to the townspeople. The cheerleaders at my high school were sluts. In fact, all the girls were sluts. No slutty looking girls were at this homecoming. There were some slight weirdos, three young girls with hair wraps and Nine Inch Nails shirts who wandered over to ask about my hair. Iris got all excited when she saw them then walk down toward the creek, because that's where she used to go to sneak cigarettes in high school. *Let's go follow them,* she cried, but first we had to go back to the car to get our pack so we could bum a light and seduce them. By the time we got there, the girls were gone. It was just me and Iris on a rock above the slow-running creek that swarmed with flies. And, up a little closer to the street, three new girls, little fifth graders who were watching us kiss. Of course you want to visit the place that shaped the girl you're in love with, watch all her stories spring up around you, and you get to walk right through them. You just don't realize how you have to undo yourself to walk down the streets. The kids started yelling at us. *Faggots! Homos! Are you a boy or a girl? Go commit suicide!* yelled the ringleader, a whiny-voiced girl with long blonde hair and babyfat. It was so precise, "go commit suicide." Not "drop dead" or even "go kill yourself." Like she'd heard the story, at church or at home, that homosexuals kill themselves because their filthy lives make them so miserable. *Come up here,* she challenged us, *come on up here.* She wasn't even scared of us. We were Big Kids, we could kick her ass, but someone had told her that people like us can't fight. You Come Down Here! I yelled, and I was prepared to dump her ass in the creek if she did. I Don't Care How Old She Is, I told Iris, and thought about how great it would be if we missed her sister's wedding because we drowned a ten-year-old girl in the creek and had to skip town.

So we'd been stuck in Georgia so long we had exhausted our tiny supply of activities. By then it was starting to feel like my hometown, too. The novelty of the Waffle House waitresses calling out my hash brown orders had faded completely. Earlier I'd been sad that we couldn't drive down to Athens to see L7 because it would interfere with the wedding. Now I didn't care. Of course we couldn't leave, of course we would remain here, in this town, Chickamauga, Georgia, forever. Lying on the couch, hiding from evil fifth graders, breathing the toxic carpet, never having sex because the television

122

had sucked up our libidos like it did little Carol Ann in *Poltergeist*. But from deep in our boredom Iris came up with one more activity. We would find Trent. Iris had had a thing with this boy when she was about sixteen or seventeen years old. Trent had been about thirteen or fourteen, and while three years is not a big deal, at that point on the adolescent development timeline it usually means someone is being corrupted. Trent and Iris would drive around in her mom's car or hang out in secret places, smoking cigarettes and making out. He was probably the closest thing to a dyke she could find at the time: a scruffy, alienated skaterboy. They never had sex, but a letter he wrote her made it sound like they did, and when Trent's snoopy mother found it she went nuts. She went down to Iris's house screaming about statutory rape, she was going to call the cops, she was yelling all kinds of names at Iris, who sat on the couch beside Trent, rubbing his back as he cried. Iris couldn't even let anyone know they were kissing, so the story was that she had befriended him and he had developed a fantastical little crush on her. She was ordered never to speak to Trent again. For a little while they snuck around, and then Iris just heard about him through her mother, a school guidance counselor, explaining to young boys in confederate flag t-shirts why it was dangerous to huff gas. I laughed at gas huffing when Iris first told me about it, but apparently it's a serious problem in rural areas. Like satanism, suspicious piles of ash out in the woods, beneath trees carved with evil numbers and goat heads. Young kids dying or going retarded from inhaling gas fumes. It sounded so *Hard Copy.* Iris's sedate southern town was festering under the surface. The sheriff was corrupt, he was having teenage boys run cocaine for him, murder was involved. One boy was stockpiling guns for the oncoming revolution, but it was hard to figure out where he was coming from. Was he good or bad. He didn't like the government, but still something was fishy.

And these were the kids Trent was still palling around with. Iris's mom was concerned for him, and Iris decided we had to check up on him and remind him that life existed beyond this small town of gas huffing and drug rings. We drove out to his house. Iris couldn't ring his bell, still scared of his mother, so I was elected to prance up to the door with some cockamamie story of who I, the green-haired boygirl, was. But when we pulled up, another car was already there, boy forms shifting around inside. *Yell "Trent,"* Iris nudged me. Trent! *Who's that?* called a voice, all suspicious. Just Come Over, I hissed. I don't know what I was expecting. Iris did have a thing for teenage boys, hair buzzed and shaggy, clothes baggy, young enough for their facial hair to be cute, flipping up a skateboard with attitude. Trent had a horsey face and whiskers that made his chin look unwashed. His brown hair was just kind of regular, and he wore a baseball hat, brim forward. Trent was so excited when he saw it was Iris, he hopped right into the mess of CDs and granola that cluttered our back seat. We still hadn't cleaned it out from our road trip. Tape cases crunched under Trent's work boots. He had been so cautious approaching the car because the cops

124

were monitoring him and his friends, sitting around in parked cars noting the traffic at his house. He told us all about it. The cops were out to get him 'cause they knew he was dealing drugs. They'd already raided his house once, on a neighbor's tip, and his mom had all but given up on him. *She's still a bitch,* he said to Iris, and to me, *Do you know we used to go out?* Aaah . . . Yeah, I replied. Iris looked mortified. She Told Me All About It, I said.

We drove over to the liquor store to buy a case of Bud. It was a fortunate score for the boys that these girls old enough to buy beer had pulled up. Trent handed me a sweaty wad of bills and coins and in I went. Dumped it in the car and we hit the road. I had no idea where we were going but at least we were off the couch. Iris swerved us through dark winding roads, nothing but fields on either side, and Trent was telling us about how he'd driven this road on a bunch of acid and didn't crash even though kids were always wrecking out there after drinking or gas huffing or whatever it is they're all doing. We pulled up to this crappy little house with a BMW parked in the dusty front yard. *He gets all this money and that's what he spends it on,* said Trent. The boy who lived in the lousy house had short dark hair and was sweet and excited about San Francisco. *Are there skaters out there?* he asked. *Man, I bet there're tons of skaters out there!* Another boy was inside, sitting at the end of the couch, not saying a word the whole time. He was extremely pretty, with filthy ringlets of hair on his head, and you could tell from the pout on his face he was probably an asshole.

So we were drinking Budweiser and watching MTV in this room with an enormous dead deer mounted to the wall, along with guns and a great big bow and arrow. There was a dad crashing from speed in the next room, and every few minutes the dark-haired boy would say, *Hey we really gotta be quiet,* in this scared voice. At one point the dad grunted from behind the door and the boy went pale and moved us into his bedroom. Could it be that I'd never been in a teenage boy's bedroom before? He had skateboard ads ripped from *Thrasher* hung on his wall in a random pattern that looked very planned. The boy knelt before an impressive stereo and fiddled with CDs. *Do you like Danzig?* he asked earnestly. *Do you like the Beastie Boys?* He had one of those glass orbs that shoot violet lightning out from the center, and after submitting to some of Trent's pot I was thoroughly mesmerized by it. Someone noticed that the light pulsated to the beat of the music and we all sat quietly and watched it dance to Danzig's growls. I was incredibly stoned. Trent kept handing me beers before I could drain the can I was working on. I was sitting on a bed and somewhere on the dark-brown bedspread a light-brown cockroach was crawling. I tried to keep my eyes on it, but I was stoned, so I kept losing it. I was dumb from the pot and just sat there while they talked about how cool San Francisco was and how boring it was in Chickamauga and school sucked and they were just going to quit and grab their boards and go west. Iris loved these boys, I could tell. She wanted to be them. She was them. I should've just gone into the

126

other room and let them all jerk off on an Oreo or whatever secret thing teenage boys do together.

Eventually we left and became one of the cars carrying fucked-up kids down the perilous road. We did not crash. We took Trent to his house and parked there. *You want to smoke some more weed?* he asked. *I've got some really good shit inside.* Not being one to turn down pot, Iris said yes and Trent darted into his house. I'm Really Fucked Up, I said. Iris nodded. *Do you think they're all doing each other?* she asked, grinning. We wanted them to be, partly because that was hot and partly because we were so starved for gay people. Trent came back to the car and lit a joint off the car lighter. I could not imagine what would happen to me if I smoked more pot. I held it to my lips and drew it in. We silently held our clouds in our chests, passing the joint around the car and watching Trent's mother watch us through the window. She'd edge up to the curtain and slowly draw it back, spy for a minute and move away. *Look, there she is again,* Trent exhaled. *Crazy bitch. Want to see my dog?* He led us over to a small pen that held a fierce-looking dog. It went wild as we approached, barking and trying like crazy to fly over the fence. Trent liked to give his dog pot and alcohol. *I'm going to give her acid,* he said rubbing her slobbery head. *She'll fucking trip out!* I turned back to the house and saw the mom's silhouette at the window. Let's Go, I mouthed to Iris. She made vague plans to see Trent again as we wobbled back to the car. *I'm going to come to San Francisco!* he yelled as we climbed in. *I'm going to come out there!* He waved to us from the lawn. That Poor Fucking Dog, I said as we drove away. I was disturbed. He's Going To Kill It. *He's fucked-up,* Iris said simply. What else could she say? She was terribly stoned and they used to be such good friends. Towns trap people, that's for sure. The rest of the world may as well not even be out there.

And the wedding, the reason we were stuck in a little Georgia town where a famous Civil War battle had been fought, the creek running red with the blood of the soldiers. This town is so small it's a shock to see it on a map, but usually it's listed, because of the battle. The night before the wedding I was crying. I wasn't going to go. They could shove it up their ass. I had been with Iris at the bridal shop, in the dressing room, helping her into the horrible dress, maroon like the color of crusty menstrual blood, long and straight, little rosettes on the shoulder. Raw silk. Classy, not one of those froofy pastel numbers. I was trying to make the best of it by getting frisky behind the heavy dressing room curtain. It's not every day that Iris looked girly. I thought I'd put the moves on her but it was hopeless. This is where everything turned sour. Iris on a little pedestal, an old woman crouched at her feet, sticking pins in the hem. It was so wrong, so obviously wrong. Iris was a boy, she was beautiful, she was Peter Pan, and they had her done up like a matron. Take a strong and noble animal, an elephant or a black bear, and throw a hat on it and put it in a circus. That's what was happening to my girlfriend. It was terrible to observe. And what about me, my hair was bleached a fuzzy blonde so that with my glasses I looked like a cartoon chick. I looked like Tweety Bird. I had caved in to the bride and scrubbed the lime color from my scruff. Hanging in the closet was a Laura Ashley dress Iris's Aunt Dixie handed over when we realized I had brought nothing suitable for a six thousand dollar Southern Baptist wedding. It would have been really embarrassing had I given a shit, sitting in this perfect country home my mother would die for, ducks and rabbits and that blue and white ribbon motif. Dixie was rushing in and out of her two perfect daughters' closets, offering me all kinds of tasteful clothing, and I couldn't even make a decision because I had no idea what was appropriate. I felt like such a pauper, but instead of blushing I got into it. What else could I do? *Dixie loves this,* Iris's mom assured me as Dixie whooshed back with a pair of navy blue flats for me to sample. There I was, selling out to ease the bride's histrionics. And know what the problem was? She didn't want everyone to be paying attention to me and my green hair on her big day. It wasn't fair. She was supposed to be the center of attention. She'd waited her entire life for it. Please. Like I wanted the collective eyes of the homophobic Baptist family focused on me. Maybe I Just Won't Go. I *Can't* Go. I was crying in Iris's bed. It's Just *Wrong.* It's *Wrong* That I Can't Hold Your Hand. We *Always* Hold Hands. I was wracked by the injustice. At a marriage, a celebration of love. And Iris, it seemed so easy for her to pretend we were pals, she could just shut it off like that. I was sobbing. Maybe a little melodramatic, maybe not.

This is what it comes down to, right? Standing up for what's right and all that. *Have you lost respect for me?* she asked, and I wanted to say no, do the unconditional love thing, you know, I Support You No Matter What, but I thought it sucked. Little tough-shit kiss-my-ass Iris, all self-righteous in San Francisco, so quick to judge, and she can't even hold my fucking hand. But it's her family, and that's a big deal, and you can't force someone out of the closet, blah blah blah. I know, and I'm telling you it was wrong. And it was a dry wedding on top of it all. Baptist. Iris and I had plotted to smuggle in a bottle of whiskey to share with her alcoholic dad and the best man, who was so far gone everyone feared he'd get the shakes during the ceremony, going so long without booze. Obviously that little plan couldn't happen.

I walked around the reception like a ghost, this dazed girl in a flowing dress. I wasn't there at all. Getting introduced to various relatives who had no idea who they were meeting. They thought I was someone else. It was awful. And Iris getting escorted down the aisle on the arm of some gentleman. I locked myself in the church bathroom and cried. All the relatives telling her how pretty she looked and how San Francisco is such a lovely city and how they're going to come visit one day. Iris was in the receiving line with the dyed-to-match pumps lying on the carpet, pantyhose webbing her toes. *When's your turn?* an aunty teased. *Oh, I don't know,* Iris laughed uncomfortably. Beside her was her dad, so robust and glowing I knew he was sipping from his own private stash. He knew what he was getting into. I was the fool who drove halfway across the country on a lark. Totally unprepared. I sat like a wallflower on a folding chair eating cantaloupe. Next to me were a couple of girls Iris's sister taught science to. They were pretty weird-looking for that part of Georgia, dark blue nailpolish, a cluster of silver hoops jangling off their ears. And they were fixated on Iris. She was kind of a legend, being the one girl who had looked weird and had played music and had been so outspoken about things like racism that she got a cross burned on her lawn in high school. These girls were gazing at her. *Are you her cousin?* one asked. No, I'm Her Friend. *You two are best friends?* I nodded. They were best friends too. Iris's dad danced with the evil bride and everyone went *Awww,* and then we were allowed to leave. Out front sat the bridal getaway car, hung with balloons and streamers. One kid was hiding balloons under the tires for a big bang when the car pulled off. The bitchy sister flung her bouquet and, alas, Iris did not catch it, her eighty-year-old grandmother did, and I suppose she does have a better chance at marriage than Iris. Everyone thought it was so cute that the old lady caught the flowers. The wedding was over and we all got to go home.

Before Iris and I went back to California, one more thing happened—Daisy's tragedy. It was the day before our departure, around 2 p.m., our breakfast hour. We never did manage to overcome our strange lack of energy. From couch to bed and back was a struggle. Depressed people sleep a lot, I learned in my high school psychology class. So it was two o'clock and Iris was hooking up the Folgers and searching the fridge for leftover wedding food, and we heard crazy barking in the backyard. Daisy. Just howls and barks and whines and we walked over to the back porch, this screened-in, astroturf place with a cozy wooden swing, and there's Daisy running in circles, frantic, crying those awful cries. I thought maybe she'd been stung by a bee. She ran around the side of the porch scratching on the wood like she wanted inside. She hopped into the window, and that's when I screamed. Look At Her Eye! It was a moment clipped from a horror movie—our screams, little Daisy who had become a monster, her eyeball hanging out of her head, red and white, grotesquely swollen like a balloon you could pop, the pupil dead and staring in the center. Iris screamed, *Oh my god, oh my god!* and we did not know what to do. We heard her scratching at the back door, a noise like this awful beast. We were scared and crying, and we couldn't open the door. Iris called her mother at work. We were really inept. Now was the moment Daisy needed puppy cuddling the most and we couldn't even look at her. But we had to. We had to get her into the car and to the vet's. It was a nightmare. We left the house gingerly, like two kids in a slasher film, and when Daisy spotted us she barked fearfully and ran. She was so confused. We had the car door open, we tried to coax her in. We couldn't touch her, I couldn't stop thinking about the eyeball bumping into me and bursting. *Come on, Daisy.* She usually hopped right in. *Daisy, get in the car,* Iris cried. She was sobbing. Daisy got

132

in the front, and I got in the back and held her still, petted her. I forced myself to look at her eye so I could get used to it, but that didn't work. Bulging right out of her head. The fact that eyes can pop out suddenly became a reality to me. My eye could pop out. So could Iris's. If My Eye Ever Pops Out, Just Cover My Face, Don't Look At It, I said. *Oh, Michelle, I couldn't look at you with your eye out of your head,* Iris said, still crying. I Couldn't Look At You Either, I confessed. It was terrifying and heartbreaking. Poor Daisy. She seemed much calmer and not in pain but sometimes she'd try to scratch the eyeball and I'd shriek. There was lint caught on the end of it. We pulled up to the vet's and Iris's sister's husband's mother was waiting for us. This big crazy-looking woman with makeup caked into a deeply wrinkled face, silvery bird-feather hair like a bad hat. She came over to the window with a smile. She was only see-ing half of Daisy, the good half. *Oh Daisy, now, that's not so—* Her face froze. She dipped her head into her arm. It was very dramatic. *Daisy, WHY? Oh, WHY Daisy, WHY?* Daisy stared at the woman with her exploding eye, very calm. She had been hit by a truck, and it jolted her eye straight out. *Daisy got her eye knocked right out of her li'l ol' head,* Iris's mom said in her sweet voice, all perky. The vet said the eye was hanging by a single nerve. Imagine if it'd snapped. I couldn't have handled that. I guess they snipped the eye off, then sewed up her eye socket. She's a spaniel, so hair grew right over it. It's kind of cute, like a pirate puppy. Just her depth perception is off, so sometimes when she chases her braid she slams into the wall.

133

10

That was the year I puked on every winter holiday. If I was lucky, I had my head jammed down a toilet, innards convulsing. If I was unlucky, the stuff went elsewhere. Thanksgiving I was at Iggy's house back when I first met her, when she was fresh to the city from Chicago. Iggy was a loud redhead who told stories so incredible you wondered if they were true but ultimately didn't care because you were so enraptured by her grand gestures and re-enactments. And they were true. Iggy drank, and she cooked tremendous gourmet meals, and she smoked tons of cigarettes. I was glad that her place was a smoking household since me and Iris were a big smoking couple. Every morning Iris would rig up the espresso machine in her kitchen and froth us up these great soy milk coffee drinks, and about halfway through the glass, weighty pint glasses stolen from The Stud or The Uptown, we'd grab our smooshed blue packs of American Spirits and light up. I loved sitting on her back porch, on the peeling grey stairs that looked on to the weedy empty lot where homeless people slept on damp mattresses. A fat, magnificent palm tree grew in the middle, its top a burst of heavy leaves like an ancient jungle. I would sit and look at the tree and smoke and think about how great my life was. I leaned back against the rickety wooden crates packed with dirt and sunflowers, tangled vines with little yellow tomatoes you could pop in your mouth. Iris's garden. She would come and sit beside me on the old wood, and the stereo from her room would leak out, Sonic Youth or PJ Harvey. PJ Harvey was ours. So tortured about what? Why were we tortured? We were in love and life was a fast current swarming around our ankles, threatening to topple us into the wet part of the planet. It was intense, that's why we were tortured. It was enormous and exploding like that palm tree. Iris was my Yuri-G, my Delilah, my Stella Marie. Strong dark women you had to love with a strong dark heart that throbbed in gorgeous pain because love is terrible. I mean, ultimately. It would go away like a needle lifting from the vinyl at the end of the song, we knew this. The music would cease, one of us would die or else we'd just break up, and this drove us to drink from each other like two twelve-year-olds sneaking vodka from the liquor cabinet, trying to get it all down, trying to get as fucked up as possible before we got caught.

But back to Thanksgiving. Iggy cooked this huge fucking turkey, draped in warm apples and all that luscious grease, and you know I don't eat meat, or I didn't, hadn't for years and I stared longingly at the bird as it was brought from the oven for basting. Iggy bravely endured the lesbian/turkey baster jokes from the boys, and I sucked in the stink of roasting flesh like a cigarette. The turkey was in everything. It didn't even occur to Iggy that some people might not eat meat. Every dish had a bit of the bird in it. The stuffing had been up its butt, the gravy had been cooked from its muscle like sweat. All me and Iris could do was eat plain mashed potatoes, drink wine and smoke. *I'm having some stuffing,* Iris said defiantly, and that was great because if she could, I could too. I don't mind doing awful things as long as somebody else does. I would totally jump off the bridge, thanks for asking. I scooped a lump of the nasty stuffing onto my plate. And what was the difference between the stuffing and the gravy, both were tainted with the deceased turkey's secretions. I glopped a gorgeous, golden puddle of gravy onto my mashed potatoes. It was a holiday. I brought the plate into the living room with my wine and sat down in front of *Real World* on MTV. I had never seen it before, and as you might guess I got very wrapped up in it. Iggy's mom was visiting from Chicago, a short and charismatic woman in a sweatshirt that said I ♡ My Attitude Problem. Everyone ate the food and I kept thinking about that tray of turkey sliced up all nice on top of the stove. Turkey had been my favorite animal to eat. The tinge of it in my gravy was making me crazy, it was so good. What would happen if I ate some. Would I lose all respect for myself? Did anyone still care about animal rights? My shoes were leather, the people were right, I was a hypocrite. I Left My Cigarettes In The Kitchen, I said and hopped up, the fatty gravy sloshing around with the wine in my belly as I approached the oven and like a bulimic adolescent stuffed slabs of meat into my mouth. It didn't taste as good as I thought it would. I was not prepared for the reality of its thick, fleshy texture, the juices that oozed into my mouth as I chewed. I was too used to eating fake meat products that, once you adjusted, gave all the benefits of real meat without the gagging fat and gristle. I choked the turkey down and went back into the living room with a fresh glass of wine. I Ate Turkey, I confessed immediately. *I knew that's what you were doing!* Iggy hooted, delighted in that way carnivores get when vegetarians slip, like they knew we couldn't live without meat and would eventually give in to our flesh-shredding instinct. Iris looked disappointed in me as she chewed the spiced bread that had been marinating up the bird's ass. Oh well.

When the food was digested as much as food like that can, we all piled, drunk, into the car that Iggy's out-of-town roommate was letting her borrow. Iggy turned the radio up loud, PJ Harvey, and we all talked about how dumb it was to be driving drunk through the city in a borrowed car on Thanksgiving. We made it to The Stud and I, for one, got more beer. I don't have a driver's license. The bartender who worked the far end, by the DJ booth, liked to give beers away to the dykes. He was this cute, bald boy who would do snaky, gyrating dances behind the bar while he poured your beer. So I had my free beer and then Iggy grabbed me as I swung by her stool and she dragged me over to the counter and said, *Have you ever had Goldschlager?* Had What? *Two,* she ordered from the bartender, who immediately dropped a couple shot glasses onto the bar and started filling them up with a thick liquid that had some shit floating in it. *Goldschlager!* Iggy hollered. *It's got fucking gold in it!* twenty-four-karat flakes. For real, suspended and glinting in the syrupy drink. I would have loved Goldschlager in high school, it would have gone so well with the glittery twinkling teenage alcoholic faerie thing I was doing. One hundred fifty proof and so glamorous with that expensive confetti in it. Is It Ok To Drink Gold? *I'm sure it is,* Iggy reasoned, *or else they wouldn't sell it.* I knocked the shot back. It was pretty horrible, had been much better to look at, shimmering in its cup on the bar like a little lounge singer in a fancy dress. Thanks, I said to Iggy, and stumbled off to my beer and my girl.

A few hours later I was laid out on my futon, the world somehow set loose and spinning in my forehead. Ooooooh. I opened my eyes and the dismaying sense of movement continued. My head swam on my pillow. Iris, I moaned. I felt that tingle beneath my ears, a kind of crawling at my throat. I wasn't even that nauseated, but I knew what I was in for. Iris, I'm Going To Puke, I said, and Iris made some alarmed noise as I struggled to my knees and threw my window open hung my head over the sill and sent a great splash of vomit down three floors to the patch of scraggle and grass that was my backyard. I heard it land wetly. *Blaaaa,* another involuntary, unflattering sound, and more chunks careened past my landlord's bedroom window. Oh, Iris. I wanted her to save me. She wanted to sleep. Somehow I made it to the bathroom, the narrow red water closet. I folded myself around the bowl and stuck my head in like I was bobbing for apples. My entire internal system clenched and released, clenched and released as I threw up forever. It smelted worse than anything. I guess it was all that meat, all the fat in the gravy, but it smelled like something already rotting. I opened the window to the air shaft but it barely helped. The smell alone inspired vomit. I would vomit, breathe, catch a whiff, and vomit again, a terrible cycle. Eventually I shuffled back to bed. I felt pure the way you feel after you vomit, kind of light and strangely holy, like having taken a sauna in hell. I was embarrassed that Iris had seen me at my lowest moment. I lay in bed and felt two-dimensional beneath the covers, and I fell asleep.

I didn't puke on Xmas, exactly. I should have. Iris invited to dinner this girl she kept denying she had a crush on, even though it was so obvious to the entire world. I should have thrown up right there at the table, as we played Truth or Dare with the tall bottle of Southern Comfort Candice had stolen from The Stud. Everyone stole candles from the place, and occasionally pint glasses, and now at

Xmas it was fun to pull plastic snowflakes and candy canes off the wall, but the brand new bottle of Southern Comfort complete with a plastic spout was an incredible prize. She had to sneak behind the bar to get it. We drank shots of the stuff and the horrible girl in the brown dress asked me questions like, *What is your relationship to "femme"?* and I gave her dares like Go Into Iris's Room And Whack Off And Be Real Loud When You Come, which Iris thought was soooo hot. Really I had wanted to dare them to make out. I could see the workings of their inevitable seduction churning in their faces, little shimmers like summer heat rising off pavement. Why was she even there? It was a family holiday, a time for feeling safe in your surroundings. *She doesn't have anywhere to go for Xmas,* Iris had whined. She's Lived Here Longer Than I Have, I shot back. Why Doesn't She Have Any Friends, Why Doesn't Anyone Like Her, What's Wrong With Her?! Iris gave me a sad quiet look that said *you are mean.* I should've vomited in my Southern Comfort. I felt nauseated enough. There was my future, in the watery balls of this girl's eyes. They bobbed in their sockets like an excitable little dog's, like they were going to fall right out and roll across the linoleum.

But I did not barf that night. A few nights earlier this girl Angela's parents had gone out of town, and Angela had thrown a party. Angela was the only San Francisco girl I knew who was a native. Her parents had this big two-story house that struck me as super-wealthy, but probably it was just regular. My places are always so shoddy that anything even approaching middle-class seems extravagant. I was sure that somewhere there was a tub, a gigantic, luxurious tub we could fill up with water and bunches of girls could climb in. There would be lathers for our skin and bubbles for the water and it would be divine. We would splash and drink cocktails. This conviction grew with every tequila drink, sitting around the extra-long dinner table playing poker with beans and pennies and M&Ms. Girls were coming from all over the city to this party, with bedrolls and sleeping bags. It was a slumber party. There was an actual fountain in the yard, you could hear its quiet tinkle as you stood on the back porch smoking. If they had a fountain they had to have a tub. I began my wild quest for it, the luxurious sunken tub. At least to find an unusually large claw foot. C'mon, We're Going To Have A Tub Party! I was grabbing random girls and tugging them up the carpeted stairs. We were going to get naked in the water and bond. Find The Tub, I was ordering these girls. They went poking their heads into rooms, looking. In some rooms people were having sex in the dark, and they would yelp when the door cracked open. One room had a shower, a normal, actually kind of shabby shower, with no bathtub. That's Impossible! I was railing. All This Money, This Wealth, I gestured around me, And No *Tub?* Are They Crazy? Don't They Know About Tubs?! *Come here,* yelled one of my little scouts from deep inside the parents' bedroom. Is It A Tub? I gasped. It was a bidet. One of those fancy toilets that shoot water up your butt. No Way. Girls gathered around, watching the squirting water like it was that fountain in the yard. It was impressive.

141

But to have a bidet and no tub? Angela's parents were weird. Girls were discussing the masturbation potential. I think we all wanted to give it a try, but Angela busted out of a sex room and herded us out. *You can't come up here,* she said, *you all have to stay down-stairs.* It felt like high school. We marched down the stairs. Angela, Your Parents Have A Bidet! *I know,* she said. Downstairs everyone wanted tarot readings. Where was my girlfriend? I sat on a couch cushion on the floor and told everyone all about their future. I give fantastic tarot readings when I'm drunk. The cards fit together so smoothly and I do not mince words. Angela's little brother wanted one, and then passed out right in the middle of it. Sitting up and everything, just sitting there, unconscious. Angela, Look At Your Brother. I read Angela's cards instead.

What a great party. I went up into the bathroom and puked. Very businesslike, I knew what had to be done and I did it, gave it a little jump start, finger poking down my throat and the convulsions began, dry at first and then I was retching into the bowl, there in the bright bathroom. I remember someone had left this beautiful knife on the clothes hamper, and I was thinking how someone could just steal it. I could steal it. But that would be wrong. I concluded my vomit session and rinsed my mouth. My teeth felt like stucco. By the sink lay a spiked belt, and there were latex gloves in the wastebasket, glistening with some girl. Angela had better remember to fix the bathroom before the butt-splashing parents got home. I went back to my little cushion on the floor and curled up. *Are you all right?* girls asked. They had heard me barfing. I lay down and my girl came and lay down with me, we curled together and slept amidst the cacophony. The party would not end. I love the party experience of everyone thinking you're passed out when you're not, and they talk about you and you get to passively soak up all this attention. It feels so noble somehow, like being a dying princess. Everyone talked about how cute me and Iris were, and how I had puked, poor thing. It is the closest you can come to the fantasized moment of your death, all your loved ones leaning over your casket reminiscing about you. It was nice. I felt a lot better after puking and eventually the party chilled out and I fell asleep. In the morning some industrious and not-so-hungover girl was flipping pancakes, and everyone needed big cups of water and sweet syrupy orange juice from a giant can. Sober now and squinting in the light, everyone compared notes from the night before. Two girls who I hadn't seen at all stumbled onto the back porch. They had done acid and spent the night locked in an upstairs room. Apparently it hadn't been pleasant, and they were still tripping. They looked pretty disturbed. Me and Iris split a cab back to the Mission with them.

And then I puked on New Year's. I had refused to get dressed up because that was dumb and I was deconstructing the whole concept of getting "dressed up" and why I was supposedly more attractive in this certain style of dress. It was about gender and about class and I was boycotting it. I was at Bobby's cocktail party drinking a can of beer and everyone looked glamorous and great and I was instantly filled with regret, cursing my overly analytical mind. I was a common pauper in the same ratty things I always wore. Bobby, Can I Wear Some Of Your Clothes? Bobby looked smashing in this short, ridiculously feminine thing, sickeningly pink and flouncy and plunging all over the place. I went into his closet. He had everything, shiny plastic things I couldn't understand how to work, tiny rubber outfits dusted with talcum powder, vinyl goddamn stockings. I selected a moderately slutty black dress with bits of netting here and there. I used a little of his eye stuff and lip stuff, I got all glammed out. And wasted so much time primping that everyone was nicely buzzed and I was sober, so I started tossing shots of booze to the back of my throat, trying to catch up. Everyone wanted to be somewhere different at midnight and it was such a big group of us I knew we would ring in the new year trying to find parking. We were on our way to a gay bar, riding in a big, crappy car, big like they don't make cars anymore, stuffed with kids. A clown car. We parked in an alley south of Market and traipsed through rubble to our club. It was a gay club, right, but the owner had died without making any arrangements to hand it over to another homo, so it got passed on to his straight brother, who put all his asshole straight friends in key positions, like bouncer. They were at best condescending and at worst actually dangerous, physically dragging kids out or slamming them into walls. This night some friends of Iris's had been pulled

144

out and flung in the street for being too young. It had been brutal, becoming one of those drunk, urgent blurred dramas with all these kids clamoring around in their outfits trying to figure out who was inside and who left, where did they go, who saw it happen, should they call the cops, should they sue, girls were crying, and we needed dimes for the pay phone, and what was the proper response to it all. *I'm not going in there,* Iris proclaimed righteously in her slight Georgia twang. My belly floated downward on a torn parachute of hope. I knew she was right, but that's where all our friends were, the ones who hadn't been beaten and thrown in the gutter, and the music thumping through the walls was good stuff, and I was smashed, wanted to dance. *Come on,* Iris said. I cannot argue with righteousness. Iris was a soldier, it's why I loved her. The faith I had in her rested like a vital organ in my body. I mean, once I got over what a sell-out she'd been at the wedding. When the revolution came Iris would lift two rifles into the air, she would throw one to me and together we would run into the streets.

We left the throbbing nightclub and went to Iris's friend's house where the traumatized eighty-sixed girls were. The girl who lived there was super-deluxe political, she'd been on SSI for years because she convinced the State that she was incapable of working with men. She'd traveled through Central America, hitchhiking rides with gun-smuggling Zapatistas. She smoked pot from a pipe, leaning back on her couch, smiling a faint stoned smirk like she knew everything. She dressed schlumpy like Iris did. They passed the pipe back and forth while I sat chilly and exposed in my tiny slutty dress, feeling like a dumb girl. I kept wondering what Iris's friend thought of me, did she think I was shallow because I was sitting there drunk in a black mesh loincloth, did she think I didn't know how horribly awry the world was, or maybe she thought I didn't care, or that I cared in a vague feed-the-stray-animals way but not in her complex intellectual way. That I was worrying at all about this makes me think I had joined them in smoking pot. But wouldn't that have stopped me from barfing? Because I barfed in the activist girl's house. Where's Your Bathroom? I asked carefully, and it was a long slow walk down the hall because I didn't want to jog and look desperate. The bathroom was messy and dim. I assumed my position around the bowl and let it fly. I was in there forever, wanting to make sure I got rid of it all. I crammed my fingers down my ragged throat and heaved and spit and wiped my lipstick-smeared mouth with toilet paper. I wobbled back down the hall in my heels. I wanted to explain to the political girl that I didn't normally wear heels. Everything carried so much meaning. *Are you all right?* they asked. Umm . . . Yeah, I said hoarsely. I Puked. I figured she'd smell it, so I might as well be honest. The two of them were talking about that girl Iris had a festering crush on. They both worked with her. *She's a poet,* I was informed. That's Great, I said, stretching a big fake smile over my mouth's barfy canyon. I'm Sure Her Poems Are Really Great. I was so sure that this girl was just really incredibly great. I was sure she never drank to the point of

146

barfing, in fact, she probably didn't drink at all, or smoke, or wear embarrassing, trampy outfits, or shoes she couldn't actually walk in. Surely she wrote stunning poems that were very deep and smartly worded and grammatically correct because she went to college. A good one, a good girls' college, and studied literature—she's very well read. I let my plasticky smile droop into a drunken frown. Iris, Let's Go, I whispered. She didn't really want to, but she did. We were girlfriends.

11

Here's a sad thing that happened about a week after New Year's. Just a little chip off the great vase of sadness. I was in this bar, a dark place with round candles in glass glowing at the tables. I was co-hosting an open mic for girls. Poetry, right, but they did all kinds of things: puppets, lip-syncs, chain saws and one naked girl playing a cello. A girl was doing a dance, I think it was supposed to be tribal, her raver idea of that. The girl was usually on a lot of drugs and trying to get me and Iris to have sex for the porn movies she wanted to make. She did acid and Ecstasy and speed, she had something like nine hairdos going at once—shaved, stripes, a few colors, a tail, all kinds of stuff. Later I nearly had an affair with her. I really tried. She'd cut out using the drugs but had this maternal girlfriend keeping her in line. But this night she was still the crazy girl who was always high. You'd see her dancing forever at a club, topless and wrapped in a feather boa, the drugs shooting off her skin like a glow. She'd been a stripper in Amsterdam. So at this open mic she danced, naked but smeared with paint like mud, paint in her fucked up hair, crusting the short bits together. She had candles and a big shell that held incense or sage, something smelly to stink up the bar. She had bunches of flowers and that was the best part, thick green stalks, long flowers like a royal scepter, strong flowers like a branch wrenched from a tree. She played some trippy music on a little radio and writhed and twitched and held the flowers, moved them all over her face, dark around her eyes. People paid attention, more than they did to the poetry. Her pubic hair was one more dark spot on her body, and the bitch who ran the bar was going nuts about her being so naked. It kept happening. You have an open mic for girls and they all want to take their clothes off. I thought it was great. I wanted to get in a fight defending it. The naked dancing girl convulsed on the floor on top of all those flowers and I winced because I was planning to take them and I didn't want them crushed. She finished up and took her little radio and the smoking seashell and padded barefoot back to the bathroom to wash off. Her back was stuck with leaves and bits of flower and stuff from the bar floor.

She left the candles burning on the stage, she left the flowers lying beaten on the floor, and I went for them like the kid who'd busted the piñata. I wanted to give one to Iris because things had been so weird. We were trying to be nonmonogamous so that she could make out with and eventually sleep with that girl I didn't like. I would be very lofty and intellectual and cool about the whole concept and then she would show up looking like something terrible had happened to her neck, and I'd collapse on the sidewalk and weep. I figured I'd give her these flowers. I looked around the bar. It was filled with women. The lady who owned the place was busy pouring beers and couldn't yell at me about the naked girl. I went to the front of the bar to this big round booth, black leather, and Iris was sitting there with that girl, the both of them in the booth's dark curve, the free beer she got off me frothing on the table. They looked at me. Here, I said to my girl, thrusting the lily at her like a sandwich or the ten bucks I owed her. I left pretty quick. Like I handed her my heart and left fast so I didn't have to see what she did with it. I didn't want to know. Her and that girl and their big empty faces. I walked back to the bathroom. This girl I kind of liked was in there. We started shoving each other around, started kissing against the wall. Joey had this big, excellent body, she was really very cute, and I was so happy she felt like kissing me. Ha, I thought with her tongue rolling in my mouth. It was pretty perfect. We pulled away and smiled hot little smiles at each other, flushed, rearranging the spit in our mouths, and then she left the bathroom, and then I did. I saw Iris against the bar, alone with the lily and her beer. Where's Emma? I asked about her floozy. I Just Kissed Joey In The Bathroom. *You did?* Her face got kind of broken-looking. She

150

was pissed. You Were With Emma! I yelled. *We weren't kissing!* she yelled back. I knew that. It was almost worse. I Came To Give You Flowers, I said, And You Were With Her. Iris was such a shithead. I was so good, picking up the bruised flower with its green blood and rumpled petals to bring to my girl. She broke my heart, so now I have to write about her forever. It made everything different. It's something that can only happen once. You will cry a thousand times but they'll only be echoes. The dancing naked girl came back with all her clothes on. That Was Really Great, I told her. She was very high. *Yeah,* she said, her eyes darting around. Later she told me she did it all for me, the dancing, the candles, some sort of ritual seduction, but it sounded like she was lying. I Thought You Liked My Girlfriend, I said then, and she said *No, you, always you.*

12

I felt like someone stuck some awful in-flatable toy under my ribs and pumped it big and puffy until all the lungs and the skinny highways of veins and all the tender nameless organs got crushed up against my stomach. I felt like I was going to faint or puke or cry. All because of Joey, that girl I made out with in the bathroom to make Iris jealous. I'd crushed myself out on her and it was making me sick. She was a big heart walking down the street, not a sweet curvy heart fit for holding nothing but melty lumps of chocolate. I mean she was like the heart she carried under her ribs, a big strong one, thick and heaving. Gory and beautiful in its honesty. That's what I saw as she swung her bicycle through the cafe door, all smiles, puffy jacket, knit hat on her greasy head, black glasses wrapped around her face like alien eyes. She looked like she was hiding from someone, on the lam. She leaned her bike up against all the other bikes and whipped off her glasses. She hugged me with the fat arms of her powder blue ski jacket, just like the one I had had as a kid. I don't have to tell you I was happy she was there. Iris had taken to sleeping with the awful wench Emma. I'd show up at Iris's house like usual and she'd not even cleaned, the dick left in its harness on the floor, sheets in a tangle, evidence everywhere. But her stereo, that was the worst. PJ Harvey, right there, a sleek vinyl scab on the turntable. She was fucking Emma to PJ Harvey, our music. It was like all the girls were interchangeable. We were the passing bodies of her landscape, we were trains or clouds and the music was Iris's soundtrack for her love affair with herself, the music and the gasps and the giggles. Valentine's Day morning I woke up early in my own bed and made a trip to Rainbow for breakfast stuff, fake sausage and fake Canadian bacon, eggs, Odwalla. I bought her a rose, bagels. Soy milk for coffee. As the 14 Mission bus heaved and jerked along its route I realized I might be surprising Emma as well. I thought about walking into the bedroom and seeing Emma's mousy head of hair poking up from the blankets, her body curled around my girl in sleep. I was glad I'd bought some grapefruits. They'd make such a great thud as they hit the wall, maybe even splatter if I threw them hard enough. The eggs would be a mess, that I was happy with. Food carnage all over that unfaithful girl's walls, knocking over bongs and spilling her putrid pot water onto the carpet. I was livid, almost disappointed when I found a single solitary Iris, her sweet drowsy face happy to be about to get fed. But I'd gotten so involved in the fantasy I felt like the scene had already happened. Too shaky to cook. *You would've flung the food all over the place?* Iris asked, kind of delighted. *Really?* I Would Have Kicked Her Little Ass, I lied. It's Fucking Valentine's Day. Iris loved the idea of girls fighting over her, it made her melt right back into her futon. *Emma's a black belt in karate though,* she warned me. *She'd probably really hurt you.* Oh, fuck both of you, I thought and scrambled some eggs.

It looked like it was about time for me to get interested in a girl who wasn't Iris, and Joey was plenty interesting. Inside the coffeehouse she took up space like a heart inside a body, like the room was a throne for her humble importance. She held a smudgy newspaper in her hands, eyes on the astrology column. *I've got to confer with you about my horoscope,* she told me, making my own heart bounce because I knew she had a real romantic horoscope that week. That's when I know I like a girl for certain, when I search her zodiacal blurb for a hint of myself inside her destiny. I hated her saying that, making me get all melty, and encouraging the hopeful *boing* of my heart. Joey needed a tarot reading and that's all she needed, but the ping-pong ball inside me kept on rattling. She held the cards in her hands, flipped them around sloppily, a dog with silver-ringed paws. She shuffled the deck like playing poker and asked if that was ok. She kissed the deck and slapped it down

154

on the metal table. I laid the cards out, thinking, she should get someone different, someone who wouldn't be looking for clues in every card. Oh, the girl was sad. I flipped them over, she had those merciless swords, sharp points tearing apart a flower. She had the murkiest water cards, she had the scarab that stole the sun and hid it beneath the ocean, and I knew if she just let me in a little more I could make the good cards come.

Outside, we smoked cigarettes in a garden full of girls. Joey was turning her petals toward all their different lights. Me wishing that I knew what her dream girl was so I could become it. Yeah, I knew that was a dumb thing to think, I could tell by the way it felt in the sad space of my stomach. All lousy, as I looked at my linty wool tights, re-evaluating my smudgy red eye shadow. She liked girls who looked like superheroes, the kind of girl superhero who required you to suspend disbelief in order to imagine her kicking ass. Like the ultra-skinny girl over there with the biggest eyes and perfect hair the color of roses. All these girls were the fanciest, as I sat on a small red table and swung my legs like a child, looking nervous. There was another girl and I guess she could've passed for Wonder Woman, her eyes were lidded with sharp blue, she had glittery barrettes in her jet-black hair and Joey's head on her lap. I thought she should appreciate it more, touch her greasy swirls or something, not just sit there like she was waiting for the cameras to go on. Wonder Woman had Dr Pepper lip gloss that she let me borrow even though I told her that I hated Dr Pepper. It made me think

155

of driving cross-country with my grandfather when I was a kid. I told them about how we'd pull into a hotel when the sun went down and he'd climb into bed with a bottle of whiskey and a single red can of Dr Pepper, smoke filterless L&Ms in the unventilated room, and stay up all night watching TV movies while I ducked my head under the covers, hiding from the glare and the thin haze of smoke that glowed like the LA sky at dusk.

God, I want to barf just thinking about it, said Joey the talking dog from her place on the superhero's lap. So I kept talking because nothing gets me going like knowing I should shut up. Oh, I should be quiet and full of potential like all those still flowers, but I know I am a weed and I've got to blow my seeds around the garden. I have such faith in words, like the right combination spilling from my mouth could've made her look at me like she looked at all of them, eyes blue and bright as a kid's. So I babbled about pot cookies and mystical experiences, the time I got so high I thought I was buddha and Jesus and had an orgasm right there on my bed just thinking about it, both hands tucked under the pillow. I knew I sounded like a lunatic and the dog grinned lazily. And when the superhero finally left the cafe, I learned that she was the straight girl Joey had told me about kissing the other night.

In the corner store we pulled fat bottles of water from the shelves. No one thinks it's weird that we have to buy clean water, and that's how I know we're going to hell. Joey needed candy. We hovered over the racks, she grabbed Starbursts and bunches of

156

chocolate and I ladled a handful of artificial fruit stuff, lollipops and colored gumballs, hard blocks of Jolly Ranchers sticky under cellophane. The stoic counter guy rang up our purchases. Outside, winter made like it was leaving, and I felt it all inside me as I took off my fluffy jacket and my tight, filthy thermal. We walked the warming February streets, this phony spring making me different, making me want to fly right out of this city and land someplace new. Do You Look At Yourself In Every Window You Pass? I laughed as she nodded. I Do Too. She sang Carly Simon. We were in a band together right then, and she was the singer. She sang like . . . I would sit inside my chest thinking it couldn't get any worse, my heart, and then I'd hear her sing and I'd beat my drums like I was driving away every feeling I'd ever had, slamming at her and the garden girls, Iris and her new Emma. *Bam bam bam.*

We entered the cool cave of the practice space with all the long-haired, goateed boys stoned on clouds of pot and playing with power tools. I tossed my fluffy coat into the hollow of my bass drum and lay on the carpet with my worn newspaper. A shirtless boy came in and told us he had to cut the power for a minute, and I thought about being alone in the cool black room with Joey. *Let's go smoke,* she said, and I grabbed the cigarettes off the amp. She started talking to me about Wonder Woman. *I feel like something big is happening, but I don't know what to do about it.* With The Straight Girl? I asked in the blankest voice possible. *With everything.* Back in the sun we walked to the edge of the parking lot where

157

a black Impala convertible sat, rusted and rotting, looking like it just got dredged from a swamp. Rainwater pooling on the floor. We climbed up onto it and sat our butts backward on the edge of the windshield, feet stretched into the front seat. Before she even joined the band, I would think of her each time I passed the car, the little round medallions with the red and black racing flags affixed to the dash. On the rusting Chevy, Joey told me about her date the other night with a girl she used to like who she maybe liked again. How her heart was shut off and it felt pretty good. How she just wanted to play around and this girl and that girl and this girl and I smoked my cigarette and went Uh-Huh. The sun made me feel like a restless country girl even though I'd never been on a farm. I knew what I stood for, even if nobody else did. I knew the piece of me on the inside, truer than all the rest, that never comes out. Doesn't everyone have one? Some kind of grand inner princess waiting to toss her hair down, forever waiting at the tower window. Some jungle animal so noble and fierce you had to crawl on your belly through dangerous grasses to get a glimpse. I gave Joey my ciga- rette so I could unlace the ratty green laces of my boots, pull them off, tug the linty wool tights off my legs. I stretched them pale over the car, the hair springing like weeds and my big toenail looking cracked and ugly. I knew exactly who I was when the sun came back and the air turned warm. Joey climbed over to the hood of the car, dusty black, and said *Let's lie down, I love lying in the sun,* but there wasn't any sun there. We moved across the street onto the shining white sidewalk and she stretched out, eyes closed. I smoked my cigarette, tossed it into the gutter and lay down beside her. She said she was sick of all the people who thought she felt too much, who wanted her to be calm and contained. Who? I asked. All the flowers, the superheroes. I thought about how she had kissed me the other night, quick and hard, before taking off on a date in her leather chaps, hankies flying, and I sat on the couch and cried at everything she didn't know about how much I liked her, and someone put an arm around me and said, *You're feeling things, that's good.* Yeah, I said to Joey on the sidewalk, I Feel Like I Could Calm Down Some. *Awww, you're perfect.* She flipped her hand over and touched my head. Listen, we're barely here at all, I wanted to tell her, rolling over, looking into her face, we're barely here at all and everything goes so fast can't you just kiss me? My eyes were shut and the cars sounded close when they passed. The sun was weak but it baked the grime on my skin and made it smell delicious. A little kid smell. We sat up to pop some candy into our mouths, and then Joey lay her head on my lap, spent from sugar and coffee. Her arm curled back around me and my fingers fell into her slippery hair. On the February sidewalk that felt like spring.

13

One thing I did that February was give up on the seduction of Joey. Another was flip a coin about breaking up with Iris. The third noteworthy thing I did that month was place an ad in the gay personals. Bratty Little Bottom, it began, Looking For Tough Girls To Rough Me Up And Boss Me Around. God, I cringe just thinking about it. Don't Want A Girlfriend, the end proclaimed, Just A Hard Sleazy Fuck. Iris didn't have so much time for me now that her affair with Emma had blasted off. Each day another lesbian nonmonogamy boundary crumbled beneath Iris's need. She needed to see this girl on a weekend, taboo. Make plans at the last minute, break plans with me, take her to the bar where we always went and dance with her to "Rebel Girl," our song. As it was, Iris and Emma saw each other all day at work, kissing in the

160

cooler of the worker-owned organic food co-op. Iris was about a day away from rent when she got that job, with practically nothing in the bank and seemingly no employment prospects. Instead of actually looking for work she was burning a green candle stamped with the word "job," bought at the Mexican grocery on the corner. It sat glowing on her television by the bong, infusing Iris's smoky room with luck. A couple weeks before rent was due, she had decided to pull the traveler's check scam with the paltry $160 she had in her account at the credit union. I Don't Know, I said. You Can Only Do This Scam Once Because They'll Have You In Their Computer. Don't You Want To Wait And Do It With More Money? It seemed like a lot of nerve-racking work for $320, but that was Iris's rent exactly. So she got her money converted and went up into the Haight to go shopping. She did it all wrong. You're supposed to spend as little money as possible cashing the checks, but Iris came home that night with a gleaming new ceramic bong from a head shop, cute knitted hats from pricey skater shops, records. Even if the scam did succeed she'd be short on rent. She tossed *Confusion Is Sex* on her turntable and fired up her new pot toy. Then she called the check company and told them she'd been held up at knife point in a parking lot in the Mission. I rolled my eyes. It was the worst story ever, and Iris sounded like a shady weirdo telling it. What was she doing loitering in a dark parking lot in the "bad" part of town? Why hadn't she filed a police report? The last thing you want your scam story to be is complicated. A simple pickpocket, something

161

the lady on the phone could imagine happening to herself. Nothing that suggests your lifestyle might be unseemly and you to blame for the theft. I once heard about a girl who didn't get her money simply because the check place found out she stripped. She eventually got the cash, but she had to go to court to make it happen. The check people told Iris to file a police report about her "attack," and to call the next day at exactly 3:00 p.m., something she remembered to do around 5:00 p.m. For a week, she just kept forgetting to call. It was clear that they did not believe her story. She gave up. She had some new gear and less rent money than ever. Then, on the way to her job interview at the food co-op, she bicycled past a phone booth with a wallet lying open on top. Hundreds of dollars inside. Iris checked the ID and verified that the owner was an acceptable person to steal from, a white-haired white man with a lot of credit cards. She took the dough and left the wallet, went to the interview and got the job. Iris. She was a beaming child of the cosmos, karma's kid sister. No matter how lazy she was, how much she fucked up, how many hearts she broke in the most careless way possible, magical things kept happening to her. Money, jobs and five sweet new girls for every one she left bitter. A halo of luck around her darling dopey head. I hated her. I realized chance was on her side, and a flip of the coin would never advise me to break up with her. I would jog alongside her romance with Emma forever, waiting for it all to end.

Nights Iris was out cavorting with Emma I went out drinking. Smoking in bars I was ok, but alone, in my room, anxiety shook me like a teakettle. I'd come home late, drunk, and check the voice mailbox for my personal ad. I was terrified that someone I actually knew might call it. Would I recognize a voice I knew? One woman left a message telling me how she would lovingly bind my wrists to her wrought-iron bed frame and tickle me with an ostrich feather. I called the number she left. Listen, I slurred, I Meant The Part In The Ad That Said "Roughed Up." I'm Talking About Some Serious Violence Here, So Call Back If That's What You're Looking For. I hung up. How psychotic. I wanted to be whipped into numbness by a stranger. I wanted to be slapped around until I left my body, slid into an altered state of consciousness. The next message started out good enough, a gravely girl's voice telling me she was going to take me into a filthy public toilet. But the fantasy disintegrated into the most ridiculous poop and pee scene ever, and I knew it was my insane friend Tatiana making fun of me. The burst of laughter at the end confirmed it. She had actually called from my house when I had run out to get cigarettes. I wanted to kill her. There were no other messages. Of course there weren't. I knew the name and face of every S/M dyke in town, and they all knew me, and this whole personal ad thing was a big embarrassing mistake. I flipped another penny and it told me to continue my masochistic love affair with Iris. I checked my pervy voice mail again and there was a new message and it sounded all right. From a girl who had just moved here from Boston, same place I was from, so we'd have that to talk about at least. I arranged to meet her. I have a sex date with

163

a stranger, I thought, hitching garters around my waist and throwing on a flouncy skirt. As long as I was able to keep my mind away from my heart, it seemed like a pretty cool situation. Brave and exciting. But my heart was a whirling, starving void that sucked and sucked like a terrible black hole, and when it gobbled up my logic it made what I was doing look lonely, and sleazy. I laced my Docs and grabbed my leather jacket.

The girl's name was Athena, and she had bleached-blonde hair covered up with a funny leather or leather-looking bandana. All black clothes, a black leather vest, kind of punky and right around my age. I couldn't believe it. Lady warrior tattoos on her arms. All right. We talked about Boston, she was a writer and a librarian, admirable things to be. We drank beer with slices of lemon skidding on the foam. I got kind of drunk and let her take me home. When she kissed me in her dark bedroom I felt a little rasp of heat, a weak memory of my first kisses with Iris when everything inside me flared and set our rollercoaster of sex in motion. Athena had that Portishead CD on repeat, it whirred in the dark for hours. *Nobody loves me, it's true* . . . She neither roughed me up nor bossed me around, though I spied whips and belts hanging from her closet door and thought maybe it was just a matter of time. She fucked me with one of those hard lucite dildos they keep in the display case at Good Vibrations, a pretty crystal of a dick. It was good until I had to fuck her back. Who was she? Should I care? Athena from Boston. I didn't feel close to her,

164

I didn't know her at all. What was connecting me to her? I felt a thin panic rise. *Nobody loves me, it's true, not like you do. . . .*

I had been thinking of buying that Portishead CD but now I knew I could never listen to it. In the morning we sat and smoked on her back porch and I told Athena all about my fucked-up relationship. She nodded warily, flicked her cigarette ash into a small glass ashtray. I told her I wanted to see her again, and when I left her house and moved back out into my life I knew it wasn't true. I walked down South Van Ness, all the crappy auto shops, fences laced with shining hubcaps. I glanced down at the sidewalk and there, carved deeply into the cement, the name Emma. I stopped. What did it mean? I bent to the ground and touched the frozen waves of cement that clumped around the letters. Emma. I walked home. I flipped another coin, and it said to break up with Iris. I Can't Do This Anymore, I cried to her later. You're Forcing Me To Break Up With You. Iris said nothing. She seemed stoned or retarded, a dull silence. I hung up the phone, or left the bar, or I left her house or she left mine. She let me go.

14

So the planet of me completed its revolution around the heart, the hot burning thing,
center of my own little solar system. In those few weeks
I became sort of a neighborhood fixture, like the Red Man, or that
tiny woman with the thick white stuff crusting on her face. I was
the Crying Girl, smoking on the steps of the Blue House I now lived
in, phone jammed against my ear. One night was marathon, five
hours I think, I called everyone but mostly Candice who had almost
all her planets in Scorpio and understood the process of death and
rebirth. One night I made the decision to call Iris, an enormous
leap, only to learn that I had just missed her. She had left to play
her drums and there was no phone at the practice space so I had
to sit on the stairs and smoke cigarettes until she called me back

at 10:00 p.m. What was the attitude? I had played all my angles, tossed my heart with a wet rattling thump onto her snare drum, I Love You I Love You I Love You. Such an impossible gift, impossible that it was just left there, a red pool on her drumset, beating its last weak beats. So I shifted to the other angle, the big strong Leonine one like Well Fine Who Cares Anyway Thanks For The Reality Check I'm Off To A Party Now. And I was, I jumped in the shower, washed it all off, put on pretty clothes and actually took a cab to the upper Haight to meet some friends at a party. I have terrible luck at Haight Street parties. The last one had me pulling off my yeasty underwear and dumping it on some guy's head. He'd been discussing my ass with his friends. This party was even worse, it was right on the corner of Haight and Ashbury, a cursed and haunted neighborhood. Some skinny guy with a skinny moustache cracked open the door and told me they weren't letting anyone in, it was too crowded. I started whining about how all my friends were inside and he gave a big sigh and swung the door open. It really was too crowded. The hallway was very traditional Haight-Ashbury, with tie-dye and trippy lights and iridescent paper covering the ceiling. Bunches of straight people, mostly men, and as I pushed my way through, a woman yelled at this relic in a floppy leather hat to please not touch her ass. It occurred to me that I would probably get in a fight with someone, filling me with a dread similar to that of having to go to work or pay the phone bill, inescapable. If I found my friends I'd be safe. I pushed through the hallway, all smoky incense and people

167

with full cups of beer trying not to slosh it on everyone. The house was an old San Francisco Victorian, rooms branching off the long hallway. I poked my head into each one, trying to spot a familiar hairdo. The first room had a DJ spinning rap music and people were dancing or sitting on cushions smoking pot. Another room was a more intense drug scene, just a bed with people sprawled out in various stages of vegetable. Then a room with live music, a guy with his dick out playing guitar, and everyone turned and smirked at me when I entered, expectant, like they were waiting for my shocked reaction, but I was so over it. At the end of the hall you could buy a balloon of nitrous for two dollars. The final room had a microphone and a guy spoke into it. *How can you tell when your sister has her period?* My friends would not have spent five minutes at this party. I had blown six dollars on a cab and I was irritated. Iris didn't love me, or loved me but didn't want to be with me, or couldn't be with me because her spongy Piscean nature absorbed my Aquarian electricity until all she was was me, or something like that. So she had to go and have sex with someone quiet and non-threatening. This was my interpretation. I made my way back down the obstacle course that was the hallway, slammed out of the horrid neo-hippie extravaganza and bumped into Tricky, a dyke. Don't Go In There, I said. Really. Please, You Do Not Want To Go In There. I Have To Get Beer, Come With Me.

Tricky was with this boy named Martian who was all done up in X-Girl drag: fuzzy skirt, baby shirt with a shiny pink heart, lots of soft

168

girlie makeup. Martian was really annoying with his toy flashlight that he kept shining in my face. I had to buy a 22 at the grocery store since I no longer had my girl to split a 40 with. Underage Tricky slipped me a five to purchase cider for her and Martian. Out front I popped the cap off my lonely 22. Tricky was talking to a skinny wired girl, beautiful in a dark Peter Pan way. She was punk and had a cane, one of the kids who live in the park. She was waiting for someone to bring her drugs. *I'm gonna get high,* she said in this really out there voice that contradicted how jumpy she was, bouncing in her boots, hitting the sidewalk with her cane. Iris had been on a cane trip when I first met her. She wanted to have an affair with an older butch dyke who walked with a cane. A fantasy lover that Iris had dreamed up. Iris also wanted a cane for herself. She was sure that one day she would walk with a cane. It was one of her life predictions that she came up with in this psychic Pisces way. Something would happen to her leg or her foot. She was also certain that she would spend significant time in jail, a premonition she talked about with this strange wise toughness, as if she'd already lived through it. Tricky liked the skinny girl with the cane, and I was thinking about how Iris would like her too. We would assume these weird characters sometimes, she the runaway boygirl who lived in the park and me the tough older coke dealer who let her stay at my place, but she had to fuck me to earn her keep. This weird fantasy would occasionally leak out of the bedroom. We'd be on the bus, and she'd be talking about the kids in the park and trying to get me to buy her a skateboard.

169

The punk girl eventually left to collect her drugs, and we walked back to the party. Tricky was all excited, saying, *She's a dyke, she's a dyke, she told me she didn't like men!* Absolutely everything was annoying me. I felt like such an adult around these two, like I was babysitting. I was filled with the aged and bitter wisdom of the brokenhearted. *I want to go back and find that girl,* Tricky was saying. Just Come Back To The Party With Me, I said. I wanted to be sure that my friends were not in there. We pushed ourselves inside, made the awful journey up the hallway and turned around to start back for the door. *We want nitrous,* Tricky said. She was tugging on people. *Hey who has nitrous, where can I get a balloon?* No one would talk to her, and Martian kept beaming that flashlight. Listen, I'm Going Outside To Smoke A Cigarette. If You're Not Out By The Time I'm Done, I'm Going Back To The Mission. I was feeling very bossy. My life was strongly out of my hands. I was attempting to control what I could, sitting on the corner of Haight and Ashbury with a beer and a smoke, reading an astrology book. The absorbent, subconscious nature of Pisces. And then up comes Iris on her skateboard. I heard the rumbling of wheels on concrete and looked up and she was there, flipping up her board with her feet. I Am So Glad To See You, I said in a direct, matter-of-fact way. I was completely unsurprised to see her there, sent by the universe to guide me out of this terrible, unfamiliar territory. And of course it meant something else—we had to talk more, something was unfinished. My heart was back in my body, and it was not throb-

170

bing. It was just calmly pumping blood, its purpose no longer passionate but mechanical. I felt very detached from Iris, this girl I had spent the past eight months with. Yet I needed her to know how detached, how over it, how completely above the whole situation I was. I had the idea that I was a very noble animal, committed to romance and passion, and if she was not qualified to share that with me, then, whatever. I Promise You You Don't Want To Go In There, I said. She looked around at the loitering straight men and knew it was true. I told her I was waiting for Martian and for Tricky, who was trying to score nitrous, and then they came out, sober. We tried to formulate a plan. Martian was pointing the toy flashlight at Iris's face, and I finally grabbed it and pushed it down, saying, You've Got To Stop With That Light, in the no-nonsense voice of a schoolteacher or dominatrix. Iris looked at me, surprised. This was my pain, my intense spiritual maturity that no one could match. Iris was a floundering child, too young to understand how precious I was. She wanted to play.

Iris had come to the party in search of the friends I hadn't been able to find. We spent a long time musing about where they could be and a longer time sliding quarters into pay phones, dialing up answering machines. Finally Vinnie answered. Of course they didn't stay at the party, they went to some awful gay bar and drank beer. I didn't even know that Haight Street had a gay bar. Vinnie was concerned about me, trapped in the upper Haight with Iris. It's Ok, I said quickly, I'm Totally Over It. We walked to the corner to wait

171

for a bus back to the Mission. I had a beer, Iris didn't. I was drain-
ing the bottle before the bus came. I bummed a dollar from her to
pay my fare. *Don't worry about it,* she said, or something like that,
something reminiscent of the olden days of communal girlfriend-
ship. I'll Pay You Back, I said, along with some phrase designed
to drive it home that things were different now. We were on the
bus. I was going on and on about Pisces, reading things from my
astrology book, and Iris seemed more and more frightened as I
expounded on how inherently hopeless it was, her nature. It was
mapped in the sky that she would never know what she wanted.
Pisces, Pisces-rising, Scorpio moon. She was a flooded river with
no substance, taking shape only when poured into another vessel. It was futile. Iris looked horrified. I'll Never Go Out With A
Pisces Again, I proclaimed. You're Worse Than Geminis. The final
astrological insult. We climbed off the bus at Market and the walk
into the Mission consisted of my trashing the fish and Iris quite
despondent, asking, *What can I do?* I think I suggested therapy.
I could not understand why she didn't want to be with me. I was
so nice to her, I really cared about her. I loved her, and we had fun
together. We had plans. We were going to go to Europe together.
I was going to get an eleven thousand dollar Astrea grant for
Emerging Lesbian Writers and take her band on tour. I was generous. I bought her a sixty dollar lava lamp for Xmas. I bought her
a pierced nipple, and that tattoo from Georgia—those twin fish
swirling around the cursed number thirteen. I increased her cool-

172

ness, I nurtured her, and she abandoned me for a bland little twit who was very invested in being femme. Humiliating.

She wanted me to wait for her bus with her. I don't know why, I was exploding all over her. Perhaps she knew what a louse she was for forcing me to dump her, and her conscience was craving punishment. We were sitting in the bus shelter at 14th and Mission. It had rained earlier, and the street was dark with it. The trash was not blowing around our ankles but lay wetly in the gutter. A woman walked up and tried to sell us costume jewelry. She was directing her sales pitch at me, as the femmier of the two, with my mascaraed eyes, or perhaps she just thought Iris was a boy. *You'll like it,* the woman promised and dug some shiny necklaces out of her pocket. No, Really, I'm Not Interested, I said. She went away. Iris said I was mean. I was still on edge, impatient, waiting for the world to spin back to the place it had been when I ruled. If only people would just trust my vision. I was mournful, but angry-mournful, and I couldn't stop being a know-it-all bitch to Iris. I actually think she liked it. Iris enjoyed being subtly dominated by women who appear older or smarter. *You're fucking with my mind,* she said. You Love It, I shot back. *I do not,* she cried, but she was smiling, a painful smile. I couldn't stop. We were really into the rhythm now, me spinning my snotty analysis of her and her interjecting a *No, that's not true,* every now and then but mostly getting up from the folding homeless-proof seat and standing on the curb, searching for the bus. We were flirting the cruel breakup flirt. She asked me to go to Europe with her. I asked her to go home with me. I smoked her cigarettes. At one point I kicked her off her seat with my boot, her back crashing up against the Evian ad. I didn't mean to be so rough but apologizing would've bunched my act, so I grinned. She sat back down on the narrow plastic seat and brought her big goofy head up to mine. She was such a boy, Iris, a boy with a crush on her babysitter and guess who that was. The shiniest blue eyes and a full mouth of snaggly teeth. I grabbed the zippered edge of her leather jacket and reeled her in for a kiss. Her tongue swam in, and it was like watching a really great re-run, like you flip on the TV and it's your favorite episode, *Happy Days* with Leather Tuscadero, the one they never show. This mouth had kissed me so much it had worn its own grooves into my teeth. It was like settling into the arm-chair that fit exactly the round of your body, only it was incredibly exciting because everything was different now, and it was horribly wrong to be kissing. It would only prolong everything. I sat there in the bus shelter, back up against the glass, hoping the bus would never come. Desperation is the sexiest emotion. She wouldn't come home with me. I wasn't begging her to. I shrugged. Whatever, Your Loss. Part of me was relieved—what would it be like to have her back in my bed? A sickening déjà vu morning. In the bus shelter it seemed like breaking up had actually rejuvenated our relationship, though it was a tough line to walk. One wrong step, and we'd fall right back into the girlfriend ditch, and there was nothing taboo about making out with your girlfriend.

174

Iris missed her bus. It came, pulled right up to the shelter in all its rumbling orange glory, opened its mouth, swallowed up a couple of passengers and kept going. Iris stood on the curb, the most pained expression on her face, and I shrugged, maybe smirked. Well, I'm Going Home, I announced, watching her bus cruise away. Iris wanted another kiss. No Way, I said. She wasn't going to get everything while I got nada. She chased me home, literally, the sky starting to sprinkle again, and I was running down 14th Street with her feet slapping behind me. Good Night, I said, digging for my keys. *Have another cigarette,* she coaxed. What was this about? She didn't want me. This was fear, this was the primal fear of abandonment, it was childhood, fear of death, the infinite void, fear of the unknown. This was not about me. That's what killed me, worked me into a cold astrological bitch. To have someone know you so thoroughly and not want you. Is there anything more painful? I was a favored piece of clothing that had lost its novelty. I was bound for the thrift store, to be bought by someone who would think I was new. I just couldn't kiss her again. I submitted to a hug, my arms around the familiar leather jacket. *Goodnight, Michelle,* she said. It sucked that she said my name like that, her sad little voice with its faint southern twang. I thought, what is she trying to do to me? I was still teasing her as I unlocked my door. Last Chance, I said, and she made an awful noise, this guttural speaking of my name, and I realized she was crying. *I really have to take care of myself,* she said. *This is really hard, I really have to go home.* Iris, I said, reality

175

breaking a bottle over my head. Are You Ok? Do You Need Anything? I had this feeling, like when I was a kid playing different characters with my sister, playing for so long I couldn't get out of it, my brain feeling stale in my head. What confused thing had been created? *I just have to go,* she said sadly. Goodnight Iris, I said, watching her go. Take Care.

15

When I agreed to play a part in the artsy lesbian porno flick, my breakup with Iris was so recent that I was actually still talking to her. Although miserable, I hadn't yet realized the depth of the cracks and fissures, wide enough to get lost in—and I would. I met up with Iris the night of the shoot, at the bar where we'd taken our affairs when we were girlfriends. It was a dive down on Capp Street that no one had discovered yet, busted-up booths with scarred tables, smoke-soaked couches and the women working the streets outside stumbling in on ground-out heels to use the bathroom. Oh, I wanted her back so badly. Iris. She was soft like a girl no one had broken and, impossibly, no one had. The girls Iris went through wound up cracked vases no longer fit for flowers, leaky dust collectors. After

Iris, girls left town or started fucking boys. She ruined everyone. I should have run from her watery smirk, but there I was all bunched up in the booth, trying to act cute and unconcerned, the only way when your heart is so big and ugly, when your brain is a cartographer mapping out her tiniest road of intention. I was wearing black skater shorts with little skulls all over them, a death metal t-shirt and a bandana over my head, which was growing in hair strangely. Just sprouting up at different dumb angles I couldn't slick down or back or anything, I could only hide it and wish it were long and stormy, blowing around my head like the cloud that hung there, flashing. I wanted dense, angry hair. *You look like such a rocker,* said Iris. Iris said she was into punk girls. Iris said she felt like she was only taking a vacation from me, surely she'd be back. What a stupid thing to say. That one sentence stayed with me at least a year, so much longer than our relationship. Maybe, I thought, maybe she's only pretending to break up with me so that I can write again. Girls always threaten or politely offer to do this for me, because I cannot write when I have a girlfriend. But I still couldn't write. I could only do sit-ups in my room, my hips bruising on the wood floor, so that I could fit into tinier and tinier t-shirts, my new fashion. Lie still on my dustball floor with PJ Harvey's erotic mourning rushing through me like a virus. Sleeping was a good pastime. I slept as much as possible, though waking was the worst. A moment of groggy delight at the blue spring sky outside my window followed by a seeping dread that roused and woke me, killed the rest of the day. At night

178

I would dream that I was old and didn't know how to dress my age. I was wearing children's t-shirts with faded '80s cartoon characters stretched across my chest, and people would pull me aside and whisper to me. I dreamed that Emma was inside my house, and my roommates wouldn't let me kick her out. I dreamed there was a newspaper filled with every good thing I had ever done, I sat in an armchair with Iris and flipped the pages in her face, crying, while outside, Emma smoked cigarettes with my mother.

I'm Going To Be In Bernadette's New Porn Film, I bragged casually. This wasn't a dream. We're Filming It Tonight At Her House, So I Have To Leave Soon. Iris wasn't so impressed. I dumped more beer down my throat. I figured I should get drunk. I didn't know what would be expected of me, but I knew it would flow better drunk, not sloppy, just loose. It would be good to have cinematic proof that I was sexy. The film would be premiered at the big gay movie festival in case anyone had any doubts. I had some doubts. I left Iris at the bar and trudged up to Bernadette's place in the Castro. I was the first girl there, and I wasn't really drunk, and Bernadette had only a single bottle of wine that belonged to her roommate. *I don't think she'll mind,* she said, and dumped a bunch into a glass for me, thick purple stuff. I sucked it down and waited for the others to arrive. Ashley and Tommy. I didn't like being alone with Bernadette. I'd sort of harassed her for a date once and then forced a messy kiss on her and felt that generally she was an echo of Iris: contained and clean, a Virgo, a shirt-tucker. The theme of the evening's film

179

was "film," and all the erotic props were to be film supplies, like cameras, tripods, metal canisters and long loops of amber film that Bernadette had unraveled and strewn across her bedroom. The room was lit by metal dishes of light and the night felt dangerous. There was Bernadette, and my bandmate Tommy, who was after Bernadette, and Ashley, who was after both Bernadette and Tommy, and then there was me. Why had Bernadette invited me? I sloshed myself a bit more wine. I knew I was louder than the other girls, and brassier, would probably take more risks in front of the camera, certainly that was a worthy role to fill at a porn shoot. When Ashley and Tommy showed up, they wanted some wine too, and I thought, there's no way that one bottle is going to get us all drunk, but it will get me drunk, and I was here first. No way. They drained the bottle, and Bernadette said, *Let's go.* Her bed was smothered in film, which looks soft and flimsy but is actually hard and plasticky. We warmed up by go-go dancing in it, kicking the plastic up in little piles like autumn leaves, holding cameras and dressing in some of Bernadette's cowboy accessories, because you know how dykes love cowboy accessories. I took my shirt off, and things felt a little looser. My bandana fell off my head, and I hoped for the best. With the old-fashioned cameras, we pretended to film each other dancing. Bernadette handed me a rubber dick, and I hung it out of my shorts and whacked it around with one hand while aiming the camera at wiggly Ashley with the other. Ashley and Tommy started making out. *Good, good.* Bernadette was a

180

friendly and encouraging director, moving around the room with her video camera growing out of her face.

What would you like to know about Ashley and Tommy? Ashley's sexiness was aimed at everyone and no one. She would have crushes on a dozen girls at any moment, and though she would never do anything about them, you, as her friend, were instructed to stay away from these girls because they were her crushes. Ashley was sexy, a broad, earthy gas that tumbled over everything. It never seemed focused, but there was a maternal, unconditional sexiness present in the way she smiled at you when she spoke—her gift to the planet. Tommy was either tightly asexual or profoundly sexy. I couldn't figure it out and recently had felt on the verge of having a very meaningful crush on her. Her sexiness was a laser, a thin beam. It was intellectual, and if it wasn't shot at you, you might miss it. Or you could trip it like an invisible electronic security system and find yourself trapped in sudden floodlights with the cops on the way. Don't ask about me. I was not drunk. I figured the best I could do was whip myself into some natural hysteria, like a hyperactive child.

Bernadette wanted us to do something with the tripod, which was difficult. All we could think of was to rub our crotches on its legs like a pack of humpy dogs, and that was not sexy. Plus, it was very lightweight and kept falling over. I crawled beneath the tripod and that felt kind of cage-like, and Ashley was inspired to tie my limbs to it with strands of film and, getting really creative, grabbed a plastic yellow spool that the film had been wound around and popped it into my mouth like a ball-gag, tying it there with more crinkly strings of film. Bernadette loved it, and I was relieved of having to move or do anything, which was good. Somehow all my clothes were gone by then, and Tommy brought her face very close to my crotch and hesitantly began kissing my thigh. *Is that ok?* she asked, and I nodded. It was a porn movie, right? Tommy looked striking in the dim light by my legs, her bleached bangs falling over one eye, and I wondered again if I should perhaps get a crush on her. It was all so competitive then, sex and romance, and everyone wanted Tommy, so I pushed the idea out of my head and rolled my eyes up to Ashley who was touching my face and beaming her little smile at me like a benevolent health care worker. The plastic spool was really too big for a gag. My jaw was cramping, and the spool kept popping out of my mouth, and the little knot of film kept coming undone, until it finally rolled spitty onto the floor, and me and Ashley started making out. I had already kissed her once, a few weeks before, in the bathroom of a martini bar. She had flung me up against the wall and kissed me violently, bit my neck like a tough piece of steak and then released me, giggling. She wasn't attracted to me, Ashley, it wasn't about that, it was simply the air around us then, pulling everyone together in a bumpy awkwardness that you tried to eroticize. Everyone was horny and bored and drinking too much. Bernadette circled our kiss like a technological vulture and I wondered if this was at all a turn-on for her, for any of them, and if it was meant to be for me or if we were simply actors. We got rid of the tripod and messed around with the film. Tommy stuffed some down her boxers and out the fly, and I got on my knees and kind of nudged it around with my tongue, trying to look seductive, but come on. I didn't know how Bernadette was going to make any of this look respectable. I dove into the bed of unraveled film and flailed my legs, like a '50s starlet, I imagined. But the film was actually painful, giving me sharp little nicks all over my skin.

And then I got it, the plan for my shining cinematic moment, the reason I had been invited to participate in this awkward soiree: inspiration, the daring act that no one else would do, pulling the whole film together. I would stuff the film up my pussy. Like Karen Finley and the American flag, like Carol Schneeman and her damp scroll, like all the women artists and drug smugglers before me who had seized on the genius of having an actual hole in your body that you can actually store things in. I rolled a single garland of film into a tight cylinder and pushed it gently into my cooch, leaving a little tongue of celluloid hanging out so you knew it was up there. *Oh my god no way no way!* Bernadette was gleeful, *Jack off with it!* She had a bottle of lube and squirted globs of it onto my crotch as I tugged the little strip of film over my clit and jerked it. Bernadette brought a dish of light over and aimed it brightly at my cooch, which was, incidentally, going through the same transition as my head, growing in from being bald, shaved, still bearing bumpy stubble and redness, and then more redness along my inner thighs where the heat rash I sometimes get in warm weather had flared. A strange tropical reaction that I picked up as a kid visiting family in the Louisiana swamplands, a sort of fungus that feels the weather warm around it and begins to rise to the surface of my skin, homesick, bursting like sweat in my thighs and armpits. I thought of how awful it would look on film and wondered if my friends now thought I had some skanky STD. Having a fungus didn't sound much better. It's Just A Rash, I offered lightly, and tried to hide that part with my hands. I felt embarrassed that mine would not be the belle of the beaver ball. For the grand finale I cautiously eased the film out from my secret hole and let it unspool on the futon beneath me. *That was great!* Bernadette crowed, and handed me something to mop up the lube with.

That everyone started fucking around in Bernadette's bed that night, where we were supposed to be merely sleeping, makes me think that for my friends the film shoot was sexy and fun and not a jingling ice cream truck offering a variety of icy anxieties. Bernadette's room was complete blackness, the tree by her window blotting out any light from the street outside, and splotchy ghosts of bright camera lights hung burned in my vision. For a second I kissed Bernadette, or maybe Tommy, and then that was done and me and Ashley were by default paired off while Tommy climbed onto our director and bucked there 'til morning. It was so silly. I should've just slept but the performancy group participation was burned into the night like the lightbulbs, and Ashley was kissing me roughly and alternately rubbing and slapping at my panties. *Bad girl,* she murmured in a Cruella de Vil voice, pulling my hair, but it was impossible to take her seriously because she was Ashley, slumber-party Ashley who lost her house keys weekly and came over to crash on my futon. Ashley who phoned me at work sobbing because her roommates rototilled the backyard when she had just planted peonies and daffodils. Ashley my best friend who lent me velvet gowns and cascading wigs of hair and sternly told me to please not ruin them. She petted and poked my crotch and pushed my own hand away from hers until we finally fell asleep next to Bernadette and Tommy's slurpy slurps.

16

I really needed a hobby after breaking up with Iris, so I decided to stalk someone. I decided to stalk Fate. Because it sounded poetic and because she said I could. So I don't know if it truly counts as stalking. I wasn't risking a restraining order, or violence, or any of the drawbacks true stalkers face. Fate grabbed me in a bar, held me tight, told me I was cute. Fate was a pretty grabby person, I'd seen her go up to girls and stick her tongue down their throats as a Hello, so I don't know why I thought I was so special. She was this really cute girl, fucked up looking in the best way, just layers of ripped-up clothes and studded leather scraps she wore in a true, punq way, not like some S/M lesbian trying to look like a bad girl. Scuzzy head of hair, blue, and a lot of tattoos. She had two Madonna tattoos, the *True Blue* cover on her forearm—head back, eyes closed, hair in perfect tousled spikes like a Nagel painting. Then on her shoulder, Madonna from the cover of *Interview*—bowler hat and polka-dot shirt, grabbing her crotch. She was going to get them covered up, which totally excused her for having them. So Fate grabbed me and gave me that simple compliment, and I went, Should I Stalk You? and she blinked and said, *Sure.* And I said, Really? 'Cause I Will. And she said, *Sure,* and let me go. That was all the action I got off Fate that night. She may have sat on my lap at some point, but Fate sat on many laps.

Fate became my art project. I made this great note, hundreds of eyeballs with the words "I am watching you" clipped serial-killer style from different magazines. I slipped it through the mail slot at her apartment on Valencia, then walked up to the Kentucky Fried Chicken and got a bucket of gluey mashed potatoes. I had just gotten my tongue pierced and couldn't really ingest anything that required chewing, and Fate herself had recommended the mashed potatoes. She had her own tongue pierced like three times, this clump of silver clattering around in her mouth. I sat across the street from Fate's house and sporked the glop into my mouth, inhaled it to the back of my throat, and swallowed. You had to be careful not to inhale it all the way or else you'd choke. I was feeling pretty stupid about my new piercing, pretty fashion victim. The other night my new roommate, newer to my new house than even I was, had had this nice lesbian potluck, and all these lesbians brought over this lesbian food, healthy stuff with rice and greens, and I was starving.

I'd been living off smoothies, so I attempted to eat some tahini-tofu thing, and I sucked it into my windpipe and couldn't stop choking. All the lesbians just stared at me. I went to my room. I had pierced my tongue so I would stop smoking and because breakups always leave me with a need to make myself different. Since breaking up with Iris, I had acquired a sailor suit, just like the one my grandfather wore when he got his picture in the paper for being the youngest boy in Chelsea, Massachusetts, to go off to war. In the picture, my grandfather is skinny and kind of sinister despite his smile, like David Bowie. His eyes glow strangely. I wanted to look like that, different, so that when Iris looked at me now she would not think she knew me, that she owned any part of me by knowing it. If she had ever known me she would not have left, and I would parade her ignorance through my own transformation. Really I just wanted a new girlfriend immediately, to show her what hot property I was, how well I got on with things, and plus I missed spending all my time with someone who thought I was really great. I figured I'd slip Fate a few more notes, she'd see how really great I was, want to be my girlfriend, and I could forget all about that last one. I chopped up some more magazines and slipped the product through the mail slot, rang Fate's bell and ran. It was pretty fun. I had some friends with me, we made a racket clattering up the street, me hissing Sssshhhh over their laughter. Bonzai, a video artist, wanted to make a movie about my pursuit of Fate. I thought I could maybe do a zine.

188

I went to a play party at a warehouse space in Oakland. The girls who lived there would throw these parties where you could walk around and watch women in various states of undress having painful things done to them. This one was more of a fetish-themed dance party, though there were people being tortured. A girl was rigged up to this wooden structure, her hands stretched up with chains, and another girl was doing something like sticking pins in her, or pulling them out or maybe burning her. Quick, jabby motions that made the bound girl shriek milk-curdling shrieks. It was hard to see exactly what was going on because they were surrounded by so many girls, all watching intently with serious looks on their faces. There was a bar serving red plastic cups of beer, and a dance floor filled with girls dancing in shining leather and latex. I was wearing this leather and chain-link garter belt I had found on the sale rack at this overpriced fetish barn and had bought even though it was a couple sizes too small and hard to breathe in. I paired it up with some tall black go-go boots, and I looked like a gigantic slut. I looked like a slut a lot right then, needing attention and pursuing it with the artistry of an abused twelve-year-old girl. My heart was broken, I couldn't be held responsible for my fashion.

Where was Fate? She was over on the couch where the porn movies were playing, with this red-haired girl she was maybe on a date with. I couldn't figure it out. She'd been flirting with me pretty hard recently, but if she was on a date I would have to leave her alone. I mean, the reason my heart was currently in such sore shape was because that slimy creep of a girl Emma had moved in on my true love in a way that I thought was just incredibly disrespectful of girlhood and lesbian relationships, and I was getting a lot out of hating her and feeling superior about her apparent lack of a code of honor. If I wanted to hold on to that feeling, I was going to have to play by my own rules. So I flirted with Fate, left, danced a little, wandered around the warehouse. I bumped into this girl I had really hurled myself at when I first moved to San Francisco. I had been in a bar wearing a black see-through dress and some shiny blue panties, and I pulled off the panties and offered them to her as a gift. I really loved crazy women and just assumed everyone was with me on that, but apparently it was not the case. *How long have you been here now?* she asked me. I Don't Know . . . Two Years? *You've really grown up,* she said. I went back downstairs and pulled Fate out onto the dance floor. It was hard to move around because a parade of girls in intense Victorian costume had emerged from the back room and engaged in some theatrical performance involving a crawling girl on a thin, glinting leash. My beer was sloshing all around the place. It occurred to me that I was drunk, and I wondered if it was a plus or minus for Fate to think I was a lush. The party cleared out at midnight, everyone having to catch BART back to the city. I attached myself to Fate and the red-haired girl of vague status, and we all got a ride with that girl I had given my panties to.

190

I didn't want the night to end. You Guys Want Tarot Readings? We stopped at my house to grab my deck, and went on to Fate's place, which didn't at all match her rough and tumble exterior. It was homey, clean, with plants. Green, living plants. I found out during the tarot reading that Fate and the red-haired girl were indeed on a date. They curled up on the couch like kittens. It was just a first date, though. My integrity went right out the window. It wasn't like they were girlfriends. I wasn't busting up a relationship, wrecking a home. If I stopped stalking Fate, I'd have nothing to do. Plus, she kept making out with me. Just grabbing me in bars and planting one of her platonic soul-kisses on me.

Ashley was having a huge birthday party. She was a Taurus, and it would be an enormous bash for all the Tauruses. Lots of lesbians are Tauruses. There was a bull theme, so I figured I would dress up like a mariachi dancer and invite Fate, a Taurus. A fact which explained her clean home with the adequately watered plants. I cut her up another stalker note inviting her to be my date, and she said ok. I was so excited. I wondered if Iris would be there to see me on a date with such a cute and dangerous-looking girl. I spent weeks searching for the perfect mariachi dress, and I found one, tight red velvet with an incredible ruffle explosion happening at the hem. I got red lace to tie in my hair, a big shawl, clunky shoes. I got ready all day long. I bought red lipstick, I bought a flower for behind my

191

ear and another for Fate's lapel or whatever raggy t-shirt she would wear. All evening I left messages on her machine. She called me back in the early evening, groggy. She had just woken up, she had had a really weird dream. She was disturbed, she'd be ready in an hour. I'll Wait For You, I said. *Well yeah, I'd hope so,* she said. She sounded cranky. I spent the hour perfecting my makeup and she showed up in leather pants, a shitty t-shirt and a black cowboy hat. The pants were new. I tried to safety pin the flower to her shirt but the pin tore the flower apart and the petals fluttered onto the sidewalk. The walk to the party was excruciating. I realized we had this flirtation based on flirting, and I didn't know how to do much but giggle and say stupid things and she just kind of nodded and looked uncomfortable and told me she was freaked out by her dream and she'd decided to quit drinking and was in a weird mood. That's Ok, I said. Could I stop acting so vacant? What was my problem?

The party house had a big art gallery in the front where everyone was coloring on the walls with crayons, and there was a big sketch of a bull so you could play pin the tail on the bull and win a prize. Not many people were there yet. Me and Fate went out to the backyard where there were trees and a bonfire. We sat together in uncomfortable silence. Was it ok if I drank? I had never gone on a date with a sober girl before, but since most of my crushes were drunks it seemed like a logical evolution. I got some punch and sipped it real slow. Then this big group of Fate's friends showed up, and she went off and sat with them on the porch. They were

192

these super-rowdy girls hugging 40s in wrinkled paper bags. I wondered if Fate had had them come to rescue her. She huddled with
them on Ashley's porch, talking low and laughing loud and rolling cigarettes. I didn't talk to Fate anymore that night. *How's your
date?* people asked. I Don't Think I'm On A Date, I said. I wandered
around the party. Some girls showed up dressed like a mariachi
band, carrying a shitty acoustic guitar stuffed with candy like a
piñata. Birthday-girl Ashley got to slam it open on the floor. The
girl I gave my panties to at the bar was there again, and somehow
we ended up in Ashley's roommate's closet. On the floor on top
of all her dirty clothes, exquisite beaded dresses swinging above
our heads. We had sex and left the used glove there in all the dirty
clothes, and later the girl found it. She was really grossed out.

Ok, so I finally got to sleep with Fate. Months and months later,
when I didn't even care anymore, which is how those things usually
happen. She was coming around my house a lot, to hang out with
my roommate Sam. Fate was drinking again, we'd all get cans of
beer at the New Star Market on the corner, drink them in my room,
smoking cigarettes, and Fate would give me shit about my music
collection. Not enough speed metal. Fate kept referring to Alcoholics Anonymous. She called it The Cult, there were all these people
in The Cult trying to get her to quit her drinking. Her face was dark
when she talked about it. Her asshole sober boss who pushed her to

go to meetings and then fired her when she "slipped," picked up a bottle again and drank from it. I don't know, I could never come up with a good reason *not* to have a beer, so I completely understood. Plus, she looked good with a beer in her hand. Now she had no job and nowhere to live. She was couch-surfing, staying up in Bernal Heights, housesitting for a girl who was on tour with her band. She had me come over and give her a tarot reading. The place was empty and she had Metallica on the gigantic stereo. She sang along in a muttery way, not too showy but you understood she knew the song well and that it mattered. I don't know which song. When I spread the cards out on the big bed and Fate sprawled out next to me, belly down, I really thought we were going to have sex. But then she started crying. All the cards were bad. I didn't know what to say. *It's ok,* she said and wiped her face. I was impressed with how easily she cried in front of me. She didn't seem at all embarrassed, her slick, reddened face was opened, soaking in the meanings of all her little destinies. I looked at her respectfully, feeling ashamed and dumb for having thought she was luring me over for sex. Did I think she was a stud? I gave her some money for cigarettes and left.

A few weeks later, at the dyke bar, Fate came on to me like weather, a front of clouds, a boozy kiss and *Can I come home with you tonight?* Finally. Sure, I said. But something was off. Fate was manic drunk, I recognized it because it's the kind of drunk I get too. When the bar closed down for the night I took Fate across the street to my bandmate Tommy's house. Tommy's new girlfriend,

Bee, was in the band too, an amazing guitarist. But Tommy and Bee were cranky punk rock snobs. They adhered to the strict Pacific Northwest girlpunk tradition, as found in Portland and Olympia. Clean, grrl-positive kids with short hair and little sweaters, pegged pants and deliberate ethics. Middle-class and youth-worshiping, but with a consciousness about classism and ageism. They did not like drunken Fate, she seemed a hesher beside their streamlined aesthetic, a bull in the china shop of their kitchen. She picked up their instruments without asking and started plucking, the big taboo. She's Cool, I kept mouthing, while they kept a mother's eye on the bass held awkwardly in Fate's inebriated paws. I think she did drop it. Onto the linoleum with a thud and a twang. It was time to take Fate home.

The fucking happened so fast that by the time I realized I didn't want it, it was over. Fate fucked me quick and rough with her grubby hands, impatiently pushing fingers into me, and I understood that she didn't want it either. She was earning her keep. She only wanted to sleep, and to cuddle. She pulled her hand out of me and curled herself around my back tightly, as if there were something between us. It seemed like a brave and vulnerable thing to do, like when she cried above my tarot cards. I lay there with her foreign arm clutching me, knowing that she thought she'd earned this rest and closeness with the brief, perfunctory fuck. I had a tangled, icky feeling like a confusing, hungover morning. When I woke up, I found blood sticky on my thighs, seeping out from where her hand had torn me.

17

Spacegirl was worried about me. She thought I was dying of cancer. We hadn't met yet, she was watching me on the cafe patio as I tipped the pill bottle into my palm and knocked back the tablets. There *was* that weird bald spot on the back of my head. I remember clearly that warm day, the medicine I was taking. I had a pussy infection. Something common enough, not gonorrhea or anything, but it made my pussy smell fishy. I was supposed to keep out of the sun, and I didn't, so I got a really bad sunburn. Spacegirl was there, watching. Now that I think about it, she probably would have fallen right in love with me had I been dying. She was the kind of girl who would do really well with a weak, cancer-ridden girlfriend. She could be self-sacrificing and carry herself with a deep and noble sadness. Spacegirl had a motorcycle. It was a piece of shit, clunky black, and she had to start it with a screwdriver. But I'm getting ahead of myself. Spacegirl stared with concern on the patio, and she cornered me later at the bar. I saw her aiming her big body at me, her boots thudding heavy on the wood floor. When I heard her speak, all her makeup made sense. I had already been exposed to the southern phenomenon of butch girls and cosmetics, so her twang explained for me the powdery film on her face, the dark red lipstick. *Are they contacting you?* she asked, incredibly serious, her fingers touching the UFOs tattooed on my arm. Aaah, No. *They will,* she nodded. Obviously Spacegirl was a prophet. She grabbed my arm and monologued me for nearly an hour, and when she was done, I went and sat alone at the edge of the dance floor, letting everything she said sink in. *It's coming,* Spacegirl had said. It was all coming and couldn't you just feel it? Couldn't you feel the end of everything, growing bigger like a hunger that chewed at your belly? Oh, I was so hungry for the end of the world right then. I was so bored. Spacegirl had been living in New Mexico where there were joint government-alien bases burrowed under the ground, enormous subterranean complexes stuffed with magnetic propulsion crafts and hybrid beings suspended in glowing tanks. Spacegirl saw them flying in the sky, she heard them pattering on her roof like elves. She left her radio on at night like that David Bowie song, and they talked to her as she slept. *I'm not scared,* she said, and nothing could do it for me like a tough girl talking shit about UFOs in a southern accent. *When they come down I'm gonna light up a cigarette and walk right in and say, "Whaddaya all eatin', I'm cookin'."*

Spacegirl was a liar. I didn't care. She lied right to my face and I let her, pushed her to unwind these stories into vast landscapes that I wanted so badly to believe in. It is a true talent, one I've witnessed mostly in drag queens, to tell lies so detailed and glorious that your victims don't even care that they're being taken for fools, gladly they become gigantic fools, and I was a fool for Shelly. That was her real name. "Spacegirl" came about because no one would know who I was talking about so I'd have to yell Spacegirl! Spacegirl! until that's all anybody called her. Shelly was tall and looked strong, like she could really kick up some shit. Her hair was bleached and greasy with long bangs that fell into her face, pasty white with all that makeup. Her nose went up like a ski slope and her eyes were tiny. I kept trying to figure out if I liked her. The makeup threw me off, but I did know that I absolutely needed to impress her.

We were together at a bar and I was explaining the bald spot on the back of my head. Usually people think I did it on purpose, shaved a hole to be weird or cool or something. It drives me crazy. I always think they must see me as such a really dumb person to think I would do that. I was glad Shelly had thought it was cancer. Really it was a birthmark, or used to be a birthmark. This mass of bumpy brown skin, sprouting hairs, bleeding when my mother ran the brush over it, really gross. They brought me to a doctor and the doctor said if I didn't get rid of it by the time I hit puberty I could

198

get cancer and die, so Shelly had something right. I had to have an operation. I remember being on a stretcher, the bright lights of the ceiling whizzing by like lines on a highway. It was one of the Shriners Hospitals, where burned people came from all over the world to get better, and I was lucky to live so close to it. I saw a small boy in a wheelchair, the doctors were building him a new nose. He had two holes in his face and some bandages like scaffolding. Big doctors pushed me around like a shopping cart. *What's her name? Swankowski?* They told Polish jokes. They had a mask of gas to knock me out. Did I want bubble gum or cherry? I picked cherry and the mask came down over my face, heavy plastic and rubber, and the doctors were liars, it didn't taste like cherry, it tasted like death, thick poison death. I kicked and swung at the guy for all of three seconds and then I was out. Then I was back again, right away it seemed like, an eyeblink, but all this stuff had happened. I could feel it. I was a flat white body in a cold empty room, sickened and aching and my head was wrapped in a big bandage. I started crying. I was about seven. I had needles and tubes coming out of my hands, stuck there with bloody bits of scotch tape. I started crying for my mother, Mama, Mama, and a little old man, flat and white on his own metal bed, said, *It's ok honey, your Mama's coming,* and I was calmed. They cut the ugly birthmark off my head, and they cut a flap of skin from my ass and they stitched it to my head, to hold my brains in, I imagined. They took the skin from my ass so that no one but my husband would ever see the scar. I

199

figured I could never pose for *Playboy*. I got to stay out of school for a while, on my stomach on the couch, while my mother changed the bandage, peeling the gauze from my ass, tugging gently where it had begun to knit to the skin. Daubing it with Mercurochrome, so bright red and liquid that I thought it was blood, that my bum was cut and bleeding like crazy. On the end table near my head was a vase of flowers, orange tongues of tiger lilies and the fat yellow head of a sunflower. I got them for being sick, like winning a pageant. When Halloween came and I was still bandaged up, my mother took the gauze and extended it down from my head and I was a mummy. My mother was so scared that the operation would make me ugly. I had very long hair, thick and blonde and it was a big concern how much would be cut for the surgery. Would I be a freak? She held her breath when the bandage came off. The trauma of the surgery was still so recent that the new skin sat swollen and puffy on my head and my mother shrieked, *It looks like a pancake!* and passed out right there in the office. That's Why I Call It My Pancake, I told Shelly.

She was fingering her lower lip. *Well, listen to this.* Shelly grew up in a trailer park near the Everglades in Florida. She had already told me about how she saw Bigfoot there, all orange and furry, swatting for fish in the creek. But when she was like two years old a neighbor's pit bull knocked her down and bit her bottom lip off her face. Did the dog eat it, or did it lie in the dirt like a bit of meat? Shelly's mom sued the guy who owned it, there'd already been complaints and he was supposed to keep the beast chained up. She won a lot of money and took Shelly to the best plastic surgeon. They made her a new lip. Out Of What? *Guess,* she said. She was gloating. It was impossible to impress Shelly because she would just make up a lie to top whatever story you told her. *They took a skin graft from my mother's pussy!* she screamed. Your Mother's Pussy? *My mama's pussy!* She Must Have Really Loved You, I said. Shelly wanted to leave the bar, looking around the bright darkness with wild eyes. *Let's make a movie.* Shelly claimed to have bunches of cameras, video, Super 8. I assumed she was full of shit, but she left the bar and came back with two cameras, old and silver like laser guns from a '50s science fiction movie. When Shelly actually delivered, it made me wonder if maybe she wasn't a liar, maybe her lips were fashioned from her mama's labia and the aliens were talking to her and the world was really going to end, soon, and shit would finally start to happen. We took the cameras into the street. I remember Magdalena Squalor was with us, and I was thinking shit, Magdalena is going to fall right in love with Shelly. Because Shelly was tough and southern and had a motorcycle and was obviously a freak. And plus me and Magdalena had exactly the same taste in girls—she was Iris's ex-girlfriend, responsible for bringing Iris to California. But I had finally decided to like Shelly, makeup and all, and now Magdalena was going to ruin it.

We went to the twenty-four-hour donut dive near my house, Johnny Donut, and sat with our donuts in the hellish brightness. The

201

help didn't care for us at all, or perhaps they were just so skilled at tuning out the clientele, the drugged and hyper denizens of 16th Street slapping down palms of begged change, the impatient kids the bars spit out lining up for pastries. Shelly sat with her strong legs spread and her boots scuffed on the linoleum. She and Magdalena both used to live in Georgia and they both loved Vic Chesnutt, so they bonded over their crusted sugar donuts and I was stuck with Shelly's roommate, this girl on a lot of Prozac. Her eyes were really weird. Magdalena seemed in love with Shelly. Well, I didn't care. Shelly was nothing but a big fat liar. The world was nowhere near ending, the world was ancient and it had no intention of stopping, would keep chugging on until it killed me, and I would never see the aliens. We made a little film about donuts. I ripped into a thick lemon one and let the sugary pus squish through my teeth. I filmed the pastry case, all the shiny greasy foods. I held the camera and pulled the trigger, heard the whir and click of the film inside. We wanted to film them making the stuff in the back, but they wouldn't let us. *But we're making a movie!* Shelly cried. It was really important. There was a black man in the donut shop, watching us fiddling with the cameras, and Shelly asked him to breakdance for her. *What?* Me and Magdalena shot horrified looks at each other. *You want me to what? Breakdance,* Shelly repeated. *Shelly,* one of us said. *Why do you think I breakdance?* Jesus Shelly, Just Because He's Black Doesn't Mean He's A Fucking Breakdancer! *What?!* she exclaimed. *When I was little all the black kids breakdanced. In the*

202

'80s. They did it real good man, it was fucking cool. You really don't breakdance? She ended up making friends with the guy. He was fresh out of prison, and Shelly was telling him a big whomping lie about having been a cook in the cafeteria of the jail he was just let out of. That food sucked, the guy complained cheerfully. Back out on 16th Street I had to pee. *Pee right here,* Shelly dared and of course that's all that needed to happen for my pants to be down around my ankles. Not even in a corner, just right in the middle of the side-walk, squatting. *Oh shit no way holy shit I gotta get this.* Shelly was crouched in front of me with the camera as I sprayed a dark fountain of urine onto the pavement. *Ya gotta go, ya gotta go,* observed a homeless woman from the donut shop doorway. *That is the truth!* Shelly hooted, shaking her head. I wiped with my donut napkin and tossed it in the trash can. I was just warming up. I figured I would scale the great brick fortress over on 14th Street, the old armory, this enormous abandoned castle. On one side skaters hang out and do ollies off the steps, on the other side homeless people piss and shit and it smells awful. The bricks are jagged, sticking out from the wall like small shelves and I'd always wanted to climb it. Shelly didn't tell me to be careful. She stood with her camera poised and I grabbed the edge of a brick and hoisted myself up the building like a rock climber. It wasn't so hard. The bricks were thick and dusty, and there were soft green carpets of lichen growing between them, as if the fortress were a thing of nature. I got up as far as the lower boarded-up windows where pigeons lived. There was a lot of pigeon shit so I

203

was afraid to touch the bricks there. *Keep going!* Shelly yelled from the street below. *Look in the window!* There were some holes and cracks in the boards, but I couldn't get close enough. I guess I was scared to. I had heard all about the dead junkies the city pulls out of there, and of course the rats. I climbed back down. *That was great,* Shelly said, hitting the camera. It was late.

I was at a bar again with Shelly. She was showing off by picking me up in the air and tossing me around, how big girls flirt with me. Petra was there that night. She grabbed me for a hug on her way out. *Be careful with her,* she said, nodding toward Shelly. What Do You Mean? I asked. Do You Know Shelly? Curious and defensive. *I just get a bad feeling off her,* Petra said, shaking her head. I hated when people pulled this psychic shit on me. Like, we're all supposed to honor each other's intuition and Different Ways Of Knowing, but don't come at me with esoteric warnings about someone I have a crush on. Petra's revelations trapped me. *Go home with her, have fun, just keep your money in your shoe. I don't trust her.* We're Just Friends Anyway. Out front Shelly grabbed me for a goodbye hug and a kiss and her tongue slid into my mouth and for a minute we were really kissing. *I'm sorry,* she said. Why Are You Sorry, I laughed. Shelly straddled her motorcycle and stuck the screwdriver in the ignition, was gone. I took a cab home with Candice and my new roommate Sam. *What was that?* they jabbed me, and I shrugged. We're Just Friends. But Listen To This. I told them about Petra's creepy warning. *I think she's right,* Candice said. What? Candice had this really final way of delivering her commentary. Like everything is decided and that's it. *I don't like her,* she said. *I don't like her either,* Sam chimed in. *She reminds me of someone who'd beat you up at the roller rink.* Now, what was that supposed to mean? Wasn't that the prevailing aesthetic? Weren't all the dykes trying to look like the mean girls at the roller rink? Maybe Shelly was just too authentic. *Do you really believe she was abducted by aliens?* Candice demanded. They Don't Abduct Her, I scoffed. They Just Talk To Her. I didn't feel like explaining the psychology of my acceptance of Shelly's compulsive lying. I got out of the cab.

For a while Shelly was having this thing with a straight girl who was on speed or heroin and had a boyfriend. It was very intense, possibly a past-life thing. They weren't fucking. Shelly wouldn't fuck a junkie and plus there was the boyfriend. They would just get drunk and make out and the girl would start crying and Shelly would kick her out. The girl came to the bar once. *She's stalking me,* Shelly said. She was this really boring-looking blonde girl, I couldn't believe that this was the person who succeeded in captivating Spacegirl, however briefly. Shelly claimed to be married. To a woman, some girl back in Atlanta. They'd been together twelve years, they were nonmonogamous. Shelly only mentioned her sometimes, and it was always different. They were in love, the woman was jealous, they were getting divorced, she was coming to San Francisco, she was staying in Georgia and building a home for them. I felt embarrassed for Shelly when she talked about her wife. It was such a sloppy lie, such an obvious one, and not nearly impressive enough to suspend disbelief for. I would change the subject, get her talking about Armageddon. *It's comin'*, Shelly promised. The sky above our heads was huge and fragile. When Shelly became obsessed with Anastasia she shut up about the wife. Anastasia was this very glamorous girl who was nonmonogamously involved with Petra, which lent some credence to Petra's psychic hunches. There was intrigue with Anastasia, again very intense stuff, probably past-life and all hush-hush because of Petra. I'm Sure Petra Doesn't Give A Shit, I told Shelly, but she shook her head, lips tight with the deep secret of her and Anastasia's love. I didn't want to hear it anyway. Anastasia was incredibly gorgeous, and sweet as well, but everyone had a crush on her and I thought it was very unoriginal of Shelly.

Weekend mornings, Shelly would pick me up on her crummy motorcycle. I would jam the extra helmet over my head, and we would fly through the streets to this faraway diner for coffee and crab cakes. *These ain't crab cakes,* she said. *You come over to my house, I'll fix you crab cakes.* I loved being on the back of Shelly's bike, like a girl on a float at a parade. We bought tall bottles of beer, Oatmeal Stout, good stuff, not malt liquor. We sat on the sidewalk and drank, making friends with all the other wandering afternoon drinkers, mostly homeless guys. Shelly threw parties at the tasteful apartment she shared with the Prozac girl. She had a tequila party and blended enormous margaritas and a cowgirl girl taught everyone to two-step. Another party was wine and Vietnamese take-out. Sam's mom was in town so she was there too, drinking wine and smoking, getting tipsy. Sam didn't know how to act around her mom and the girls all at the same time. Shelly had bunches of dildos, enormous glittery ones. Girls were putting them on beneath their clothes, and then Laurel let hers hang right out, this gigantic pink schlong, right next to the mom on the couch. The mom touched the dildo. Everyone was drunk and everything was dangerously possible, or so it seemed. The mom touched the dildo, lifted it and let it flop dully back onto Laurel's thigh. *I like mine a little harder,* she laughed. I was sitting on the floor playing a private game of Truth or Dare with Melanie. We were talking about cuttings and knives and blood. Melanie was this intense girl with a dark past she would occasionally refer to in this passive way, a little worm I would suck into my mouth, hook and all, just like I did with Shelly. These girls were like thick novels with a binding you can crack. *I dare you,* she said to me, *to go into the bathroom and kiss the first person who comes in.* Ok, I said, But Not Sam's Mom. Shelly's bathroom was small with no light and no door. I sat on the edge of the tub and smoked, listening for footsteps. I heard some and got ready. Melanie walked in. Oh, I laughed, flicking my cigarette in the toilet. Melanie kissed me with a hard tongue and we went back to join the party. Eventually we would have an affair and it would totally ruin our friendship.

I stopped seeing Shelly because she was working twelve hour days, for Anastasia. To save money, to take them to Europe. *We can't be together here,* she said bitterly. She talked about some intense, romantic moment on the beach with "someone." Who? I probed. *I can't say,* she said, and gave me a meaningful look. *Is Shelly clean and sober?* Petra asked me one afternoon. No Way, I laughed. Well, she told Anastasia she was seven years sober. I shrugged, embarrassed for Shelly and for myself. Her messy lies were making me look bad. *Are you fucking her?* Petra asked, and I shook my head. We Just Kissed Once. *I always thought,* Petra started, *that of all my friends, you would be most likely to sleep with a serial killer.* Thanks A Lot, Petra, I said, thinking that of all the people I had ever slept with, Petra was most likely to *be* a serial killer. *Anastasia is freaking out,* she continued. *She's about to get a restraining order on that girl if she doesn't back off.* Really? Shelly called me about a week later, she was moving back to Atlanta. *I had this dream,* she said in a heavy, trembling voice. San Francisco was crashing. It was sliding into the ocean, people were dying. *It's the big one, Michelle. It's coming. I've got to get out of here. I saw it.* So Shelly left. I never heard from her again.

18

Scrumptious stood on the corner in a vinyl outfit that spread black like an oil slick across her body. It wasn't hers. None of it was hers, not the clothes, not the hair—a wig—and not the leather jacket. That leather jacket was Iris's, those stickers peeling on the back, the thick, crinkled arm I'd hung on for months. Who was this girl wearing my ex-girl-friend's leather jacket? She was Scrumptious, but not yet. Her real name was Stella, she didn't become Scrumptious until later when we were all so high. Stella drove to San Francisco alone, on her motorcycle. All the way from Canada. She was supposed to stay at this notorious pervert house that had a red basement hung with rubber slings and photos of girls with carved skin on the walls. But the place was already packed with perverts, so she was shunted to

Iris's house, to sleep on the pull-out couch. That's My Ex-Girlfriend's Jacket, I said, filled with dread at the thought of looking at it all night. It was the night of the Dyke March, that's why Stella was so done up, the brilliant silver wig that bobbed in synthetic swirls at her shoulders, the slick second skin of vinyl. She looked like she wanted to get laid, and I guessed that she would have no problem on that most bacchanalian of nights, when girls grow fangs, and hair sprouts on their chests, and no one goes to bed before six. I wasn't planning on going to bed at all. I had a bag of crystal in my wallet and my heart was still smashed. This time last year I'd had Iris on my arm, licking her mouth in the street. Now she had the other girl, and I would spend the night in fear of bumping into them. I couldn't wait to do the drug. I had done it once before and wanted that feeling inside me again, like needing to hear your favorite song, an external experience made internal, made intensely personal. Blood zinging through your body like pinball and you own it, the king of your own glowing kingdom.

Right away I saw Iris. I was at a little convenience store that was so packed they were only letting people in two at a time. I had a Coke to dump my whiskey into plus a granola bar for dinner and there she was, with her annoying girlfriend. They actually looked alike, physically. It freaked me out. Hi, I said quickly, and scooted away with my food. I was sure they were laughing at me, both of them in their creepy matching faces. I dumped some Coke into the gutter to make room for the whiskey. Standing amongst ten thousand lesbians I was suddenly a lot more conscious of littering. Girls were winding slowly through the streets, not so much marching as plodding. Thank god no one was chanting. Let me tell you right here that it is just so sad what a year can do to you. What a girl can do to you. It had just about ripped the life right out of me. I smoked cigarettes and walked through the Castro with Stella, the tower of glamour, and with Magdalena, who carried an enormous bouquet of daisies, cradling the thick green cluster. When she saw a girl she thought was cute she'd tug a single stem free of the bunch and hand it to her. She had the white and yellow blossoms pinned in her hair like little smiles. Everyone with a camera was snapping pictures of Stella and Magdalena. I hung off to the side in my unremarkable outfit, keeping an eye out for my Iris and her shiny paramour. I'd spent the past few weeks beginning bunches of little affairs and then bailing, and those girls were all milling about as well, a tiny army of girls I needed to avoid. I was feeling slightly under siege and was thinking maybe it might be time to leave San Francisco. Let's Do Drugs, I hissed at Candice, who had gone in on the bag with me. Let's Go. We rounded up some kids and tried to find a good place to debauch. Laurel was there. We're Going To Do Speed, I told her. Speed has such a bad reputation. You can't play around with it without everyone thinking you're on the skids. *I cannot be around that*, Laurel said. *I hate speed energy.* She had her hand held out like, *talk to the hand.* People are terrified of the thought of me on speed, but the truth is it makes me feel strangely calm, like I've bundled the whole world up to nurse at my breast, grand and serene, all my daily manic energy concentrated into a fine point that sits in my belly and I am god. Oh, Laurel, I'm Fun On Speed, I protested, but she was not having it. And now my speed partners were tense because I had implicated them, and now everyone would think they had drug problems, but I just cannot be discreet about drugs. We walked up one of the shadowy streets stretching up from Market and huddled together on the steps of a Victorian. I pulled the goodies from my wallet. *Did you cut it?* someone asked. Uh . . . No, I said. I didn't know I was supposed to. I dumped some of the crumbled white stuff onto my ID and tried to chop it into a fine dust with my ATM card. *You're losing it!* someone gasped as tiny crystals pinged off the card into the darkness. Well, You Do It Then. Someone more worldly than me took the drugs and went to work, while the rest of us watched fearfully for cops or the residents of the Victorian. *Can I have some?* Stella asked. *I'll give you money.* Stella took a tightly rolled bill and lifted it to her nose. She was really something, her fake hair glittered as dazzling as the crystal she breathed into her nostril. She tipped her head back and sniffed, silver hair cascading down her neck. The drug shone pretty like snow and I was anxious for my turn. Stella was going to ride her motorcycle in the parade the next day and she didn't have anyone to sit on the back. I Will, I said and dipped my nose to the drug, sniffing hard. It seared a chemical path through my sinuses and dripped bitter and gritty down the back of my throat. I drank some whiskeycoke. *Yeah, you should ride with me.* The more you talked to Stella, the more you could see how that outfit wasn't hers. She looked great in it, but it was a costume. *This S/M woman in Vancouver let me borrow it,* she said. *I don't dress like this at all.* She laughed. What did she normally look like? Who was she? I felt the pleasant rush of speed like an excellent tide, and instantly I was fascinated with Stella. Her eyes flickered at me like the tongue of a cat and I forgot about all the girls out to get me. Around the corner was the steady roar of every dyke in the world. We gathered our stuff and joined them, then met up with more friends who also wanted to do drugs. We searched out another hiding place, the vaguely wooded area behind the Harvey Milk school. There were a few trees, cement stairs we sat on as I busted the stuff out like a big dealer, chop chop. I did a little more. Tommy swallowed some Ecstasy and Stella said, *Can I have some? I'll give you money.* We sat in the relative hush of our scrawny forest and chattered our speed chatter, squatted to pee against the skinny urban trees.

When did this big lightning bolt happen with Stella? Dancing by the DJ booth they erected in the middle of the Castro, in the street there, Prince, "Erotic City." Stella yanked me into the sweating throng of dancing girls and started dancing at me in that sexy way I hate, all grindy, with the strategically placed knees, but for some reason—the drugs, certainly—I was able to do it. I gripped Stella's squeaky vinyl hips and churned her on my knee, straddled hers, and on the sidelines my excitable friends jabbed and poked at each other. Me and Stella stared deeply into each other's dilated eyes and gyrated. I hoped Iris was seeing this. It was so sick that Stella was wearing her jacket. The speed offered me terrific powers of concentration as I maneuvered my legs beneath her. Right before we kissed, my eyes snagged on this girl I'd had sex with recently, a girl whose calls to my home were going unanswered. I'd be checking voice mail and there it was, this unfamiliar, girlish voice streaming out from the receiver. I'd feel something, it was panic's little sister. I'd jam my finger on a button like squashing a bug. *Message erased.* The feeling evaporated like sweat from my skin. Now this girl was at the edge of the dance floor, glaring. I snapped my eyes shut and dove into Stella's mouth. It was like falling into a warm bath, or a swimming pool if you're sweaty. God, speed is so great. I was in love with Stella. She was magnificent, so tall and strong and wrapped in that plastic outfit. She was like a bendable figure you'd pick up in the toy aisle at Walgreens, some glamorous girl warrior. What would the night give us?

We walked to a party, a short walk, and crashed into a living room crowded with topless girls dancing to Depeche Mode. One with a little pierced-up face grabbed us and barked, *Take off your shirts, take off your shirts,* pulling on the fabric. I peeled off my tiny Boston Red Sox t-shirt and stuffed it in my back pocket, starting to dance with Stella. She was probably Scrumptious by now. Tommy called her that, and it really stuck. That party was being thrown by this really sex-positive S/M dyke who was always trying to get an orgy going at other people's parties. I grabbed her as she moved into the kitchen. Hey, Can I Have Sex In Your Room? *Sure love, with who?* She was British. I pointed to Scrumptious, dancing nasty between a new set of thighs, and the British girl went and threw down this really impressive spread in her room, gloves, a bucket of lube, shiny square packets of condoms, a holiday. Scrumptious came into the room, grabbed me and looked very deeply into my eyes. *Do you believe in destiny?* she asked, and flung me on the bed. It was hell getting those vinyl pants down. Stella's wig was gone now, one of the topless girls in the other room had ripped it off her head. She was bald beneath it, just a tiny fuzz of blonde, her makeup stark on her face without the halo of hair to soften it. Stella talked a lot during sex, and I was glad. I was on all that speed, and I didn't want to have to stop talking just because the night had taken this turn. My enormous jeans, barely held up by my belt, fell easily to the floor. *Do you like this?* Scrumptious asked. *Do you like that?* Before I could answer or even consider it, she'd zoom off to some other part of my body. Everything was frantic and crazy and she kept, I don't know, telling jokes or something because we were both cracking up and talking and people kept coming into the room to get their coats from the foot of the bed. Tommy walked in and grabbed my jeans from the floor, picked my wallet from the pocket. Don't Do It All! I hollered as she walked with it into the bathroom.

Stella left to get some water and came back with a third girl and we had sex with her too. We were like a pair of deranged lawnmowers. The third girl had this gnarly belt, metal rings looped together with bits of leather, and she was kind of going to town on my ass with it, and I could barely feel it with the many chemicals coursing through me. I liked the sound it made, though, a fleshy *whap*. My body was like a ball of light, it was supernatural. My friends were banging on the door, *Come on, let's go, we want to go.* We Should Go, I said to Scrumptious, Before They Do All The Drugs. *You guys are on drugs?* asked girl number three, weaving her belt back into her jeans. Out in the living room shirts were still off, and the British girl was on the couch, an arc of glinting pins pushed through the skin around her breasts. Tiny creeks of blood dribbled out the holes and pooled in her bellybutton. *Bye, love!* she shouted as we left her apartment. *Be safe!*

Ok, so the plan was to not sleep, to stay up until the sun rose and make first call at this shitty boy bar in the Castro. By four o'clock I think we started to realize what a really meritless idea that was, but no one wanted to back out, and no one was capable of sleep, so we trudged on. To another party. A rave thing, right, so we figured, great, everyone would be as wired as we were, all drenched in awful synthetic noise. When we got there, it was liquid calm, an opium den with kids decomposing on pillows, looking up at the herd of panting elephants busting into their mellow. Another girl I had slept with recently and then needed to never talk to again was there, on

216

Ecstasy. I ran back down the stairs and hid in a doorway until my friends got nervous and came looking for me. The only place we could think to go was Club Universe. An awful all-boy techno club with that terrible, repetitive headache music, thousands of fags with no shirts bumping into you with sweaty, steroid torsos. *It costs like a million dollars to get in,* someone protested, and I said, Don't Worry. Deep in the dark alleys South of Market you could hear the club's loud thumping for blocks, a dull bass beat pulsing through the pavement. We paused on a deserted corner and dipped the tip of a house key into the tiny pouch of speed, held the metal to our nostrils. We had acquired a youngish, sort of nervous girl at one of the parties, she was just there for the ride. We were like those guys from the *Wizard of Oz,* people could tell we were going nowhere fast and they wanted to come. She wanted some of the drugs. *Can I have some?* she asked, tentative, then, *No no I can't I can't. What if I just did a little?* I Guess You'd Get A Little Speedy. When we were done she took the key and licked the fine dust from its crevice. *I had to try it!* she gushed. We approached the mammoth dance club. It was something like fifteen bucks to get in. I tried Club Courtesy on the door girl, to get us in. *Do you have a laminate?* She was jaded and bored. Um No. I told her all about the little open mic for girls I hosted, a noble thing, maybe she'd let us right in, but the female minion of this throbbing cash cow was not impressed. Well I'm Also With The Film Festival, I said, whipping out a laminated card with my dopily smiling face on it. *That's nice.* Listen, I commanded, pulling out my ammo. I Write For The *San Francisco Bay Times,* I'm Writing A Piece On Enormous, Alienating Dance Clubs And I'd Like To Get In As Press. This had actually worked for me in the past. I could see her hesitate, mesmerized temporarily by the Svengali of Media. *Do you have a press pass?* she asked, snapping back into door-cop. No, But I'm On The Masthead. *Do you have the masthead?* Well, No, I Don't Carry The Goddamn Paper Around With Me! Behind me my friends shuffled awkwardly and twitched. Listen, How Many Dykes Are Inside There? I demanded of the door cow. None, Right? Maybe Like Two Dykes Are In There, But That's It, Because Your Cover Is So Fucking Expensive We Can't Afford To Come In! It's Classist! There's A Bunch Of Gay Boys With Too Much Money, Two Dykes, And That's It! There's No Diversity! It's Goddamn Dyke Night And None Of Us Can Afford To Come Into Your Club! She looked at me, boredom sitting on her face like age. *Hold on,* she said. She went away, whispered to the guy in the hallway. *You can get in for five,* she said, *and that's it.* I turned to my people, they looked pained. What Else Are We Going To Do? I said helplessly. We dug into our wallets. In my haste I yanked out the speed, the bag fell to the floor with a splat. *Michelle,* hissed Candice. Oops.

Inside was a factory of men. It was like they were being mass-produced in another room, hundreds of buff and shirtless homosexuals dancing stiffly to monotonous rhythms. We dumped our stuff behind a podium, and Scrumptious grabbed me. Let's *dance,*

218

she said. I Hate Dancing To This Music, I whined, I Don't Know How. Scrumptious hopped up onto the podium and pulled me up beside her. Her wig was back on her head and she looked regular. There was a moment back at that party when I had looked at her ghastly bald head, the dark creases of makeup and realized she looked like a female impersonator after the show. I had felt a bolt of panic. The thought Who is this person? bubbled up my throat like unexpected puke when you thought you were just burping. But now I felt fine. Scrumptious was dancing. She danced good, and she was wearing those clothes. Fags clustered around the podium, hooting up at her, and then Tommy jumped up and took off her shirt, I took my shirt off, forget it, we were like a birthday cake plop in the middle of a dinner table. And I *can* dance to that shitty music on speed, I can do anything on speed, I'm fucking Jehovah. It was so moist in that club. Sweat rose from our bodies, condensed into a cloud that hovered by the disco balls, and rained back down on us. I took a break. Speed and water. *You have to put your shirt on,* some guy said, grabbing me. This happened to me a lot that summer. I couldn't keep my shirt on. It was a hot summer, and I was very angry. I looked around at the sweaty naked chests of a thousand gym queens. What About Them, I demanded. He shrugged. *Look, I'm sorry, it's not me, I—* It Is You, I snapped at him. You Are Part Of The Problem. I laid into him, I was on speed, my argument was finely honed and swiftly delivered. I could have stood there for hours debating with him, hollering above the impossible sound system. *Put your shirt on or leave,* he said and walked away. Fucking Asshole! Scrumptious rubbed my sweaty back, she was so excellent. She helped me tug the small t-shirt back onto my sticky body. It nearly strangled me. The summer I only wore children's t-shirts. So cheap, sixty cents at Thrift Town, and they made me look like I had tits. We roamed around the boring club, bored. Downstairs was cooler and nearly empty. Industrial music, a little better. We danced. It was actually great, speed being a drug that turns all boring and repetitive tasks into something marvelous. I moved my body back and forth, back and forth, a glowing machine. I did it for hours, we all did, pack of androids.

I have to go, Scrumptious said finally. *My feet hurt.* She was wearing heels with that outfit. We stopped at a twenty-four-hour donut shop for donuts and coffee. Why bother with the coffee, right? But the drugs were running low. We walked the long walk up to Market Street, Scrumptious's arm wound round my waist like a vinyl belt. Scrumptious was a physical therapist. She had a beautifully furnished apartment in Canada. *You'd love it,* she said wistfully. She had just broken up with her girlfriend, and her dog, Plum, had just died. *This was her collar,* she said, fingering the studded red leather she wore around her neck. Everybody loved Scrumptious, all my friends. *You have to move here,* they begged, *we love you!* It was like we'd all gone to high school together. *Don't you want her to move here, Michelle? Oh, she swept Michelle off her feet! In like, what, two hours! You have got to move here.* My friends

220

were completely ready to marry me off to Scrumptious. It was like we'd all forgotten we were on drugs. Scrumptious blushed. A bus dropped us off at the Castro, and we met more friends at a diner there. Vinnie and Bruce. I tried to tell them about our night, but I just couldn't. It was too much. The sun was up and the air smelled like someone had cleaned it. The dykes had really made a mess of the Castro, there was shit everywhere. *Jesus Christ,* said Vinnie, surveying the carnage. Vinnie, That's Scrumptious, I whispered to him. She's . . . She's Incredible. I'm In Love With Her. *Really?* said Vinnie. We sat down at a long table inside the diner, and everybody ordered toast. The boys ate real breakfasts, big steaming plates that made us sick to look at. We nibbled our toast and pushed it away. Nobody could eat. Just chewing felt unnatural. Smoking was good. The drugs had made us synthetic. We were polyester. How gross bodies are, so needy. Swallowing, ugh. We gossiped about which waiters used to be waitresses and vice versa. We paid the check and left, through the thrashed neighborhood to Castro Station where everyone was on speed like us or else had just woken up and was drinking the bad bar coffee. Gay Pride Day. We leaned against the wall in the sunny part of the bar open to the street, drinking whiskeycokes. A guy from Oklahoma started talking to Tommy, who was also from Oklahoma, and they got close over that. The guy was pretty drunk and kept hitting Tommy's glass with his own, saying, *We got out, we got out!* It was about nine o'clock. Soon the parade would start up, boys were already walking out into the morning debris of the Castro. We went to Tommy's house to take showers. I was still sticky down there from sex with Scrumptious, whose motorcycle I would soon be stuck on the back of.

I feel like I'm not telling you enough about Scrumptious, particularly since by now we were in love for real. Her outfit looked even better at nine in the morning. The day looked lazy around her, like it wasn't trying hard enough. The simple streets and all their houses. *I've got to go back and change,* she said. Oh, I said, Do You Have To? *Yeah,* she laughed, looking down at herself. *And I don't think I can ride my bike.* My heart slumped in my chest. Really? *Yeah,* she said, *I'm wrecked. Are you disappointed?* She touched my cheek. We kissed passionately in the street outside Tommy's, and Vinnie took pictures. Upstairs I begged Tommy for something to wear. Something clean and not gross. I got to wear her one-piece Team Dresch bathing suit, with Mariel Hemingway leaping a hurdle on the front and tour dates on the back. I felt better after the shower and the fresh outfit, but we were all crashing. The beginning of the end. We dumped the rest of the speed onto Tommy's drawing table and cut it up fine, divided it into lines. Vinnie and Bruce wanted some. You Don't Understand, I told them. This Is To Keep Us Alive. We gave them a little. Where Is Scrumptious? Scrumptious was taking forever. We phoned the home of my ex-girlfriend. I had forgotten all about her. Scrumptious, Hurry Up. Irritated. No one could decide whether to ride with Dykes On Bicycles or skateboard or what. *Ride a bike with me,* Tommy begged. I Can't, I said, I'm Dying. The bell

222

rang. It was Scrumptious. Her face was blank and uneventful with no makeup or hair. She wore a tank top, neat shorts, sneakers, and . . . freedom rings. *Freedom rings!* everybody shouted, *Freedom rings!* Everyone wanted to wear them. As a joke. Stella didn't get it. You couldn't really call her Scrumptious now. It didn't work. She looked like eight hundred other lesbians, she looked normal. She was normal, she was a normal lesbian from Canada with a very nice apartment and a job as a physical therapist. She kept talking about how much better Canada was. They had socialized health care and no guns. We should all move there. *You'll come and visit, right?* I wondered if her Ecstasy was still working. *What's so funny about freedom rings?* she asked. You couldn't really explain it, you just got it or you didn't get it, though Tommy did launch into a brief monologue about capitalism and assimilation and the marketing of homosexuality. She was like Linus going on about the true meaning of Xmas and wrapped it all up with a passionate plea to please let her wear the freedom rings. How could Stella say no? They jangled on Tommy's bony sternum as we slopped to the parade. *I'm Gay!* she kept yelling, delirious. *Happy Gay Day!*

Brand new girls were with us. Bonzai was on acid. She took one look at the tiny band of protesting Christians clustered around the Muni entrance and started having a freaked-out bad trip. They had their big bleeding signs, hell this, sodomy that, and Bonzai started crying real tears, her big brown eyes all swirly and pained. The Christians were surrounded by a blue fence of policemen.

Bonzai turned and ran back down Market Street the way we came, and Ashley, who had done no drugs and was very clean and well-rested and centered, turned on the heels of her little boots and ran after her. I couldn't deal with Bonzai or with the Christians. I sat down on the pavement, and Stella wrapped her arms around me from behind. I had a 40. I thought it would somehow help. I drank it and watched the parade float by. Everyone had so much energy. Who was this girl hugging me? Sleep deprivation makes me question my relationships to everyone. I get really confused. The sun was so hot beating down on our heads and when the gay cops passed we booed them and everyone around us booed us for booing them. *A good person is still a bad cop!* Tommy shouted. She seemed to be holding up pretty good. *Barbie oppresses me!* she screamed at a pack of drag queens, clunky and hung with the dolls. We all got nuts when the mayor rode by in a limo. He Is Not! I shrieked. You Are Kidding Me! We gaped at him. Such a bad man, he looked totally *Weekend at Bernie's* with his bloated hand propped up and that dead little smile. Mayor Jordan. Remember when he got naked with those DJs? Bonzai came back to the fold, her eyes haunted and dilated. Oh God, We're All On Drugs, I moaned. Bonzai looked at us accusingly for not feeling the pain of the protesting Christians. I know what it's like to be struck by injustice while you're fucked up, it's catastrophic and isolating, but there was nothing I could do. I could barely make it to the giant mob scene shopping mall eatery in the grassy area. We waited in line for food and tried hard to eat it. I lay in the grass with Stella and attempted to sleep. All these people with life inside them kept coming up and taking our picture. I couldn't talk. I couldn't form sentences. I could breathe and I could twitch, that's about it. And I had to co-host the open mic that night. A band was booked to play, and I expected it to be packed. Somehow I made it back to the Mission on a bus and me and Stella separated, each to sleep and freshen and meet that night for my gig. Finally home, I lay in my bed and thought about every horrible thing I could think of: poverty, my own and the world's, Iris, who didn't love me anymore, all the people who didn't love me anymore, plus all the people who never did and never would. I thought about loneliness and all the years my fast-paced lifestyle was shaving off my life, how my lungs were blackening and how my teeth were falling out because I had never been to a dentist. I thought about all the people who didn't like me because I was loud and I never stopped talking. I never shut up, never let people get a word in, and probably I drank too much. And my writing was self-indulgent. I was vain.

When I exhausted my misery I got out of bed, showered, changed and went to meet Stella. She was waiting at 16th and Mission in a pair of white jeans. Thank god Tommy still had the freedom rings. Stella couldn't stop asking about them. And her sunscreen, which Tommy also had—when could she get it? Later, I promised. I couldn't believe she was wearing white jeans. You are such an asshole, Michelle, I continued with the self-flagellation.

Why do you care what color jeans she wears? You are shallow. Nobody came to the open mic. Nobody. Just the band and a couple of girlfriends and my co-host, Iggy. And Stella. I tried to hold it together for the band because they were all clean and sober and I didn't want them to know I was on drugs, but I kept nodding off or slipping into hallucinations while talking to them. I Haven't Slept, I apologized. I'm Sorry Nobody's Here. I was full of apology. When would the endless day end? After the pathetic show, me and Stella went for greasy tofu burgers at the twenty-four-hour donut shop and then we went home. My home. We did not have sex but we kissed and it was weird. Kissing was an expression of affection—what was this affection based on? My mind chugged like a scientist over a mysterious tube. I didn't know this girl at all. My tired spun-out head whirled with it. I barely slept. I do speed once, I'm up for three days. Stella slept, no problem, snoring in short, delicate snorts throughout the night, which of course didn't help. In the morning she had to go shopping. In the Castro, a part of town I could have lived without seeing again for a few days. Into the used leather store to try on dozens of leather chaps, none of which fit. There was an enormous pile of discarded cow outside her dressing room door, and I was sitting on top of it when Candice walked into the store. She gave me a face. I guess I must have looked funny, sprawled out half-dead on top of all that leather. I'm With Stella, I shrugged. *Really?* Candice wrinkled her nose. Candice didn't like her, but Candice liked few people. She had only recently decided

I was ok. I shrugged again, helplessly. I had only wanted to have a little fun and now I was married and would perhaps never sleep again. We moved on to a trendy thrift store, and Stella put half of it on her credit card. She started to fuck me in the dressing room, but she was just teasing. What could I do but endure? I kept hoping she'd buy me something. She seemed to have a lot of money. Back at my house my roommate Sam was stressing out about the flyers for her club that she still hadn't made. *I know—you two!* She had us get naked and crawl around like animals and pounce while she took pictures with her clicking little camera. We were moving around the filthy linoleum in my bedroom. I hadn't cleaned since the breakup, just kept moving my bed around and pushing things into different corners. In a lame attempt to make myself feel alive again, I'd painted my walls blood red. A passionate shade, but I woke each morning filled with rage, like those inmates they did color and mood studies on in prisons. Red makes the angry angrier. We moved into the bathroom and took a very silly picture of Stella up on the toilet licking the lightbulb on the wall and me underneath her licking up at her snatch. I kept trying to kick-start the excellent feelings I had had for her the other night, but if you want to feel like you're on drugs, you have to do drugs.

Stella got sick. Just a cold, but she couldn't ride back to Canada on a motorcycle with a cold. She felt dizzy. She was spread out on my couch picking through old Ursula Le Guin paperbacks from the ancient bookshelves filled by past roommates. My current roommates brought Stella glasses of orange juice. Make Yourself At Home, I said weakly and left for work. I had managed to get a job raising money for an environmental outfit that was trying to save a bunch of trees up in Mendocino County. These trees were so old and valuable that if you chopped them down you could get like ten thousand dollars apiece for them. There's This Girl At My House, I said to my friend Jay during our fifteen-minute cigarette break outside. Jay was adorable, he looked like a little Kurt Cobain with a pierced dimple, a little silver ball stuck where his smile hit his face. *Who is she?* Jay asked. I Don't Know. I didn't. Stella kept asking for her freedom rings, but I couldn't get in touch with Tommy. Before leaving, Stella handed me her dead dog's collar, the one with the round silver studs she'd worn the night she was Scrumptious. *This was Plum's,* she said. *I want you to have it.* Stella, I said. I had nothing of comparable value to give her, or at least nothing comparable that I wanted to part with. I grabbed a black leather bracelet off my cluttered bureau. It was one half of a pair of wrist restraints, useless now, but I had to give her something. I had just given it to a different girl a few weeks before, and she'd returned it the day before the Dyke March, when I told her I couldn't see her anymore. Here, I said to Stella. Stella left the next day while I was at work talking about nature on the telephone. I came home to a note on the kitchen table, and I was washed with relief. It was the closest thing to alive I'd felt since the march. She had been a living hangover, sitting in my front room, coughing. The night could not end until she

228

left. Then I slept. I got letters from her, sweet at first—*Show me your soul.* I didn't answer. Then the letters got mean. She wanted her goddamn freedom rings back. And her sunscreen. The rings were hanging from the rearview mirror inside Tommy's battered VW Bug. Stella Wants Her Stuff Back, I said weakly, riding shotgun. *Unh-unh!* Tommy yelled with animation. *These are mine! You can take the sunblock though.*

19

Cecilia was a recovering alcoholic bike messenger with a long mane of tangled, streaked hair and a fabulous sneer. It wasn't a snotty sneer, it was how she smiled. Like she really wanted to smile, but something in her face was holding her back. I thought it was one of the sexiest things I'd ever seen. I almost blew it with Cecilia, right off the bat. The whole alcoholic thing. I was actually trying to bond with her, over sandwiches at the Baghdad, about how I came from a long line of alcoholics. My birth dad had been a raging alcoholic, so bad that he got himself fired from his job at the post office, and many of the men in his family wound up dead from drinking, their livers soaked through, rotted to nothing. My maternal grandfather was a happy and occasional drunk, but neither happy nor occasional enough to prevent my grandmother, the daughter of a violent drunk, from flinging corned beef and boiled potatoes all over the walls when he bumbled home late for dinner with his sloppy, charming grin and a fumbling whiskey tap dance for the kids. And my stepfather, there were enough bad drunks in his family to fill the local Moose Club, with him being a shining example. But he was recovered now, sober. *Does he go to meetings?* asked Cecilia. She was eating a hamburger. I had decided we were on a date even though my roommate Sam was along for the ride and we were only at the Baghdad, looking out on the throngs of gay folk clotting the Castro. No, He Doesn't Need To Anymore. *What do you mean, he doesn't need to?* Cecilia asked, suddenly tense. *If you're an alcoholic, you're an alcoholic for the rest of your life. You have to keep going to meetings.* Well, He's Still An Alcoholic, I agreed quickly, glad that I at least understood that part. Once an alcoholic, always an alcoholic. But my stepfather had hated A.A. He'd gone for a little while, but found the way everyone relied on the meetings irritating. *Just trading one addiction for another,* he said, shaking his head. And he didn't believe in god. He hated the whole "powerless over my addiction" mantra. *I got myself into it,* he'd said to me, *and I got myself out of it. Goddamn right I did.* Made sense to me. You did all that work staying away from booze, and then you were supposed to give all the thanks over to some abstract force? But at the Baghdad I sat with my grilled cheese and wondered if maybe my stepfather had pride problems, maybe he should still be at the meetings

231

with the other alcoholics. Maybe *I* should be in Al-Anon. My little sister loved it. She'd figured herself out and forgiven the jerks of our family everything. *It's a disease,* she'd explained to me earnestly. Alcoholism. I couldn't imagine spending another minute of my life dwelling on all those people, these alcoholic men. Fathers. I didn't want to sit in a circle and talk about them. They could all go and do whatever they wanted, I was through.

I flicked the subject away, talked to Cecilia about her pet rats. They lived in tall cages like rat apartment buildings. The two pink-eyed ones had enormous tumors that dragged from their bodies, they hung like udders or marsupial sacks and were grated raw from the cage's metal floor. Those poor white rats, even if they weren't born in labs, their ancestors were so they were all doomed to tumors. A third rat, brown-eyed and brown-spotted, was a slinky, healthy little rat. Cecilia would let it loose in the folds of her bedding while we lay around on pillows. The rat's quick nose would bump up against my ankle, my ribs, its tail in my hair as it frantically searched for a way off the loft bed and down onto the world below. Cecilia would grab the rat by the middle and hold the twitching head close to her face. *There's nowhere to go, ratty,* she'd say in her rat voice. *There's nowhere to go.*

After the A. A. conversation came another awkward moment when my roommate Sam launched into her favorite fantasy of me having children. Me sending my spawn down to the liquor store at 16th and Valencia, where the big guys working there would pack-

age up a couple 40s and send "Little Tea" back home to her alcoholic mom. Heh Heh, I laughed uncomfortably. Sam was always
blowing it for me with the sober girls. Like the time I brought the
older, sober writer I worshiped over to our house, and Sam was sitting wasted in the dark, empty bottles at her feet and a half-empty
half-pint of Jim Beam in her fist. *I hate girls,* she croaked. I steered
the worshiped sober writer down the hall and away from Sam's
boozy angst. Cecilia had all these little tests for me. Like, would
I leave a beer half-full on the bar when the place closed down?
Would I leave it sweating there or would I pick it up and slug it
back? *That's a perfectly good beer,* Cecilia encouraged me shiftily.
You're just going to leave it there? What a waste. I'd leave it. I hated
chugging shit, unless it was a drinking game and that was the point.
Another time we walked into her house, into her bedroom, and she
lifted a heavy dictionary and flipped to the word "alcoholism" and
read it out loud. *"The habitual excessive drinking of alcoholic liquor,
or a resulting diseased condition."* Ok, I thought, I get it.

And I guess I was passing the tests, because we were becoming girlfriends. Just spending more and more time together and
having weirder and weirder sex. Really theatrical hooker and serial
killer sex, with weapons and costumes and psychotic notes left on
the windshield of her excellent run-down Chevy Nova. Cecilia was
great because she was a bike messenger, which meant she could be
anywhere at any minute. I would be walking down a street and she
was suddenly there, her feet in those kamikaze shoes that clipped

on to the pedals. An unexpected makeout on the corner of 16th and Mission when I was just on my way to get a bagel. Mornings Cecilia would climb from her bed, down the wooden ladder and into all these stretchy, shiny clothes, her uniform. Little shoes, special gloves on her hands, she was going into a certain battle. All that tangled hair, a sputtering radio clipped to her bag, she was out the door, her bicycle held up in one hand like a body she'd saved from drowning or pulled from a flaming building. She was a hero. Only superheroes wore such shiny outfits and crossed their cities with such speed. After she left, I lazed in her bed, played with the enormous vibrator that lived under her mattress, fed the rats some pellets. They were slowly dying, one of the pink-eyes was already gone, buried in the backyard by a rose bush. Cecilia's rats. They would clamber excitedly to the front of the cage when she came home, squeezing their skinny snouts into a square of mesh, their spastic, sniffing pulses wracking their little bodies. *There's nowhere to go,* Cecilia sang to them gently. *There's nowhere to go, little ratties.* Cecilia, I started, What's The Worst Thing You Ever Did? She hardened right up, moved away from me. *I don't want to talk about that,* she said coldly. You can never get into anybody as deep as you really want to. There's nothing to be done about it. Every night Cecilia gave herself up to me, my hands became rats and I whispered into her ears all the terrible things the neighborhood men would do to her, how I would sit in a chair and watch. Every night she pressed knives to my throat, or called me on the phone and invited me over to cuddle, her snug warmth, her long cloth of hair at my neck, and still I went home and wrote poems about how it wasn't enough. Something gaped in me, stupid and puckered like the maw of a fish, that ugly. In old notebooks I found scrawls of poems about Iris and was shocked to learn that she hadn't been enough either, at least not while she was there. Later the sky was full of her, a pagan force that energized the world around me, everything was Iris. But back when she was just a girl, I'd felt these sad stirrings and worked them into restless verse. I read them, stunned. I'd forgotten I'd written them, forgotten I'd felt that at all. Change the names, they could be about Cecilia. They could be about Willa, or anyone at all. I shut my old notebook, glittered dust-bunnies and whorls of dyed hair clogging its spiral binding. I slid it back under my bed. There's nowhere to go, I thought. Outside my window was the flat grey sky, hard as a rock. The air smelled like sauce from the sausage factory around the corner, the one that kept burning down or getting pelted with red paint bombs by animal rights activists. The factory gave each day a teriyaki flavor. I opened up my window and lit a cigarette. So many flies filled my room, they chased each other in happy circles like real animals, dancing in the air. It brought tears to my eyes. You have PMS, I calmed myself, that's all. It's Ok. There's nowhere to go, I smoked. There's nowhere to go.

20

I haven't been fucked in a while, I thought, belly up on the futon. I didn't much care, either, and that's what concerned me. Cecilia was right there next to me and it's not like she wasn't looking good. Her recently cut hair had settled into a cute, sloppy shag, quelling her desire to chop it entirely off, thank god. We don't need any more girls with bleached crew cuts. We may not even need any more girls with crew cuts, period. Bring back the hair. Cecilia was curled up on me all nice and then she had to get up and get ready to go see her therapist. Outside, the sky was as grey as the scum in my tub, pissing rain and it was so sad to imagine going out in it. All I had eaten that day was half a bagel with a smear of cream cheese, and I was feeling pretty shaky like I do when I don't eat. I figured I'd go to the health food store around the corner. Something really good, maybe some fake meat. I grabbed a pair of dirty socks out of the empty computer box that worked as my hamper, pulled them up over my legs. Good long socks, wool ski socks, blue with red trim. My girlfriend layered herself up and so did I. We went down my dark stairway to the rainy day. Cecilia had her bike chained up to the parking meter, a little red bike. It was real small because she was. She grabbed me and kissed me good, squishing me with her thick arms. Cecilia was short but she was real muscley. Big bulging arms covered with tattoos. I liked kissing Cecilia, but it made me feel guilty because I'd been thinking for weeks about breaking up with her. We broke up once before but only for about twelve hours and we were together the whole time we were broken up, lying sobbing in her sturdy loft bed, clutching each other in tight, desperate hugs, my orange slip a mess of salty snot. Cecilia talked about the ebb and flow of a relationship, and how we were in the ebb but certainly we would flow again. We spent all day breaking up and then we changed our minds and went to Taco Bell. I was supposed to read that night at this bar and I couldn't, I was so weak and puffy. I could only wander around the big dark room and let everyone buy me drinks, light my cigarettes. So there I was in the ebb again, impatient. I tried not to think about it. I gave myself furtive tarot readings and then disregarded everything they said. Occasionally I would have these outbursts with my close friends, spurting out how I didn't know, I wasn't sure, something was missing, I loved her so much, it was hard, I needed something else, what, a writer, another art-ist, someone crazy? Cecilia was kind of crazy—maybe I needed a different, more literary crazy? I would instantly regret these con-fidences, because I knew I wasn't going to do anything. I wasn't going to break up with Cecilia because she was so nice and I loved her, and now all my friends would look at me and think that I didn't like my girlfriend. I did like her, I liked her a lot. She was a big soft bed to curl into, she was warmth and sadness, green vegetables and really perverted sex.

Later I went over to the Mexican place on Valencia with the bad food and the good margaritas. I had eaten there once with Iris, after I had taken us shopping at the cheesy leather store across the street. We got nachos and slushy margaritas and we chewed and screwed, ran laughing and out of breath from smoking down this little alley and I hit her with our new riding crop. This kind of public sex and general scamming would never happen with Cecilia and I knew that was part of the problem. I was looking for someone who got into more trouble than I did, or who at least was open to getting into whatever trouble I could come up with. No trouble for Cecilia. Those days were over. She told me bunches of stories, about riding home on her bike with a beer stuffed in every pocket, slugging one back as she rode. All the times she smashed her car and kept go-ing. Now she was in the Twelve Step program and being good. She was being more and more good each day. She had quit her bike messenger job and was working as a yoga instructor. She dressed a little tamer, no more wild dry mane of black and red rocker girl hair, scruffy sweaty clothing. I was glad Cecilia did what she needed to do to save herself, but I couldn't shake the feeling of missing out on something. She wouldn't have sex with me in public bathrooms. Little things like this haunted me. I was only twenty-five.

In the margarita place I found Rachel eating nachos by the pinball machines at the back. She had a glass of water and two books, *On Being a Jewish Feminist* and the Bible. Rachel's thin brown curls had gotten long since I last saw her. She'd been going out with some really insecure woman from Marin who wouldn't let her have friends. She got a new job at a methadone program and stopped smoking pot because she felt guilty—why should she have her high when others couldn't have theirs? Rachel was an Aquarius. People kept popping in for margaritas, people we knew. Rhonda showed up, full of complaint about this girl Leona, me and Rachel knew her too. Rhonda bitched about how Leona was so weird to her the other night, and we all talked about how weird Leona always was, and I offered that she had been really unsupportive of my writing and everyone agreed that that was really lousy. Whenever people had a complaint to offer they would take a greasy tortilla chip from the wooden bowl on the table and place it on their shoulder. The margaritas were beautiful, thick and cold, pale green. I took the lime wedge from my edge of the glass and scooped up some icy froth, sucked it into my mouth. A shallow plate with a thin layer of creamy guacamole, a plastic bowl of watery red salsa, chunks of onion and soggy leaves of cilantro. Rocco stopped by, and told us how he had had a tantrum about his roommate, and the phone was off the hook and she was still on the line and heard everything and now she was moving out, which was great because now Rhonda could take her room. Rocco wasn't sorry. He sold cars, Saturns. He really loved it. He toasted me and called me "Comet" and I felt like a poseur. I wasn't a comet. I was a wife. I was drained and jaded and I was only twenty-five. How did it happen? The tequila was working its unpredictable intensity on me. I wanted to Fuck Shit Up. We paid the bill and walked over to the open mic at the bar down the street, some girls we knew were reading. Actually just one girl since the other girl had canceled with a hangover. The girl reading seemed ill at ease, like she wished she hadn't gotten herself into it. She gave me a drink ticket, which was great since I only had two dollars left. I got one of those beers with a lemon. The bar was dark and crowded, lots of red, shiny stars hanging from the ceiling, velvet paintings. The stage where the poets stood had fire painted on the wall. The girl poet stood up there and smoked furiously and read her poems. *I hate reading because it interferes with my smoking,* she said. I remember last winter she was sick forever and everybody was worried about her because she kept smoking and smoking. I was smoking too. Other people's cigarettes. I knew I was drunk when my reactions to the readers got so violent. I loved that one

240

boy so much! Really great. I tried to explain why he was so great to all my friends but they didn't get it. His simple beauty. I gulped my beer. Most of the readers were bad. I tried heckling but I was off, I was being sarcastic but people thought I meant it. Kim read, and that was good. Kim was this really cute girl, short black hair, shiny, bangs cutting across her forehead. Some makeup but I think she was butch. I mean, I was attracted to her so I figured she was. But her shirt was always tucked in, which made me think she was probably a Virgo or some other incompatible sign. Kim liked me back when she had a girlfriend and I was free, and now I had one. She would read at my open mic, drunk lesbian sex stories, my favorite. You could tell she was young, and probably a mess. Just the other night Sam and I were trying to figure out if she was always blacked out at the bars. There was something weird and unfocused about her, and every week she would introduce herself to me all over again as if she had no memory of the week before. I watched her sit against the bar and drink beer and smoke long white cigarettes. There was an aura of anxiety about her. She was attentive to all the readers, you could tell she really believed in poetry. I drank my beer and stared at her more and more openly. I thought about going out with Kim. What would it be like? Being drunk all the time, real passionate about writing. Lots of making out in bars and bathrooms, then sloppy drunk fucking at home, late. Or not, because she would be in a blackout. Can you fuck in a blackout? Her friend saw me staring. She whispered to Kim. Kim seemed to be using the corners of her eyes, she looked nervous. I just continued to stare, harder and harder, until she turned her resistant head and looked straight at me. I smiled a lazy smile. She turned away quickly. I bummed another cigarette. I imagined Kim grabbing me and kissing me. I decided I would kiss her back. I had never cheated on a girlfriend, I was very righteous about it, but then I thought, what if it was something I was supposed to experience in this life? Cheating was a very common experience. I would kiss Kim a little and then push her away and yell No! having it both ways. A moment of indulgence before coming to my senses. I had a girlfriend. A really nice one. A good, miso soup when you're sick, you need a backrub kind of girlfriend. I was an asshole. A drunk one, the worst kind. My beer was over and I had no more money and all the girls I knew were leaving. Including Kim. I got up to hug her goodbye. *Here.* She gave me a little scrap of paper. *I still want to have coffee with you, and write. Here's my number.* Oh, Yeah, I said. I'm Always Going Writing Alone, I Need Writing Buddies. She pressed the scrap into my palm. *And I'm not hitting on you, I know you really like Cecilia.* Oh, I laughed, punched her arm. Bye! I walked down the street, kicking the trash in my path. I was so fucked up. I looked at my reflection in the shop windows. My hair looked really good. Green, and kind of big. The wind flipped it all over my head. I imagined Kim on the sidewalk behind me, watching me walk away. At home Sam was just waking up, groggy in the hallway in her blue Superman bathrobe. I showed her Kim's number scratched on the torn

242

paper scrap, and boom, another outburst. I Don't Know, I'm So Confused, If Only I Really Knew. Whenever I Think About Breaking Up I Think No, I Love Her, But I Think About Staying And I Feel So Restless. Sam looked disturbed. I'm sure she did not want to hear this. I hopped in the shower and when I got out Cecilia was there, in my house, and again I felt like an idiot. Maybe I would stay with her forever. She was so nice. We sat in my bed and talked about writing, I untied her shoes and yanked them off, little black canvas things. We curled up into each other on my crummy futon, under my blankets. My room was filthy. We went to sleep.

—

21

I need to bring you back to my first date with Iris. It seems that I'm not done with her yet. It wasn't really a date, we were both too skanky for dates. We got a big glass jug of beer, malt liquor for a buck and a quarter, and sat on the curb outside the rock show, trying to figure out a way to replicate the admission stamp with spit or a sharpie. Before we got on the bus that dragged us into the fog-soaked Haight she'd said, *I'm really selfish,* and I looked at her pretty wet eyes and laughed like she was a skinny girl bitching about the fat on her hips, because she was much too cute to be an asshole and plus I am a fool for love.

Iris ran away from the South in a dust cloud of drama. Magdalena Squalor had brought her to San Francisco from Georgia. When Iris and Magdalena were girlfriends they had driven in a van across the whole country and never spoken. They'd sat in the thin ice of silence and slept on the shoulder of the road. In Santa Cruz they found a room way up in the trees, and Iris got a job at a vitamin factory and Magdalena worked at a cafe, and there they stayed with nothing to do. Together they cooked cauldrons of vegetarian chili and sold it to hippies at Dead shows; they combed the woods behind their house for brambles and wove wreaths to sell to catalogue companies. They seduced this girl who looked like k.d. lang and the fallout had driven Iris deeper into her destiny, to my city where she left her van in the street to be cracked open and dragged away. Magdalena Squalor hadn't let Iris drink, hadn't let her smoke cigarettes or pot from a bong, so I got to be the bad girl who freed her, the good nasty girl, the whore with a bed of pills and cherries. The grandmother who doesn't have to live with the brat, who comes and takes the brat to bowling alleys and the bright aisle of a Woolworths with a pocketful of dollars. I took the brat through the dark streets of the city I had owned first and we sucked from glass bottles, hands twisting the sacks around the necks into paper flowers. We fucked in bathrooms and alleys bold as boys, bent over porcelain sinks that creaked from the wall with the weight of her hand inside me. The rustle of clothes and rats, clink of belt buckles and feet on broken glass. When someone saw us by accident, I let them be embarrassed. Shame was like a dirty tampon pulled from my body and flung in the bucket when I was with Iris.

Early in our affair I had gone with Iris to the outdoor cafe to meet Magdalena Squalor. I hadn't needed to talk at all, I was so smug. My scrawny arms had dangled like bones in my shitty t-shirt and my hair was terrible. There sat Magdalena and I hadn't wanted to like her. She was the birth mother who maybe wanted her baby back, and even though the baby wanted to stay with me you know the justice system sucks. I kept her and fed her as long as I could, and when she went away it wasn't Magdalena she ran to but that other rotten girl, and only Magdalena knew what it was like to have this baby ripped away when your tits were still heavy and leaking and aching to feed.

One day, months later, me and Iris and Magdalena Squalor sat with plates of eggs and bread and thick gloppy sauce. Me and Magdalena needed love. Real love, not the watered-down shit that Iris squirted out. Iris was diluted, she had too many girls. Me and Magdalena wrote our personal ads on notebook paper with a purple pen. She had moved herself up from Santa Cruz, and was living in a little pink room in the Tenderloin. We laughed and talked dirty and made fun of Iris, who sulked and drank her coffee. When a cute girl tells you she's selfish, you better be listening. You better not blink and giggle to show how cute your smile is. When me and Iris roamed the summer, I had hatched plans like hungry children that I could not support alone. We would fly in the sky to other countries, we would crawl along the dust of our own, we would rule the nighttime streets of every city. Those places mewed and scratched at my thighs and now I had nothing to feed them. Magdalena Squalor became my friend. She told me things that made my burning ears sting sharper, but I didn't want to feel good anyway. I wanted to feel terrible and I did. She told me how Emma took photo booth pictures of herself with no shirt on and gave them to Iris. She told me about a performance where Emma read words from a page while Iris sucked the dildo that hung out of her pants and it sounded so dumb but I was hot with envy anyway. She told me about the pink princess gown Emma wore to the street fair, and how Iris followed her from curb to piss-run curb. Me and Magdalena were in a special club now, and I knew that rotten girl Emma would one day need to be in it too and I for one would slam my door on her. Iris went through girls like a slash-and-burn farmer. All I had to do was lie still as dirt and wait for someone to bounce seeds off my chest.

Magdalena Squalor walked into my house and made me want to paint my eyes. Hers were black as oil beneath the hood, swooping up like wind. I looked at her and knew I must change my clothes because Magdalena Squalor knew true glamour. A thick beauty that is hurt and needing, a syrup too sweet and heavy to drink without liquor. I dressed in my closet, we were going to a party. I spread cards on the floor to tell Magdalena her future. Magdalena looked hard at the cards but they didn't tell her what she was looking for. Magdalena needed paper pictures of green things growing, of big-bellied women, because she was trying to have a baby. For real, a secret. *I'll tell you my secret,* she said, *but if you don't like it you have to shut up because I don't want to hear it.* She was tracking her belly's dark comet so that she knew when to do it. She planned to seduce the man who gave her tattoos, breathe on his neck as he leaned between her legs, his gun at her breasts. A prayer like black ribbon across her skin. The man was a gangster, had pointed true guns at shopkeepers and left with bags of cash. He had a little boy so you knew his parts worked ok. But there was nothing like a baby in Magdalena's cards. We walked to the store and bought the worst drinks we could find, malt liquor flavored with synthetic pineapple and cherry. I wanted to be there when Magdalena's baby came, hold it wet and confused, beating against my chest like a bird. Magdalena told me about all the girls who hated her, all her enemies, the catty girls who hissed in each other's ears when Magdalena trailed her scent past them. Junked-up girls who would beat her up because someone told someone that she was a little bitch, a crazy bitch, and those girls were just sitting there high with nothing to do. Magdalena was going to tease her hair into a bubble like the cholla girls do, with evil-edged razors slid in like bobby pins, and I would dash my bottle at the tip of the curb

248

and hold its liquored edges to some girl's throat, I swear I would. Me and Magdalena drank our awful bottles and went to the party and Cecilia was there. She didn't know that my heart was a sandstorm waiting to open her skin in a desert of cuts. She didn't know the animal that waited in my stomach, silently shredding the walls. For her my heart wore small white shoes and carried a purse, went to bed early. I wanted to shoot myself into her arms so she understood the need to crash cars with me, to tear up pavement because we were beautiful.

Magdalena Squalor lived in the worst part of town. All by herself in a little room, and outside her window the terrible things people do were demonstrated nightly in the streets, while immigrant families slept close on pushed-together cots. I walked to her apartment with bottles of that sweet awful drink. One for me, one for Magdalena. She was moving away. Back to the South where the houses had big porches and you could sit with a baby and rock and rock. She was selling everything. When I got there girls were loading shelves into the hall, pulling the fat lazy futon across the floor, dismembering the frame. I sat on her floor and stacked books. I took the bedsheets that bitch ex-girlfriend gave her. Not that one, a different one. Aren't they all bitches. I took a green sweater too scratchy to wear, and the worn country shirt that slipped off my shoulders. I took the thick-heeled jelly shoes that didn't fit me. I took the black shoes she had worn on her wedding night, when she married the gay boy who needed to stay in the country. The black shoes didn't fit either, but I wore them. I took a little aquarium for my roommate who caught cockroaches and kept them as pets. I took Magdalena's little blue suitcase with a mirror on the inside, and I took her curling iron. One day my hair will be long like Magdalena's, and I will wind the locks around the hot stick and listen to them sizzle. One day I will braid my hair stiff at my neck like Magdalena, who is never happy. In the South she slits her wrists daily and drips the blood into the tank of her Camaro. She takes care of other people's babies. Magdalena Squalor, I will meet you in the dirtiest city you can dream of. We will drink cocktails so sweet they pucker our cheeks, as we perch on cracked leather bar stools. I will buy you plates of calcium and protein and we will run through the streets in excellent danger.

acknowledgments

Millions of thank-yous go out to Jennie, Kate and all the lovely ladies at Seal, to Inga Muscio, to the most amazing Eileen Myles, to Sash Sunday and Sini Anderson, and to Ginger Robinson.

© LYDIA DANILLER

about the author

Michelle Tea is the author of several books, including *The Chelsea Whistle* and the illustrated *Rent Girl.* Her novel, *Rose of No Man's Land,* was declared "impossible to put down" by *People* magazine. Her writing has been published in *The Believer, The Best American Erotica, The Best American Nonrequired Reading,* and *The Outlaw Bible of American Literature.* She was voted Best Local Writer of 2006 by the *San Francisco Bay Guardian.* Tea is the founder of the all-girl performance happening Sister Spit, and artistic director of Radar Productions, a nonprofit that stages underground, queercentric literary events in the Bay Area and beyond.

Selected Titles from Seal Press

For more than thirty years, Seal Press has published ground-breaking books. By women. For women. Visit our website at www.sealpress.com.

Word Warriors: 25 Women Leaders in the Spoken Word Revolution edited by Alix Olson, foreword by Eve Ensler. $14.95, 1-58005-221-5. This groundbreaking collection of poems and essays, the first all-women spoken word anthology, features the most influential female spoken word artists in the movement.

Cunt: A Declaration of Independence by Inga Muscio. $14.95, 1-58005-075-1. "An insightful, sisterly, and entertaining exploration of the word and the part of the body it so bluntly defines. Ms. Muscio muses, reminisces, pokes into history and emerges with suggestions for the understanding of—and reconciliation with—what it means to have a cunt." –Roberta Gregory, author of *Naughty Bitch*

The Chelsea Whistle by Michelle Tea. $14.95, 1-58005-239-8. In this gritty, confessional memoir, Michelle Tea takes the reader back to the city of her childhood: Chelsea, Massachusetts—Boston's ugly, scrappy little sister and a place where time and hope are spent on things not getting any worse.

She's Not the Man I Married: My Life with a Transgender Husband by Helen Boyd. $15.95, 1-58005-193-6. Taking up where My Husband Betty left off, this moving account of a wife's examination of her relationship with her cross-dressing partner proves to be the ultimate love story.

Whipping Girl: A Transsexual Woman on Sexism and the Scapegoating of Femininity by Julia Serano. $15.95, 1-58005-154-5. Biologist and trans woman Julie Serrano reveals a unique perspective on femininity, masculinity, and gender identity.

Working Sex: Sex Workers Write about a Changing Industry edited by Annie Oakley. $15.95, 1-58005-225-8. A proud community of sex workers write on race, class, gender, labor, and sexuality—and give perspective on what it really means to work in the sex industry today.

CPSIA information can be obtained
at www.ICGtesting.com
Printed in the USA
LVOW12s2255070517
533652LV00001B/20/P